The Whitsun Gallop

Emma Batten

To Kate, Happy reading, Emma x

First published in the UK by Emma Batten 2022

Printed and bound in the UK

A catalogue record of this book can be found in the British library

ISBN 978-1-7399854-1-7

Edited by Debbie Rigden

Cover painting by Zoe Beardsley

www.emmabattenauthor.com

To my sons, Zac and Kim, with love.

About the Book

In this sequel to *But First Maintain the Wall*, I move forward four years to 1762. As always, I strive to make the area recognisable and historically accurate. The racecourse at the Warren, New Romney, was first mentioned in 1735 (Told in Tom Miller's Diary extracts as shown in the book *The Gift of the Sea, Romney Marsh* by Anne Roper). This book also mentions that in Georgian times the Corporation of New Romney presented a gilded cup at an annual race meeting. My naming this race the Whitsun Gallop is entirely imaginary. I am not sure if the racecourse was circular (as I describe it in the book) or a straight length. There is a painting in the New Hall, Dymchurch, which places it where the golf course is today, but there is no detail. Back in the 18th century, two horses raced, with the successful rider winning the best of three heats. For the novel, I have assumed that another pair competed, and the two winners then raced each other to find the overall champion.

Warren House, the hospital for infectious diseases, still fronts the A259, its back to the sea and facing the Romney Marsh Visitor Centre. It was built in 1742. Now a private home, it closed as a hospital in the first decades of the 20th century.

Later in the story, my characters visit Lydd for another event. Humphrey Fletcher is a fictional character but his Match Against Time was inspired by a real 18th century gentleman jockey, Toke Simmonds, whose family kindly shared their research with me. I liked the name Toke so much, that I used it elsewhere in the novel.

I mention the Shepherd and Crook in Burmarsh to make a recognisable scene for readers but am aware that the building was not used as a pub until 1801. Also in Burmarsh, Rothschild Farm stands in a prominent position facing towards Dymchurch.

I hope you enjoy following the story of Harry and Phoebe, who will be joined by old friends and foes, as well as new characters, when they gather to watch the Whitsun Gallop.

Emma Batten 2022

References: *The Gift of the Sea Romney Marsh* – Anne Roper (Birlings (Kent) Ltd, 1984)

They're Off! Horse Racing at Romney Warren – Susan Scullino (Cinque Ports Magazines, May 2019)

Thanks

The inspiration for this novel came from an article in the Cinque Ports magazine by Susan Scullino. I am grateful for all her research.

Many thanks to Alison and Peter Cordon Dilley who invited me to their wonderful historic home, Warren House, and plied me with delicious coffee and cake.

Thank you to Sue Barclay who shared family stories about Toke Simmonds, eighteenth-century gentleman jockey.

My thanks to Colin Walker from the Dymchurch and District Heritage Group who explained the roles of the Lords of the Levels, bailiff and jurats within the Corporation of Romney Marsh.

Thank you to Maud Matley for our lively conversations about French traditions and for drafting the French for me, as well as checking the novel before print.

Last, but not least, my thanks to Michael Golding for the first edit on the novel, to Debbie Rigden who has done a superb job of editing and proof reading, and to Liz Hopkin for the final checks.

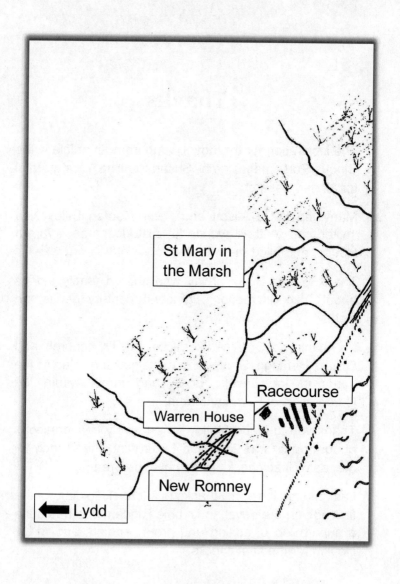

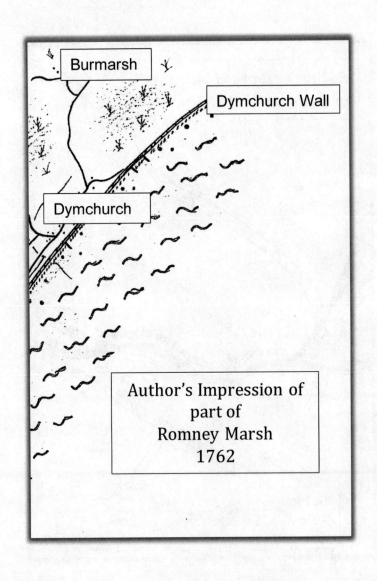

Burmarsh

Dymchurch Wall

Dymchurch

Author's Impression of
part of
Romney Marsh
1762

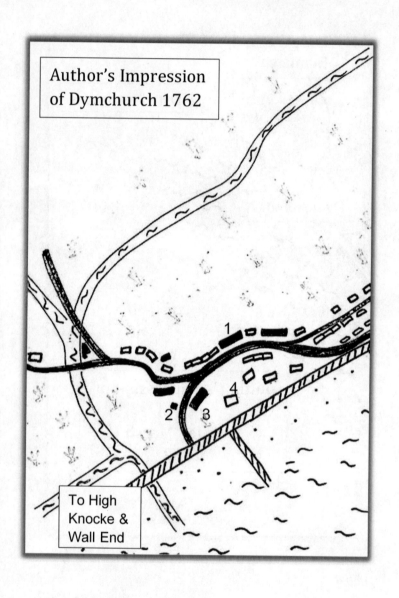

Author's Impression
of Dymchurch 1762

1

2 3 4

To High
Knocke &
Wall End

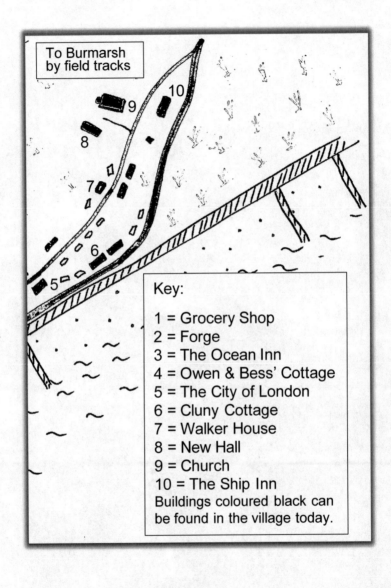

Chapter One
Harry
Whitsun 1762

A thundering beat of eight hooves permeated the ground, sending vibrations through the straggling line of expectant spectators. Incessant pounding of iron shoes echoed across the hillocks and sandhills towards the coast, as the magnificent beasts – one bay and the other chestnut – galloped side by side. Straining to see which was taking the lead, the racegoers murmured amongst themselves that the chestnut appeared to be winning by no more than a breath. Upon this scene, the sun shone boldly, and a ribbon of sea sparkled.

Harry, standing beside his wife, felt the light touch of her hip pressing against his breeches. While keeping his eyes on the race, he reached for her hand, and she gripped hard. It had been four years since they first met: he a newcomer to the village and learning the ways of Dymchurch through his labours on the seawall, she serving customers for her aunt and uncle in their general store. Now he was treated with respect, not with the distrust shown when he was a stranger and newcomer to Romney Marsh.

In the first set of races that day, King's Sovereign of New Romney and Dandy Dancer of Appledore ran the second of three heats. The event drew the bewigged and beribboned landowners and wealthy businessmen from local towns, who all welcomed an opportunity to have a flutter on their favourites and parade amongst acquaintances. They congregated, as if on show to the world, on the raised benches provided by the Corporation of New Romney, organisers of the annual Whitsun Gallop.

Harry, his luxurious brown waves powdered, sideburns trimmed and face cleanly shaved by the barber that morning, momentarily took his eye off the race. With a fingertip, he brushed the beauty spot painted on Phoebe's cheekbone. Raising her eyes to his, she gave a smile. "I'd rather be right here – feeling the ground shake. It's more exciting!" She referred to the fact that they had been invited, for the second year in a row, to be seated amongst the notables of Romney Marsh, yet chose to remain at the trackside.

"Imagine racing like that. Putting all your trust in the horse when this place is riddled with rabbit burrows." Harry knew why she preferred to keep away from the benches and the gentry of the Marsh but didn't refer to it. Aaron Chapman was sauntering about the place with his pale and weary wife in tow, their baby daughter in her arms. The young landowner still had an eye for Phoebe, despite their both being married for the past three years.

"Perhaps the keeper went about filling them all?" Phoebe suggested, knowing the task to be near impossible. This area of land was known as the Warren due to the number of burrows.

"He would need a band of men to help him," Harry continued with the theme. "Sir Julian Craythorne may well have dragged the boys of New Romney from their beds to help the young rabbit keeper tidy the course, but I still fear for the horses."

As these words were exchanged, the beasts circled the far end of the track and galloped, nostrils flaring, along the stretch parallel with the shingle bank and close to the sea. At the benches set upon wooden staging, the influential menfolk and their ladies stood to watch the race progress while, alongside the track, the onlookers' views were limited and they jostled about, searching for that rise in the land which would give them a chance of viewing the whole race.

Not far from the roadside, Harry's mobile forge was set up with his assistant, Jesse Alder, ready to re-shoe a horse at a moment's notice. In the meantime, he had a pan of drop scones baking over hot charcoal, giving him the opportunity to fill his purse with coins by the end of the day. Also hoping to benefit from the visitors and jovial atmosphere were a couple who had produced a makeshift stand selling ale and cider. 'The Warren Inn' had been daubed on a piece of wood and raised as a banner above them. Between the races, a pieman would mingle with the crowds, offering warm pasties oozing with rich gravy, while other local traders emerged, taking their chance to ply fripperies and trinkets on those attending the Whitsun Gallop.

As King's Sovereign and Dandy Dancer approached once more, on their third and final lap of this heat, the trackside spectators focussed on the race. Now they could see the muscles defined on these powerful beasts, the slick of sweat on their necks and flanks. The jockeys, with every sinew of their bodies taut, had all their unblinking focus on the path ahead, and hands so tightly wrapped around the leather reins that their knuckles showed white. The chestnut inched forward by half a length.

No sooner had the horses passed, nearing the coast for the final time, than new sensations rippled through the crowd – disbelief and fury. Then confusion, as whispered words were distorted, and each person along the line of race-watchers heard a different version of the truth.

"The cup has gone! Vanished!"

"The gilded cup has been stolen!"

"And the prize money too… from the bailiff's purse."

"It hasn't – the bailiff wouldn't allow it!"

"Snatched by a vagabond!"

"The race will be stopped – there is no prize."

Harry frowned and looked back to where the well-to-do gathered on the raised platforms. In this final lap of the heat, those who should have been watching intently were now moving from their seats or turning towards each other. Sir Rupert Bannerman of the New Hall in Dymchurch and Sir Julian Craythorne from the outskirts of New Romney had separated from their families and were clearly deep in discussion with the bailiff and jurats – all of whom upheld law and order on Romney Marsh.

"I should go," Harry said. He placed his hand on Phoebe's arm and gave a quick squeeze. "Hopefully it is nothing."

Before she could reply, Harry was finding a path through the rabble who had now lost all interest in the race. Their enthusiasm was concentrated on this tale of theft. *There must be some truth in it – but stolen! How? In front of everyone.* As a jurat, Harry must go to learn the truth, but for the moment he would wait to hear it from Sir Rupert or someone else also with a steady mind and not prone to gossip.

"Ah, Harry Farrers!" The bailiff, Jeremy Parris, raised his hand in greeting. As he did so a raucous cheer rang out amongst the few still watching the race. The bay had won. *Strange – I expected it to be the chestnut.* Harry shrugged. It was not the time to wonder about the changed fortunes of the horse which had taken the lead from the start. He nodded his greeting to the bailiff.

"Did you see anything?" Jeremy Parris asked, his ruddy face full of expectation.

"See anything?" Harry repeated. "I was over there with my wife when they started to say that the cup…"

"The cup has been stolen," Sir Rupert announced, approaching Harry and the bailiff with long strides. "It was there on a table in front of us all. Whoever took it was a chancer – and a damned foolhardy one!" Had the Leveller of the Marsh Scotts been able to run his hand through his hair to express his frustration, he would have done so. But his wig was a mass of fixed curls, so instead the gentleman raised his hands, then indicated to the carved oak table standing directly in front of the staging where he and his family had been seated to watch the race. "Blazes! I'd like to know how he did it."

Harry's gaze lingered on the table. The velvet cloth, once squarely draped over it, was now askew, and the cup, so admired by all passers-by that morning, had vanished. He looked at the stands and long benches and imagined the wealthy families of the area watching the race… looking out across the Warren's sandhills and rough ground. *Perhaps their eyes were dazzled by the sparkling blue of the sea?* "If someone were swift – and brazen – they could dart in and out while the horses galloped by," he suggested. "It could happen while everyone's attention was on the race?"

"A chancer!" Sir Rupert repeated.

"Indeed," Jeremy Parris agreed, as they walked back to the gathered group of jurats and Sir Julian Craythorne.

"Both brazen and stupid," Harry suggested. "The risk of being seen is high."

5

"But did *you* see anything?" the bailiff asked, just as he had done when Harry first approached. "Did anyone attempt to hide in the crowds? Or push through?"

"I saw nothing. There was no disruption," Harry stated, recalling that moment of anticipation when the horses pounded upon the ground, and he could almost feel the heat coming from their bodies as they thundered by.

Now they were amongst a group of twelve other men, including the two Lords of the Marsh Levels and several jurats. That Harry had been invited to hold the prestigious role of jurat had come as a surprise to him when Sir Rupert had made the offer. A year later, and he was still slightly bemused by his change in fortunes since arriving in Dymchurch four years previously. At twenty-three years of age, Harry had worked tirelessly for the good of the village, which placed him in high esteem amongst the local people and those in neighbouring settlements. This was coupled with sudden and unexpected wealth, enabling him to mix with the more affluent of his neighbours, and adding to the respect they offered him.

However, there were some who did not appreciate the high regard given to a man who was neither born nor raised on Romney Marsh, and Harry knew to be cautious when around these men. One was Aaron Chapman, who now stood beside him, a hint of a smile on his face. *Why does he smile? Does he think being with these men makes me uneasy, and that is why I chose to watch the race from the trackside?* Harry resolved not to make eye contact with his adversary. Their dislike for one another went back to when Aaron witnessed a hint of friendship between Harry and Phoebe, at a time when the young woman had spurned his own interest in her.

"What do you know about this?" Aaron spoke directly to Harry, his words unexpected.

Harry kept his face expressionless. "I know nothing. Did you see anything from the stand?"

"Not me! My attention was all on the race. Whoever took the cup was a wily fellow, wouldn't you say? As fast as a whippet and someone who would attract no attention while he lingered amongst us and made his plans."

"I hadn't considered it," Harry stated. He looked again towards the stalls and the table now holding only a dishevelled velvet cloth. There was space for someone to crawl under the platform, but there was still the matter of creeping out to snatch the cup. "You are right, of course – he would need to be fast if there was a chase."

"Do you know anyone who fits the description?" Aaron probed.

"The description?"

"Smart enough to attempt to outwit us," Aaron reminded Harry, "and fast."

"It could be any number of young men." Harry shrugged, then grinned. "You describe yourself to start with."

"But I have no motive," Aaron snapped. "None at all."

The men separated, and now Harry could hear Sir Rupert and Sir Julian speaking about the race, agreeing that the day must continue regardless of the loss of the gilded cup. "There is still the prize money," Sir Julian was saying. "Someone must go to speak to the riders – explain what has happened and tell them to prepare for the next heat. I didn't even notice who won. The chestnut, I presume?"

"No, it was the bay," one of the jurats responded.

"I've lost a guinea then!" Sir Julian gave a short laugh and sauntered off.

Sir Rupert and the bailiff began to organise the jurats, suggesting they work in pairs, searching the area from the pestilence house to the pits and copses on the far side of the road. Then they should hunt along the main road for several hundred yards in each direction, and across the undulating land through which the racecourse cut, before reaching the coast. In the meantime, the bailiff would move amongst the spectators, asking if anything suspicious had been seen.

Harry, with his companion from the inland village of St Mary in the Marsh, set off towards the west, scanning the land for anything untoward. They walked at first in silence, taking in the stalls and the vendors hoping to tempt racegoers to part with their coppers. The ground beneath their feet was sandy, with ribbons of beach pebbles which they kicked with the toes of their shoes. It undulated gently, covered in most part by dry, ragged grass and weeds. Before long, they crossed a drainage ditch and neared a substantial property.

"If I had managed to secure the cup, I'd not be lingering by the pest house," William Payne commented, as if the very building itself emitted offensive fumes. "I pray to God that myself or my family will never set foot in such a place."

In stark contrast to its purpose, the pest house – officially named Warren House – was an impressive property fronting the main road between New Romney and Dymchurch. Passers-by could not help but appreciate its generous proportions, neat rows of sash windows, and the tiled roof which slid low over the single storey area at the rear. Its chimneys stood tall, and the brick walls were straight – not yet bowed by age nor through feeling the burden of the sick who suffered there. If it served some other purpose, then any person, from landowner to tradesman, would be proud to press on the panelled door and step inside.

"We'll walk around the place and if we can catch the attention of a nurse or maid, then it would do no harm to ask if they have seen anyone hiding out or acting strangely," Harry suggested. They were nearing the property now and could see movement at the doorway to one of the storerooms. He quickened his pace and hollered a greeting to the worker, who they now saw was pushing a barrow of logs.

Pausing from his work and mopping a furrowed brow on the scruffy cuffs of his collarless shirt, the man gave a nod and waited.

"The cup has been stolen!" William announced, with a touch of drama in his tone. "The prize cup for the race," he enlarged. "Have you seen anyone running past or some scallywag hiding out where they shouldn't?"

"I've seen nothing but the log pile and buckets filled from water at the well," the man replied. "But you're welcome to look about the place."

Harry glanced at his companion and answered, "Not if you've been out here for the last hour. We'll walk past the front and take a look."

There was an obvious rise in the land, just beyond the wetlands on the far side of the road. The two men trailed along a path and stood on this high point, its being by no means a hill but merely a yard or two higher than the surrounding area. To the south-west, the windmills, cottages, inns and shops of nearby New Romney crowded the parish church with its stocky Norman tower. Inland, there was nothing but mile after mile of pastureland, with a random farmhouse or cottage, and occasionally a church spire piercing the skyline. The sun was now at its highest point and the horizon shimmered between the cloudless sky and countryside, blurring the details of buildings and trees.

"He could be hiding under our nose, and we'd know nothing of it." William nodded towards a reed-lined waterway, one of many which wound their way through the flatlands to the coast.

"He could," Harry agreed. It was an unspoken fact that a man could scuttle along these creeks for miles with his tax-free booty and not be spotted by the riding officers.

In unison, they turned their gaze back towards the road leading to Dymchurch. It appeared to be empty – at least there was no sign of a scallywag scampering away with a gilded cup.

"No point in chasing here, there and everywhere," William said, and Harry couldn't help but agree. They turned and walked back to the racecourse.

"Just in time!" Sir Rupert greeted Harry. "You had no luck, I assume?" With his usual impatience, he didn't wait to hear an answer before continuing with, "The second race is about to begin. It's a damned shame about the cup, but people have travelled for this event and the Corporation must put on a show as best they can. There's to be no more talk about the theft until afterwards."

The seats on the staging were filling once more with the wealthier residents of Romney Marsh and their guests from further afield. Harry wandered over to check on his assistant, Jesse, and the young woman whom he was courting.

"We've done a good trade!" Jesse announced as Harry neared. He gave a wide smile, and produced a leather pouch, heavy with small change. "All this excitement has got everyone wanting to fill their bellies with our drop scones between the races. But no shoes lost, which will keep the horses racing without delay."

"There's enough disruption without a horse losing a shoe," Harry referred to the missing cup.

"Damned funny business." Jesse gave a slight frown, a contrast with his naturally cheerful demeanour which made him an excellent choice of assistant. "Maybe it will turn up. What does anyone want with a cup they haven't won fair and square for themselves?"

"I don't know." Harry turned his attention to Lucy, a Dymchurch girl who had recently been walking out with Jesse on a summer's evening and a Sunday afternoon. "This was a good idea of yours." He nodded towards the pan of batter. "There are people here today with money to spend and why not make a few shillings from them? At least the fire isn't wasted if there are no hooves to be shod."

"It was good of you to let us, Mr Farrers," Lucy replied, a slight blush forming on her fair cheeks.

"I don't stand in the way of someone trying to make an honest living," Harry responded.

"I've told Lucy how you treat me fair. It was a lucky day when I asked for a job." Jesse wiped his hands on the coarse apron he wore and offered a big smile. Harry noted that despite the rough work clothes, his assistant was clean shaven, hair neat, and nails clean. This young man knew how to please the woman in his life and that boded well for them.

"It was a good day for me too! I like people I can trust around me." Harry stepped away. "Make the fire safe and come and join us at the trackside if you like."

Harry joined Phoebe as the second race began. "No sign of it," he said in response to her unvoiced words. She frowned slightly and turned her gaze back to the horses. This time it was a grey and a black who were picking up speed as they approached. For a moment, all thoughts of the missing cup were swept away as the muscular beasts, with their gentleman owners crouched forward on their necks, dashed by. Once more the ground throbbed beneath the pounding of hooves, adding to the sensation of exhilaration amongst the crowd.

As the horses passed, the onlookers dispersed, attempting to watch the horses as they progressed, circling the edge of the sandhills and following the track as it ran parallel with the coast.

Harry and Phoebe now stood with Jesse and Lucy, when yet again whispers and rumours began to spread amongst those viewing the race. No sooner had the words reached Harry's ears, than he turned to see Sir Rupert and Sir Julian bearing down upon him, and he stepped towards them fearing there was some truth in what he had just heard.

Chapter Two
Phoebe

One moment the spectators' attention was fully focused on the horses. They moved about, straining to see the action, each of them with an opinion as to who the winner would be. The next, whispers were flying and soon those hushed words became facts bandied about without thought.

"The cup has been found!"

"Found?"

"I'd have expected it to be halfway to Ashford by now!"

"Someone will hang for this!"

"At least there will be a prize to be won!"

It seemed as if the news beat a rhythm in time with the pounding of the horses' hooves. The same exclamations were repeated over and over.

"Blazes!" Phoebe heard the word burst from Harry and she followed his gaze to see Sir Rupert Bannerman and Sir Julian Craythorne approaching. He reached out, placing his hand on the small of her back, and murmured so only she could hear, "I fear there is trouble for us. Take care." Then he kissed her lightly on the forehead. Phoebe felt that kiss sitting there for the hours to follow.

Harry walked away, ready to face whatever news was coming to him, while Phoebe was left confused, trailing behind.

At that moment when the men met, the horses approached once more. The crowd followed their progress, but someone caught Phoebe's eye: standing on a sandhill within the loop of the track was a tall dark-haired man. Even from this distance she could see he had several weeks of hair growth curling about his face and neck. At first glance he appeared to be following the race, hands on hips and legs parted, but then Phoebe realised that he was watching the action unfold amongst Sir Rupert, Sir Julian and the jurats. The next thing she noticed was that this character was laughing to himself.

Phoebe turned her attention to her husband. As she did so she spotted the bailiff and several jurats swarming around one place. "No! It can't be!" She felt a wave of horror flood through her slim body. Quickening her pace, Phoebe moved further from the trackside. Whereas at first it seemed as if they were searching around all the food and drink stalls, it was now clear their interest was with the blacksmith's cart, tended by her husband's young apprentice. Harry had reached the stall, and something gleamed golden as the Whitsun Gallop cup was shown to him.

Only a few words were exchanged between the men before Harry was running back towards the racetrack. He covered the ground at speed, leaping over the hillocks and rabbit holes with ease. Phoebe knew he was trying to reach Jesse who had been tending the cart throughout the morning. She scanned the crowds, searching for the young assistant and his companion.

Unexpectedly, a commotion broke out amongst the spectators. Someone was working his way through the gathering, pushing men and women aside without care until he reached his goal. Now Aaron Chapman claimed his prize, grabbing Jesse and forcing both arms behind the young man's back. Jesse was both young and strong, and well able to fend off an assault. However, Aaron was from a wealthy land-owning family and held the status of being a jurat. Jesse submitted, allowing himself to be driven through the crowd and towards the men assembled at the cart.

Despite the heat of the day, Phoebe felt her body chill. Although it was too soon for her to understand what excuse Aaron had to treat a hardworking and good-natured young man in this way, she knew at once this was a scheme to discredit and harm her husband. A plot had been hatched by Aaron Chapman and carried out to perfection. Jesse Alder was the scapegoat for no other reason than the fact he worked for Harry. Even then, before the facts were known, Phoebe knew Jesse may well hang for this. After all a prize cup had been stolen.

"What's happening?" Lucy stood beside Phoebe. "Why would Jesse be taken away like this? He has done no wrong."

Phoebe, twenty-three years of age, turned to the girl and felt a need to mother her. At this moment, Lucy's future hung uncertain: The natural step from courting was marriage and setting up home. In Jesse, she had found herself a man whose apprenticeship would lead to a steady job, and, unbeknown to them both, Harry already had his eye on a cottage which would suit them when married. If Jesse were to be wrongly accused of theft, all their hopes would be dashed.

"I don't know," came Phoebe's honest reply. Some of the thoughts forming in her mind remained jumbled and to voice them could only cause more distress. She began with, "I believe the race cup has been found at the blacksmith's cart or close by."

"Jesse wouldn't take the cup," Lucy stated. "He couldn't have taken it. He was with me all the time."

"All the time?" Phoebe repeated, although she knew the jurats would take little notice of the words coming from a girl with romance on her mind.

"Apart from when a boy came and asked him to look at his master's horse. Jesse said he couldn't find the gentleman or a horse in trouble, so he soon came back."

"A boy asked for him?" Phoebe considered this for a moment. "If someone wanted to make it seem as if Jesse stole the cup, then perhaps they needed to make sure he was taken away from the cart," she suggested. "To make it look as if there was an opportunity."

"Why would they do that?" Lucy's voice rose and tears began to form in her blue eyes. "Who would want to cause harm to a decent man like Jesse?"

Instinctively, Phoebe wrapped her arms around the girl. Her dark hair rested upon Lucy's blonde waves. Their dresses pressed against each other – one of good primrose linen with lace trims, the other of a beige linen threaded with ribbon at the cuffs and neckline. *Aaron did it… he did it because he still hates it that Harry is liked and respected in the village. Aaron resents that I chose Harry as my husband, and he has waited three years to take revenge.* The words screamed in Phoebe's head, yet to Lucy she murmured nothing but, "I don't know. All we can do is wait and see if Jesse is to be accused of theft and, if so, you can be certain Harry will fight for justice on his behalf."

Lucy released herself from Phoebe's embrace, then brushed away her tears. "Thank you. Jesse couldn't wish for a better employer," she said, her words unsteady. She took a deep breath and straightened her back. "It won't come to that. There will be nothing to accuse him of. Everyone knows Jesse is an honest man."

"I pray you are right," Phoebe replied. "We must put our faith in the good sense of Sir Rupert Bannerman."

Walking towards the blacksmith's cart, they became aware that the mood of the spectators had turned sour. Men, who had been happy just an hour beforehand with the prospect of spending money, filling their bellies and enjoying the race, now had a new sport – throwing insults to appease the frustration felt. The final contest of this set was to be delayed. If their day was ruined, then there was only one person to blame: the lad who had stolen the cup and been foolish enough to let it be found. They despised him doubly for he had spoiled the race once by taking the gilded prize, and then again by being stupid enough to allow it to be so easily spotted. Phoebe and Lucy found themselves within a surge of bodies, all closing in on the cart.

Thankfully, they were right to trust Sir Rupert, Leveller of the Marsh Scotts. He stood upon a box, a splendid bewigged man, in a ruffled shirt and burgundy waistcoat, a horse whip held in his hand, but resting upon his breeches. "Stand back," he bellowed. "This is not the sport we have come for today." Then lifting the whip, he pointed it at one man, then another, before continuing, "Do you – or you... do you have anything to tell me relating to the crime? I think not. Go back to the trackside or take refreshments. If anyone thinks they can come here heckling without cause, then my servants will be summoned to ride amongst you and will not hesitate to be free with the whips."

Mutters of discontent flowed through the crowd, but the people knew better than to voice their displeasure. Men and women sidled away, none of them wanting to find themselves at odds with one of the most important figures on the Marsh. Phoebe and Lucy now stood in the emptiness between those gathered at the blacksmith's cart, and those who had retreated. They walked on, Phoebe's hand at the younger woman's elbow.

Jesse sat on a stool, his back hunched, and head lowered. Harry stood to one side, a hand on the shoulder of his friend, the accused man. While the bailiff kept keen eyes on Jesse, the other notables of the area were in deep discussion. Their words flowed unheard by Phoebe, but gestures made their intentions clear as they turned towards the track.

The race must continue, she realised. *Of course it must. There is money to be made today! The Corporation is collecting a fortune as people gamble on the outcome. These people with stalls selling food and drink will make more today than they usually earn in a week or two. There is something about a fair, a travelling show, or a horse race which has people parting with their coins whether they can afford it or not.* Phoebe glanced at Lucy, recalling the money Jesse had earned through selling drop scones. If it were on Jesse's person, then he would be relieved of it by the gaoler. When returned, most likely the money pouch would be lighter for its time spent away from its owner.

"I must speak to Harry," Phoebe murmured to Lucy. She knew she had been spotted walking towards the cart, but Sir Rupert's threats of a whipping did not extend to this lovely young woman whom he both liked and respected.

As she approached, the group of dignitaries parted. Sir Julian led the way back to the stalls and racetrack. Most followed, leaving only Sir Rupert and the bailiff to keep a close eye on the accused man.

Jesse raised his eyes to Phoebe as she neared. She gave the warmest smile she could muster, not daring to speak but wanting to convey her trust in him. Harry looked tired beyond his twenty-three years; he gave a slight shake of his head, showing his belief that the situation was hopeless.

"There will be a purse of coins," Phoebe whispered. "They earned well today, and Jesse's family rely on the shilling he gives them from his wages. He would not want them to suffer for this. If he is taken away from us, then his belongings will be put in safe keeping. I have no faith in them being returned."

Harry nodded his understanding and spoke to the bailiff, "You won't mind if I relieve this man of the coins he carries? They are the earnings taken while working at my cart."

"Do as you wish," Jeremy Parris replied. "The money was earned here, and I want no part of it."

Jesse barely responded as Harry knelt to release the purse from his belt. Phoebe could see it was heavy with coppers. She crouched a little and said, "We'll take care of this and see your family do not go without, but I pray I will be handing it back to you within the hour." A flicker of appreciation showed in Jesse's eyes.

Sir Rupert approached and announced, "This is a shambles. The Corporation are determined not to suffer for the disruption and rightfully so. The race will begin soon. Lord knows who won the last heat – it is over for me, but no doubt someone will know the result." He paused for a moment and surveyed the scene before him, from the defeated man to Harry Farrers and Jeremy Parris, Phoebe and the girl, Lucy, her fair face blotchy and blue eyes heavy with tears. "As this man, Jesse Alder, is Dymchurch born and bred, Sir Julian has left me to watch him."

"Watch him?" Lucy repeated, her voice shrill. Phoebe once more wrapped her arms around the girl.

"Sir?" Harry began, his tone clear and steady. "I am, as you know, the employer of this man and can vouch for his honest nature. Can you tell me what evidence there is that he stole the Whitsun Gallop cup?"

"It was found amongst his belongings."

"But Jesse was working here and had no chance to steal the prize," Harry declared. "I would suggest that someone else placed the cup here – either to retrieve later or in order to see a good man punished for a crime he did not commit."

"Your faith in this man will stand him in good stead," Sir Rupert asserted. "But he was seen lurking by the stalls, not far from where the cup was displayed."

"He was called to see to a horse," Harry insisted. "He told me himself when we spoke at the trackside. If you will excuse me, sir, I believe that is the reason why Jesse left the cart."

"Find me the man who asked he tend a horse, as he may well be able to speak for him at the trial. For the moment, he is no more than a figment of our imagination."

"I cannot find him," Harry retorted. "It was a boy, and I am convinced he had no horse in need of care. He was sent to remove Jesse from the cart; sent, most likely, so Jesse was seen near the cup, making it all the easier to point the finger of blame."

"If Jesse Alder is as honest and well-liked as you declare, then why would someone want to see him in gaol?" Sir Rupert asked, and not without fair reason.

"Perhaps it is not Jesse's good name they wish to slur, but mine?" Harry suggested. "If my employee and friend is seen to have stolen the cup, then I will be in poor favour with the many who have had their sport spoiled for the day."

"This is a talk for us to have in the comfort of my study," Sir Rupert suggested. "For this moment, I can only use the evidence before me. But I have respect for your opinion, as you know. If this man is accused, then come to see me tomorrow and I will spare you as much time as necessary."

"Then can I ask that Jesse returns to Dymchurch in my care?" Harry ventured to ask.

"Were he suspected of taking a shilling, I would be hard-pressed to give my permission. But a prize cup... You know better than to ask."

"I had to try," Harry conceded.

Watching this exchange with interest, Phoebe was struck by the regard afforded to Harry by one of the most influential men on Romney Marsh. She felt a quiet pride in the way her husband spoke with Sir Rupert – he neither cowered before the great man, nor attempted to persuade him to change his views. She saw Harry step away and knew he could do nothing more.

Now they stood in limbo while jurats moved amongst the racegoers, asking questions and seeking the evidence needed to either detain or release Jesse. Lucy flopped on the ground at Jesse's feet, and they allowed her to remain there. Phoebe reached into her reticule and pulled out a fan – it was a day with little breeze.

Not far away, a pistol shot rang out. No one flinched. The horses – winners from the first two sets – took off at a gallop. Now in the final heat, one of their gentleman riders would soon be journeying home with the Whitsun Gallop cup and a generous cash prize. Instinctively, Phoebe turned to watch the horses race the first length for the first of three laps. Even from a distance the drumming of their hooves could be felt through the ground. The horses swung in the direction of the coast, and once more the crowds moved their positions to secure a better view.

Phoebe noted that the lone figure of the man still stood high on a sandhill. It was a prime position to view the race, yet it seemed his interest lingered on the crowd. Her attention turned to someone moving away from the trackside. This person was grasping a boy whom he pushed forward by the scruff of his neck. The moment she recognised this swaggering figure, Phoebe knew Jesse's fate was sealed.

Chapter Three
Harry

The purse of coins pressed against Harry's thigh – an uncomfortable reminder that despite the words of reassurance he offered Jesse, there were doubts his innocence would be proved that day. He resumed standing with his hand on the shoulder of the accused and remained there while Lucy sat on the dry grass at the feet of her beloved.

For the spectators who had journeyed from the nearby towns of Lydd, New Romney and Hythe, or from the numerous villages set amongst the pastureland and winding drainage ditches, the race continued as before. These men and women were expecting a well-deserved reprieve from the tedium of their lives – they were determined to be both entertained and well-fed. Harry gazed across the ragged lines of onlookers. His eyes followed the line of the track, then moved to the lone figure who watched from a sandhill within the circuit of the racecourse.

While he observed the scene, other images flashed before him: Jesse tending the cart, grateful for the opportunity; Lucy in her best dress and with a slight flush of excitement to her cheeks; an unknown boy, scruffy and desperate, luring Jesse from the stall; Aaron taking his chance to humiliate Harry at a public event.

'Whoever took the cup was a wily fellow, wouldn't you say? As fast as a whippet and someone who would attract no attention while he lingered amongst us and made his plans'. Aaron's words leapt into Harry's mind. He had lost no time in approaching and suggesting that Harry may know something about the offence. In doing so Aaron had betrayed his own involvement. 'As fast as a whippet and someone who would attract no attention while he lingered amongst us'. When he said those words, he described himself! Proving it is a different matter. In fact, even if Sir Rupert Bannerman, Leveller of the Marsh Scotts, were to know of this, he would turn away and deny it. He's not a man to stir up trouble amongst the landowners.

In the four years since Harry had come to Dymchurch, his fortunes had changed from being a lowly labourer upon that great seawall of hawthorn faggots and clay-earth, to being well-liked and respected. He had married the gentlest woman in Dymchurch and played a part in the scheme to reunite her with her father who lived across the sea in Wissant. To his surprise, Harry had been offered the position of jurat, and was now one of a team of men who oversaw the rhythm of draining the low-lying countryside and ensuring that the incoming tide stayed on its side of the wall, as well as being called upon to act as juror when needed by Sir Rupert. Life in Dymchurch was good for Harry, despite him never quite feeling at ease after dusk, when the gentle slap of the tide upon the wall carried on the night air, and it seemed that the simple village folk would lurk about the place for no good reason.

Just as life had taken good turns for Harry since he had arrived in Dymchurch, so had Aaron Chapman, his adversary since those early days, gone up in the world. Already the son of a minor landowner, with a fine home on the road leading out to St Mary in the Marsh, Aaron had inherited large tracts of land near Burmarsh and was in the process of modernising an imposing house from where he would look out upon his acres. He too had been bestowed with the title of jurat, and he too had married. Here we come to the crux of the bitterness directed at Harry – this young landowner had set his sights set on the beautiful Phoebe. Most likely he would never have married her, for she came with no fortune, but Aaron would have liked to make that decision for himself. Instead, Phoebe had at first spurned him, and later shown a preference for Harry.

Shaking himself a little, Harry returned to the present and spotted the person who had been at the forefront of his mind. Swaggering along, while grasping a lad by the scruff of the neck, Aaron was stepping free of the trackside crowds and heading towards the farrier's cart. Those standing around Jesse, waiting for the next part of the drama to unfold, watched every step in silence as the man and boy approached.

"This is the lad you were wanting to see," Aaron announced to Sir Rupert, before running his gaze over the assembled group. There was a clear sense of triumph in his words and his eyes gleamed. He prodded the boy, causing his scrawny frame to lurch forward slightly.

With no further prompting, words gushed from the boy: "I seen him looking about the stands where the posh folk sit, and he had his eye on the gold cup – I'll swear he did!" He looked to Aaron, as if seeking approval.

"What's your name?" Sir Rupert asked.

"Toke," the lad piped up. "Toke Browne from Burmarsh, sir."

"Well, Toke Browne from Burmarsh – what's your father's trade?"

The boy considered this for a moment, while his eyes darted about from one person to another. "I don't know about trade, sir, but he does a bit of digging out the ditches and he keeps the hedges nice and tidy so there's plenty of wood for the seawall. And in the summer, he's busy fetching clay for the wall."

"So, he's a true Marshman!" Sir Rupert concluded.

"He is! He is!" Toke beamed. What a glorious moment it was! First, there was the shilling tucked tight into his fist, and a promise of more if he pleased Mr Chapman. Then there was this grand man smiling down at him and taking such an interest.

"And you... you help your father?" Sir Rupert enquired.

"I do! I finished with my schooling a year ago, and I'm a hard worker. If I come home a bit mucky, then it's from an honest day's work."

"Young Toke, we have established you are from a local family and a hard worker," Sir Rupert said, "Now tell us more. You said you saw someone looking at the prize cup. Can you see that man now?"

"I can! I sees him there!" Toke Browne pointed a grubby finger towards Jesse. "It was him, sir!"

"But did you actually see him take the cup? There is no crime in looking, is there?"

"Of course not." Toke bowed his head a little to show his respect, then elaborated, "I saw him running off with a sack of something in his hand."

Sir Rupert and the bailiff glanced towards a piece of discarded hessian resting against the wheel of the farrier's cart. Harry and Aaron followed their gaze, both knowing this was the sacking in which the gilded cup had been nestling when it was found.

At that moment, a roar of applause erupted from the crowd.

"The race is won!" Jeremy Parris declared unnecessarily.

"The whole day is a shambles, and Dymchurch will be to blame for it," Sir Rupert complained, sounding more like a petulant child than a mature man in his fortieth year.

"Not Dymchurch, sir," Harry interjected. "And certainly not yourself. Look towards the stands – there is a handful of jurats missing, but most people are enjoying the day as they always do. The weather is fine, and the horses have run without incident."

"You're a sensible man, Harry Farrers," Sir Rupert boomed. "I always thought it, although others said otherwise. It's a shambles right here, nonetheless, and I have no choice now but to order that this man, Jesse Alder, be taken to the New Romney gaol."

"New Romney?" A horrified squeal came from Lucy's lips, and fresh tears began to well in her beautiful eyes.

"The offence happened on Romney land," Sir Rupert confirmed. "Sir Julian Craythorne would have sharp words to say if this man were returned to Dymchurch while his back was turned."

Harry said nothing more. They would have to wait now for the cogs of the law to slowly turn as evidence was gathered. Sir Rupert had already suggested Harry call upon him tomorrow and he hoped that in the privacy of the study at the New Hall, the matter could be discussed openly.

"If you want to remain here, then I will accompany the accused to gaol," the bailiff proposed.

"Thank you, Mr Parris." Sir Rupert glanced towards his family who were amongst the gentry now milling about by the stalls. "I believe my servants have brought a fine feast, and the children will be eager to tuck in. It will take no time to deal with this nasty business in the town, so do join us on your return."

"I will do that and be glad of it!" Jeremy Parris replied.

Harry listened to this exchange, his hand still resting on the shoulder of a man he knew to be honest and trustworthy. Jesse had uttered nothing since hearing that his fate was sealed, and Romney gaol beckoned him to its chilly depths. Harry looked over to where the wealthy of Romney Marsh gathered and saw servants setting up trestle tables. Before long, these would be covered in cloths of starched linen, topped with dishes of cold meats, pies, pickled vegetables and fresh salad. Servants prepared to uncork wine, and the good man, sitting in the gaol with his bowl of gruel, would be forgotten as Sir Rupert's and Sir Julian's families feasted and spoke of the next race to come.

"I'll walk with you to the town," Harry said to Jesse.

"Thank you, but no," Jesse responded without hesitation. "Stay with the women. Take care of Lucy for me."

Harry nodded his agreement. It was what he would wish for if parted from Phoebe.

No idle chatter flowed between the three defeated characters who walked back to Dymchurch. Harry led the horse who in turn pulled the cart which on this return journey was all the lighter for the fire cage being left to cool and await collection the next day. The women walked together, sometimes at the rear of the cart and sometimes beside the horse. The road from New Romney to Dymchurch was generally in good repair and wide enough for two carts to pass with ease. It gradually neared the coast, finally meeting the beginning of the seawall, and continued alongside this impressive defence that stretched for a couple of miles until it met the shingle banks near Hythe.

The seawall was a wide and solid bank. At its core there stood a frame of oak stakes and pressed between them were bundles of whippy blackthorn branches. This was covered with clay soil brought from the land to the north of Dymchurch and pressed into the structure. The task of maintaining the wall was ongoing, involving a team of labourers all year round. But today all was quiet along its length, and unseen to Harry, Phoebe and Lucy, the tide rolled lazily towards the upper reaches of the sandy beach. On another day, they might be tempted to scramble up the bank and take in the view of the bay, but all they thought of was Jesse and their concerns that his innocence could not be proven.

The cottages, shops and taverns of Dymchurch began to take shape before them, and soon they were approaching the farrier's. All was peaceful in the village. Even the collection of men gathered on benches outside the Ocean Inn supped quietly on their tankards of ale as they turned to see Harry guiding the horse into the yard behind his workshop.

"The talk will start now," Lucy muttered.

"It can't be avoided," Phoebe replied. "I'll walk you back home."

"Thank you," Lucy replied, then she turned to Harry, "I know you'll do everything you can to help Jesse, and all I can do is pray that Sir Julian and Sir Rupert find the true thief."

"I'll go to talk to Sir Rupert in the morning," Harry told her. "Come and see me or Phoebe whenever you need to."

Lucy attempted to smile her gratitude. The women continued, passing a junction which gave the option of heading into the open countryside or continuing towards the row of low cottages where Lucy lived with her family. Harry, resting his hand on the horse's shoulder, watched them depart before removing the harness and leading his faithful little steed to its paddock. He pushed the cart into a covered shelter and, out of habit, entered the forge building from the rear, casting his eye about the place, just to be sure everything was in order.

The only light came from the open back door and filtered through the gaps in shuttered windows. Had he been working the double doors would be flung open to the front and the shutters swung back. The heat would have been almost unbearable. Even now the space was stuffy – the air thick with the slightly sweet aroma of metal and the pleasing scent of burned wood. All day long, he and Jesse took every opportunity to step through those open doors and to breath in the fresh sea air. From here they could look across to the Ocean Inn and the grocery shop, then to the seawall beyond. The forge was the last building people would pass as they left Dymchurch on the road to New Romney. An ideal position to watch the comings and goings of local people and visitors.

However, Harry had no plans to work, and it seemed unlikely Jesse would join him that week. He didn't open the double doors but retraced his steps to the yard and back to the High Street. From here he intended to walk home but found himself drawn towards a wooden cottage sheltered behind the hulk of the seawall. Bess and Owen Bates lived here – a couple who had taken him into their home four years previously and were as close to Harry as his own family had once been. As he entered through the open doorway, it was of no surprise that Phoebe had arrived there ahead of him. They both relied upon the older couple's advice and affection during challenging times.

"Come in, lad," Owen beckoned, as Harry knew he would. "Sit yourself down. I've heard the beginning of this sorry tale and I can't say it makes much sense to me."

The longest day of the year neared, and the sun rose early over the top of the Dymchurch Wall. Already the labourers would be walking the lanes and tracks to make an early start on the inevitable maintenance needed on the great bank or knockes while the tide was low. The early morning light settled upon the orange tiles and bricks at the front of a modest, but well-constructed house not far from the church.

In the bedroom, the curtains remained closed, but the light seeped through as Phoebe sat in a chair and pulled on her stockings. "I thought you were going to see Sir Rupert?" she queried.

Harry was fastening his rough breeches and already had a soiled waistcoat to hand, although his shirt came fresh from the clothes press. "Sir Rupert doesn't breakfast until nine o'clock, and will not be in his study before ten," he pointed out. "By then I shall have journeyed to the racecourse, returned *and* eaten a second breakfast. I'll ask Janey to save me some porridge and be ready to present myself at the front door of the New Hall by the time the clock in his entrance hall is chiming half-past ten.

"I knew you would have it all planned." Phoebe gave a brief smile, but her dark eyes remained solemn. She stood, allowing her light summer dress to fall to her ankles.

Harry kissed her lightly. "I'm going to take a piece of bread and a slice of cold ham, then I'll be gone." He stepped towards the door, but paused, his fingers on the handle while he considered his next words. "Are you worried about Jesse... and Lucy?"

"I am..." she replied. "I'm more concerned about them than anything else. It seems wrong to even think of my own problems..." She looked towards a small bag containing the rags used when she suffered her monthly bleed.

Harry stepped towards his wife once more and put his arm around her, showing his affection whilst being careful to keep a distance between his waistcoat and the pleated bodice of her dress. He said nothing, knowing it wasn't his place to advise her, and unable to express his own disappointment that after three years of marriage they had not been blessed with a child. Phoebe had no mother to confide in, and Aunt Peggy was too full of her own opinions. *I expect she speaks to Bess about these things,* Harry reflected as he walked down the stairs. *Perhaps there is something to be done, a remedy... or perhaps it is a case of waiting?*

Before long, Harry was leaving by the front door and walking down the short path to the road. He glanced up and down, taking in the Norman church and larger properties to his left, and the mixture of terraces and cottages to the right. Having nodded to the butcher's lad, he set off towards the forge at a good pace, his leather bag containing the early morning snack and a flask of small ale.

The horse was soon secured to the cart and Harry led it out of the yard. They turned towards New Romney, once more taking the coast road. The beast needed little encouragement, and Harry became lost in his thoughts. His gaze followed the line of the seawall and he wished he could stride along the top of it, taking in the view across the sea and along the crescent of the bay. Nothing could wash away the difficulties ahead of him this day, but for a while he would feel the tension ease. The Dymchurch Wall was wide enough for a cart, but it hardly seemed fair on the labourers to have to move aside for him when there was a decent road for his use, so the chestnut horse and his owner ambled along on the lower ground.

Few travellers were using the road, but once Romney Warren came into sight it became clear that he was not the first to make use of the cooler hours of the morning. Men who laboured for The Corporation were taking down staging used for the dignitaries, then lifting the wooden planks and benches onto low-sided wagons. Some of them turned to watch Harry's arrival, but their minds were most likely on returning to New Romney and filling their grumbling stomachs with a hearty breakfast.

After running his eyes over the metal basket where yesterday's fire had burned and prodding at the embers with a poker to ensure none were still glowing, Harry recalled a conversation with Phoebe the previous evening. "That man who tends the rabbit traps – he was there watching," she had said. "Did you see him, standing up on the sandhill? He had a good view." She was right and whereas all the other spectators had been crowding in upon each other from the outside of the track, the keeper had stood alone within the circuit of the racecourse, looking towards them. Harry had seen him at the time and considered him to have the best view of the track, but the with the subsequent drama unfolding the lone observer had slipped from his mind.

"He's a foolish fellow," Harry murmured to himself, "But perhaps he saw something of interest."

The remains of the fire would come to no harm if left a little longer, so Harry headed towards the sandhills.

Once he had passed the racetrack, he kept a sharp eye on the coarse grass where the traps were set. From them New Romney was supplied with a steady flow of rabbit meat. To have his own foot snared would be both painful and an inconvenience at a time when releasing Jesse from the gaol was of utmost importance.

There had been no reason for Harry to ever venture upon the Warren, but it was known that the keeper lived in a home crafted from the upturned hull of a boat, which in turn lay buried within a sandhill. The place was reported to be well-hidden, and it was said that the keeper lived a solitary life, only venturing to the town to sell the rabbits and to buy his own provisions.

With some curiosity, Harry took a zigzag route until he came across the person he sought. Seated almost on the ground, on a low bench, a dark-haired man was snatching greedily at bread and dripping. As he ate, pieces of bread fell away, dropping into his lap from where they were swiftly picked up and rammed back into his wide mouth. He was so absorbed with his breakfast that at first Harry went unnoticed, but then he turned and gave a grin which led to more crumbs falling.

"Good morning. Sorry to disturb you," Harry began. "I'm Harry Farrers of Dymchurch. I was at the race yesterday and wondered if you could help me... there was a theft, you see..." At this Harry let his words trail away.

The keeper began nodding frantically and laughing, and it dawned on Harry that this young man could not speak. Some noises were uttered, but none that could be deciphered. Yet, just as Harry despaired of how he could determine if the keeper had witnessed the crime, the man jumped up, knocking back the bench he had been seated upon.

Now he raced back and forth, turning sharply in the sandy ground and reaching out as if to grab an imaginary object. He paused, his large eyes darting to and fro, then tucked the make-believe item – presumably the gilded cup – under his arm and ran off across the sandhills. Harry could only watch and wait for him to return. "You saw the thief?" he asked at the first opportunity. But the man merely stood there, his eyes shining and a huge grin on his face.

Chapter Four
Phoebe

Whereas Harry usually stayed within the confines of his forge, occasionally venturing out to farms and cottages nearby, Phoebe frequently walked between Dymchurch and the outskirts of New Romney. She carried a flat-bottomed basket and, cushioned between some worn rags, were jars of honey. Sometimes there was a clay flagon of fortified wine, or bottled fruit, but she always took the honey.

On this day, while her husband stood watching the rabbit keeper, Phoebe moved with ease from the village road, passing along pathways which trailed between cottages sitting snug beneath the seawall, then up the bank and onto the wall itself. Here she walked at a brisk pace, offering a friendly greeting here and now, while appreciating the clear view to the Dungeness Point ahead of her and, if she turned back, to Hythe behind her.

Strolling along the top until reaching Wall End always filled Phoebe with happiness. She gained so much pleasure simply looking out to sea, watching the fishing boats and searching for those distant hills of France. Her beloved father and other family members lived in Wissant, a small town which she and Harry visited every summer, despite her suffering from seasickness for hour after hour as they crossed the Channel.

Today there was little wind, and already the sun's warmth gently penetrated her bare forearms. She carried a straw bonnet, its ribbons trailing down the tiers of her skirt. Soon it would cover her dark hair as the heat of the day became uncomfortable. If the breeze was brisk, as it so often was, she happily accepted it whipping around her. If combined with rain or a bitter chill, then Phoebe took the road, appreciating the protection given by the Dymchurch Wall.

Before long, the seawall ended as a manmade structure and continued as a natural barrier. She took a sloping track, dusty with dry clay soil, and smiled to see Harry approaching. *Perhaps he has some news already. A good man like Jesse should never have been taken to gaol. He's bound to be freed by the end of the day, and this will all be forgotten.* Phoebe picked up her pace, certain that even at this early hour, there would be some words to bring hope.

"I went to see the keeper..." Harry launched straight into his account. "He can't speak – did you know?"

"I've only ever seen him in the distance, and no one has said... no one has mentioned him at the pest house." Phoebe referred to her destination – the imposing brick house on the main road, so close to the rabbit colony that it was formally known as Warren House.

"He was cheerful enough," Harry declared, "and appeared to understand what I asked of him because he put on a show for me. I am certain he saw the theft and I will speak to Sir Rupert as soon as the horse is stabled."

"A show?" Phoebe asked.

"Snatching at the imaginary cup and running off with it," Harry elaborated. "It won't be easy but there must be a way of finding out what he saw."

"There must be," Phoebe agreed. "I'll tell Lucy after I've been to Warren House. Good luck and see you soon." She raised herself onto her toes and kissed Harry lightly on the lips. "Farewell."

Soon the pest house was ahead, and Phoebe glanced at the contents of her basket, knowing it would be appreciated. Her involvement with the house for people suffering with infectious diseases began when a close friend was admitted there two years previously. Ellen had been the first in her family to suffer a fever and no sooner than the pocks began to appear on her skin, she was moved with haste to Warren House. Within the week her younger brother had joined her in one of two upstairs rooms, where windows could be flung open to the front and side to allow the bad air to be blown out by the coastal winds.

Ellen was among the lucky ones. One of the few survivors. *If only there was something that could be done about it,* Phoebe thought as she pictured her dear friend's face, now so badly marked. *At least she had regained her strength, and John continued to love her.* Ellen, as fair as Phoebe was dark, had gone on to marry her sweetheart and was the mother to a little boy.

She had spent three weeks in Warren House – shivering under thin blankets and enduring the blood-letting from her weak body. Once her pocks were fully dried out, Ellen was able to return home, and Phoebe saddened by the misery caused by the illness, resolved to do something to offer comfort to those experiencing the despair of contagious diseases. Unable to nurse the patients or do anything which would bring her into contact with the bad air or fluids emitted from those who were sick, Phoebe tended her beehives with extra vigour and offered soothing honey to the hospital. As a balm it was known to reduce the risk of infection in the sores, and in a drink it soothed the throat. The sugary content offered much-needed energy for those in a weakened state.

Before reaching the front door, Phoebe took a path towards the rear of the building. Glancing up at the window of one of the upstairs rooms, she wondered how many poor souls lay on the thin mattresses and for their sakes hoped for a warm breeze to be drifting through the open window. There was a movement as a nurse went to stand at the opening for a moment, and they acknowledged each other with a slight nod. Then as Phoebe rounded the corner of the house and approached the back door, she instinctively raised her summer shawl and held it firmly to cover her nose and mouth.

She never entered that cluster of kitchen, stores and scullery all set under the lowest point of the catslide roof or ventured too close to the collection of brick outbuildings. Who knew what may be lingering in the corners where the salty sea air had not swept through? There was always a maid, nun or nurse on hand to take the honey, and if not, then it would be found soon enough if left on the bench in the sheltered area where herbs were grown.

With a welcoming smile, one of the nuns greeted her – a round-faced woman with fair curls straying from her wimple. How this woman remained pock-free was a wonder to Phoebe. *Perhaps her prayers to St Nicaise are heard?*

"Good morning!" The nun kept a respectful distance. "I thank the Lord when I see you coming with your sweet nectar. On some days it must be the only pleasure to be had for those unfortunate enough to be here."

"I wish I could do more," Phoebe admitted. "But to spread the disease back to my home would be unforgiveable."

"It would." The nun nodded, and the rogue ringlets bobbed about.

"Do they… the sick… do they fare as well as you can wish for?"

"We feel hopeful all seven here will survive. None of them are aged, and that gives us hope. Robin West of Old Romney will be buried tomorrow – he passed to the good Lord on Sunday. Remember him in your prayers, will you?"

"I will," Phoebe confirmed. "I pray for both the sick and you dear nurses." She glanced towards the ridge of the tiled roof, knowing that one of the nurses would be sleeping in the stuffy attic room, having tended the ill through the night. Then passing the two jars to the nun, she continued, "I must make haste to Dymchurch. There was trouble at the racecourse yesterday, and Harry's young assistant is in New Romney gaol for a crime he did not commit. His family need our support."

"Then my prayers will be with them," the nun responded. "We sensed there was unease."

"Thank you, sister. I'll return in a few days," Phoebe smiled and stepped away, finding a path between pots of healing flowers and herbs. Before picking up her pace, she glanced back at the building. There was something reassuring about the way it stood solid and upright in its lonely spot.

The walk back to Dymchurch was pleasant and Phoebe allowed her thoughts to flit between the annual journey to Wissant and Harry's meeting with Sir Rupert. *But if this business with Jesse is not resolved, then Harry will be needed here.* As she scampered up the bank to join the seawall track, the fishermen were preparing to take the boats out. The small vessels were pulled up on the shingle bank at Wall End, awaiting the tide. Brothers,

Walter and Joshua, turned as they noted movement on the wall, and Phoebe waved to them. These were the men who took her to Wissant and back on Walter's boat *Louisa Ann* – for long hours she would sit hunched in the bow while waves of seasickness engulfed her – then all would be well when she arrived in the town of her father's birth. *I will go on my own if that is the way it must be.* Mild mannered and gentle, Phoebe had a determination to see her family every year and an adventurous streak which was not often apparent.

With the basket swinging at her side, she continued along the wall. *Harry will have met with Sir Rupert by now. At least I hope so. Will Sir Rupert have ordered for his horse to be saddled and be preparing to ride to New Romney?* She scanned both the seawall track and the road, but there was no sign of the Leveller of the Marsh Scotts sitting astride his bay gelding. *He will have to make plans,* she reminded herself, *perhaps discuss the matter with someone else. Maybe the tide will reach the top of the sands before he is ready.* Phoebe turned to look behind her and saw the small collection of fishing boats were being pushed towards the sand, gliding on wooden skids, and awaiting the tide which would carry them out as it retreated. *It will be a while before Sir Rupert sets out,* she told herself.

The day was already warm, and the breeze slight. With her straw hat now pressed down on her dark hair, Phoebe's thoughts once again returned to her family in Wissant, as she watched the team of men labouring on the seawall. They were re-enforcing the wooden uprights on one of the knockes – a structure extending from the wall and down the beach. *Before the fishing boats have launched, these men will be withdrawing.* Phoebe knew the pattern of Dymchurch life as well as she knew the cycles of her own body.

The cycles of her body – if there was one sadness within her, it was that after three years of marriage Phoebe had not yet been blessed with a child. Her monthly bleed was as predictable as the waxing and waning of the moon. Only that morning, she had placed yesterday's soiled rags in a bowl of warm water and grated a little lye soap, watching it fall and mingle with the folds of linen. On her return, she would agitate them with a wooden paddle, then ensure they were well-rinsed.

Phoebe was almost, but not quite, resigned to her childless state. She cradled Ellen's son in her arms and remarked over his growth and progress from early smiles to eating his first solids. Then she congratulated her friend upon the announcement that a second child was due to be born less than a year after the first. "It is too soon," Ellen had said over and over. "How will I cope?" But as the months passed, and her friend's body expanded, Phoebe had none of her own news to share. Ellen stopped complaining about the child keeping her awake as it twisted and turned through the night, or the fact that a vein in one leg had become prominent and throbbed.

The impending birth played on Phoebe's mind as she took the track from the seawall past the Ocean Inn. With the forge opposite, she glanced up and down the road before crossing. Ellen could be seen balancing her son on one hip and holding a basket against the other. She passed through the open doorway into William Parris' grocery store. *I should go and help her,* Phoebe thought. *No, I must think of Lucy and Jesse today.* As she turned off the main road and into the yard behind the forge, there was a tinge of guilt in knowing that she was glad of the excuse to shy away from the expectant mother and her child.

Other than the horse shuffling about in her stall, all was quiet. Phoebe pressed on the back door of the forge, and peered in. There was no sign of Harry being there recently. *He will be with Sir Rupert.* She left and set off along the street, passing a couple of shops within a terraced row before turning into one of them.

"Here she is – just when I thought me poor legs couldn't stand for another moment!" Came the greeting from Aunt Peggy. "Your uncle has been off on business all morning and left me here on me own. I don't know where Anne has got to – we haven't found anyone reliable since you went off and left us."

Phoebe couldn't help smiling to hear the well-worn complaints. Nothing had made Aunt Peggy and Uncle Giles prouder than the moment when she had married Harry in the small parish church. In leaving the daily drudge of working in their village store and being at their beck and call, she had married a man who had recently come into wealth and was using this for the good of the village in creating a new school. All recollection of any previous distaste towards Harry on the part of her aunt and uncle had been brushed aside along with the spilt flour, oats and mice droppings on the brick floor of the shop.

"Anne's sister has dysentery," Phoebe reminded Peggy. "She is wise to stay away, and we must pray that the poor girl doesn't succumb."

"So she has," Peggy admitted. "Well, it doesn't help me get the sacks from the store or reach the jars from up there." She nodded towards the highest shelf behind the counter and the nearby stepladder.

"I'll make a pot of tea," Phoebe suggested. "And when it's brewed you can sit down and rest your legs for a short time, but I can't stay long because I need to find Harry. You've heard about the trouble with Jesse, I suppose. He needs our help."

"A pot of tea!" Peggy winked. "I don't know what's got into you nowadays. Do you think impoverished shop keepers can afford to keep a caddy full of tealeaves from foreign lands?"

Phoebe smiled as she slipped behind the counter, through the dusty hallway and into the kitchen. Her aunt's words drifted behind her: "Now if you'd married Aaron Chapman like your uncle and I hoped for, you'd be drinking tea all day long and warming yourself with a nice French brandy in the evening…"

This was followed by the scrape of Peggy's stool on the floor, and then its knocking against the shelving. A customer must have entered the shop, for now her voice could be heard as friendly and obliging, while food was weighed and wrapped, and coins taken. A moment later, when the precious tealeaves were brewing, and the caddy hidden behind the dishes in the dresser, Peggy shuffled through. She slumped in a low, cushioned chair.

"I'll mind the shop," Phoebe suggested. "But I can't stay for long – we have to do what we can for Jesse."

"Your uncle always said the lad was a bit shifty," Peggy observed.

"Oh, he never said such a thing!" Phoebe couldn't help laughing. "Jesse is nothing but hardworking and honest. He'll be out of gaol by the end of the day. Harry is with Sir Rupert now, and it will soon be resolved." She took an apron from behind the kitchen door and moved through to the shop. "Don't go falling asleep. I'll only wake you, and it will put you out of sorts."

It was mid-morning, and a steady flow of customers came through the open shop door. Having cast aside their winter shawls and heavy boots, and with the sea breeze nothing more than a whisper on this late spring day, there was a cheery atmosphere. Each one of them stood a little taller and their skin was less weather-beaten than a couple of months previously. Casual greetings and a brief exchange of news flowed between the women as they stepped forwards in the queue while scanning shelves and barrels for anything new or offering a good deal.

This moment, back in her old place behind the counter, offered Phoebe a respite from her worries. She enjoyed the familiarity of the heavy wooden shelves with their variety of jars and packets, the fresh food in baskets, and even the dust which hung in the air as flour and grain were scooped and weighed. The light was dim, filtering through thick squares of glass, which were decked with the many posters Uncle Giles made and propped up against the windows to tempt the customers.

"The boy will deliver it this afternoon," Phoebe was saying to a maid from Sycamore Farm when her aunt returned, still muttering about the lack of a girl to help that morning.

"You'll be off now," Peggy grumbled.

"I'll be off now," Phoebe confirmed. "I'm going to see Lucy." She moved through the tight gap in the counter wondering, and not for the first time, how her aunt managed to manipulate her fulsome body through the space.

"Any news?" Peggy asked, her voice a little high, almost eager.

Knowing what her aunt referred to – she made the same enquiry every four weeks and had been doing so for the past couple of years – Phoebe forced a smile, and replied, "No news."

Chapter Five
Harry

The half-hour spent closeted in Sir Rupert's study had been amicable, with both men seated in leather armchairs and savouring coffee served by the housemaid.

"It's a damned awkward business," Sir Rupert concluded. "I'll vouch for Jesse Alder's good name alongside you, but to lay the blame at the feet of another Dymchurch man – and he both a respected landowner and jurat – well, I don't see how it can be done."

"Wealthy landowner and jurat," Harry dared to correct the Leveller of the Marsh Scotts. "I'd say most would admit that Aaron Chapman is a devious man, out for his own good not that of Dymchurch, or the Marsh."

"They can say or think what they like," Sir Rupert responded. "There's not one man who would want to cross him. People prefer to keep quiet and turn their backs."

"Or they might find themselves incriminated for something they did not do?" Harry countered. "Such as stealing a gilded cup?"

And so the conversation flowed, with Harry gently suggesting Aaron had somehow removed the cup – or most likely rewarded someone else for achieving this dangerous and difficult task – and Sir Rupert insisting that a jurat of Romney March could not be accused of such a thing unless the evidence was compelling.

"If there's no evidence to connect Aaron," Harry suggested, "then we can at least try to prove Jesse's innocence. He will hang for this within the week if nothing is done to help him."

"There's no doubt about it," Sir Rupert agreed. "And with Sir Julian Craythorne as head magistrate, I can do no more than speak up for Jesse as being an honest law-abiding man of Dymchurch, just as you will. Neither of us will be on the jury."

"Can we also ask that Aaron Chapman is not on the jury?" Harry enquired.

"Yes, I can deal with that." Sir Rupert's words were abrupt as he stood and stepped towards the door, opening it to call his footman. "Brown! Ask that my horse is saddled, and the grey mare readied for Harry Farrers. We are to make haste to New Romney." Then he turned to face Harry, "Let us find this keeper at the Warren. I would like to know if I can make any sense of what he saw that day. He was, as you say, at an advantage on his sandhill looking over us all."

Sir Rupert never allowed himself to be rushed into anything. The talk of the last half-hour could have easily been completed within ten minutes, and within five of those a call made for the horses to be saddled. It was with some relief that Harry rose from the comfort of the armchair. "Thank you, sir."

"Blazes!" Sir Rupert exclaimed. "I really don't want a good man to hang. It would make me most uneasy." He strode from the room muttering something about needing his riding boots while calling for Brown who was most likely still in the stable yard.

Before long, both men were astride the horses and heading for the Dymchurch Wall, which they deftly ascended. Once on top of the seawall they pressed with their heels and both beasts broke into a brisk trot. Passing the length of the village with ease, Sir Rupert and Harry reached High Knocke before allowing the horses to slow to a walk.

Labourers who worked long hours repairing the blackthorn and clay bank, or strengthening the knockes, were retreating from the incoming tide. They spilled onto the top of the wall but swiftly stepped out of the way of the horses and their riders. Harry raised his hand in acknowledgment or nodded a greeting to many of the men. This was John Waller's team who worked the last stretch to Wall End, all of whom Harry knew well. He had toiled alongside them for six months as a penance, when wrongly accused of theft the day after he arrived in Dymchurch, and continued in the role for a further two months by choice.

At Wall End, Sir Rupert and Harry joined the road to Romney. Once more they prompted the horses to trot and when Warren House came into view, they began to search for a track through the sandhills which lay between the road and coast. Aware of the rabbit keeper's traps, the safety of the horses was utmost and once a wide track was found, the men dismounted. When they came across a secure upright pole, the horses were tethered and left to graze. Walking on, the men focussed on searching the rough ground with every step and little conversation flowed between them.

Uncertain as to where the keeper lived, Harry's brow creased with a frown. "There are no landmarks," he muttered. "We'll come across him with no warning. He was outside his home earlier, but now he could be anywhere – who knows how many rabbits were snared in the night, and the keeper will need to find them before the foxes do."

However, it was not the keeper they came across, but two others - a couple of men between thirty and forty years of age, both dressed in breeches of brown hemp, and the beige linen shirts so often worn by farm labourers or those who worked in a trade. The scarves at their necks were loose, for the heat of the day was reaching its peak, and their skin glistened.

The look of surprise on their faces was clear as they spotted Sir Rupert and Harry, and relief expressed in their voices. "Sir!" the taller of the two exclaimed. "How did you know?"

"Know?" Sir Rupert replied.

"The keeper is dead!" the second informed. "And only just, it seems."

"Dead?" the word exploded from Sir Rupert's lips. "But we had come to see him!"

Dead! The word ricocheted in Harry's mind. *Dead! But I only saw him... it must have been less than two hours ago...*

"By what means?" The boom of Sir Rupert's words interrupted Harry's thoughts.

"Bludgeoned," came the brief reply.

"For what reason?" Harry almost whispered. "What trouble did he cause to anyone living here in the dunes?" No one responded. He didn't expect them to.

"We covered him up," the taller man offered, as they began to lead the way to the body. "It seemed only right,"

They were taken to the keeper's home, where outside on the sandy ground the bulk of a large man lay covered in a rough blanket. Sir Rupert hooked part of the cloth on the tip of his riding crop and pushed it aside to reveal a bloodied shoulder and the back of a head. "Attacked from behind," he declared. "Murdered by a coward!"

Harry had seen enough. Without doubt, this was the man he had seen earlier, and he was certainly dead. The blanket fell back on the body, scattering flies. In the heat of the day, the bloodstains had dulled, and the pool of blood soaking into the sand surface was already congealing.

The keeper's humble home had no wooden door, merely a curtain covering the entrance. Curious to learn more about the man, Harry stepped towards it and tugged at the material. The place was hidden, almost fully, by the sandhill covering it, complete with tufts of withered grass to the top and sides. Once the curtain had been pulled back, it took a moment for Harry's eyes to become accustomed to the windowless hovel. He saw that it was, as rumour told, the upturned hull of a boat with roof beams curving down to the ground and the darkest depths of the one-roomed home being the point of the bow. The floor consisted of sand, with matting of rushes, and the bed was made of a low wooden frame covered with a tumble of blankets. It appeared that any personal belongings were stored in an open trunk. The tools of the keeper's trade – traps, knives and rope – hung from hooks on the wall.

Turning away from the spartan scene and back towards the sunlight, the men and the body, Harry realised he had been holding his breath. He took a great gasp of fresh air. It filled his lungs, calming him for a moment.

"It looks like this is the weapon," one of the men was saying as he kicked at a stout pole.

"There's no doubt of it!" Sir Rupert proclaimed. "Leave it there. Someone will come from the town to take notes of the scene, and the body must be removed. It will be a pauper's grave, I assume."

He is so abrupt… so practical… Harry pondered. *I can't help liking the man, but I am sure he hasn't realised the repercussions. Our witness is dead. How can I go to Jesse – if they allow me to see him – and tell him that I had been so careless as to find help, only to go and lose it?* He was about to turn away when he became aware of Sir Rupert speaking to him.

"Harry – we must make haste to New Romney and report this to the constable. Or rather you could do it, as I need to speak with Sir Julian Craythorne about the matter of our imprisoned friend." Sir Rupert began to stride away, seeming to suddenly recall the rabbit snares, for he stopped abruptly and scanned the ground before continuing, "Take the details of these men." He then proceeded at a slower pace.

"Of course." With his mind full of Jesse in the miserable cell, Harry tried to focus on the matter in hand. "Are you from New Romney?" he asked the men as they followed Sir Rupert.

"We're cousins and neighbours from North Street," the shorter of the two replied.

"North Street." Harry repeated, hoping to embed the information in his troubled mind.

"Just ask anyone for John and Bob Wright and they will point you in the right direction," the taller one continued. "The Rose and Crown or the New Inn, most likely!" He gave a snort of laughter.

"Thank you," Harry responded, giving no recognition to the joke. "Our horses are here, and we must make speed to the town. Someone will come to speak to you about this and very soon, no doubt." He reached out to the grey mare, stroking her neck, and finding a comfort in her solid presence.

Leaving the cousins behind, Sir Rupert and Harry rode to New Romney, passing the land where the racegoers had assembled, and crossing a bridge to join the road near Warren House. It was no distance to the town – the rooftops, windmills and church tower emerged before them, and soon they were reaching low cottages with reed-thatch roofs. The men parted where Cannon Street joined the main road at the Dolphin Inn with an agreement to meet at this same spot when the church clock chimed two o'clock.

Sir Rupert planned, no doubt, to be dining at the home of Sir Julian, where they would speak of the disruption caused at the Whitsun Gallop, while supping on fine wine. Harry was left to scour the streets of New Romney for the constable and then attempt to speak with Jesse in the gaol. There was little time to make progress in either matter.

The role of parish constable was an annual appointment – a man of some standing in the community, chosen by Sir Julian Craythorne to enforce the law and deal with petty crime. It was a part-time position and usually held by someone who had his own trade to run in conjunction with the task. *Who is it this year?* Harry frowned as the street became crammed with buildings butting up against one another, and stalls offering wares crowded the pavements. He looked towards the Town Hall – it offered no clues. *I should know. It was the wine merchant last year and… this year… Mr Edward Woodall. That's it! Mr Woodall, the cordwainer, with his two shops and two apprentices in each – he must be hard-pressed to cope. Is he likely to be pacing the streets looking for trouble? No – if anyone was to need him then they would know to find him at one of his workplaces.*

"Mr Woodall?" Harry enquired as he entered the shop. On a three-legged stool, pressing a needle through leather, sat a young person, barely more than a boy. Behind him was a tall, slim man with a neatly groomed head of fair hair. He wore a leather apron and had an air of authority about him. They were making the most of the sunlight beaming through the front window and positioned a small work bench in the bay. In the shadowed areas, a counter stretched across one side of the shop and behind it shelves rose to the ceiling. It was an orderly space with samples of the shoes and boots on offer, along with selections of leather, fastenings and soles. Baskets displayed polishes, brushes and shoelaces. The air was rich with the overpowering smell of treated animal skin.

"Good morning," the man responded. "Or did I hear the church bells strike noon?"

"You did, sir!" Harry smiled. If this was the town constable, then at least he was approachable. "I'm Harry Farrers from Dymchurch and I've come to speak with you in your role as constable."

"I'll ask my son to oversee this," Mr Woodall indicated to the work in progress as he passed through an open doorway to the rear of the shop. Looking into the next room, Harry saw a long bench in the centre, with a wealth of tools and materials arranged on shelves. There were at least three men working, and one separated himself on hearing his father's call for assistance. Some instructions were given, and the constable turned around to Harry. "Let us go upstairs to my office."

He led the way through the workroom, up a staircase to the first floor, then to a small room at the rear of the building. It was a pleasant, orderly space with views towards the green beyond the High Street. Edward Woodall gestured for Harry to sit down, then sat at his desk, pulling forward a large leather-bound ledger. "This one for my work in the parish," he said. "Now, Mr Farrers of Dymchurch, what brings you to New Romney?"

"There's been a death – a murder," Harry began. "I don't know his name. It was the rabbit keeper at the Warren. Bludgeoned to death only this morning." He paused.

"By God!" Mr Woodall blurted out, "I barely know the chap… but why? And how did you find out about it?"

"I think I should start at the beginning, sir." Harry recounted the tale of the stolen cup, which of course the constable knew about, and moved onto the suggestion that the keeper had witnessed the crime. "And now he is dead, which is a tragedy in itself, but doubly so when I believe he was the person who may have been able to free Jesse."

"If Sir Julian is aware, then it leaves me to fetch the doctor to confirm the death and I'll organise a couple of men to remove the body. The rector of St Nicholas must be informed too."

"What about the dead man's family?" Harry asked.

"There is no family," Edward Woodall stated. "I am almost certain of it – he grew up in the workhouse with a sickly mother who died several years ago."

Harry reflected on this for a moment. *What a sorry start he had to his life – and what a lonely existence living on the Warren. But he looked happy, only to have that snatched away from him. For what reason? Did anyone else know of him witnessing the theft of the prize cup? I can only guess they did.* "If his death is connected with the theft of the cup, then we have a truly cruel and devious man running free on Romney Marsh," he said.

"I don't know if we can link the two?" Edward Woodall responded as he stood, pushing his chair aside. "I fear for your apprentice who has already spent the night in gaol. I hear he is to go before the magistrates this afternoon."

"This afternoon?" Harry felt his skin tighten and his mouth dried. "This afternoon? I had no idea. What chance is there when I have no evidence to clear him? Would you like me to inform the rector? Then, if you will excuse my impatience, I must see Jesse or at least enquire after him." The men clattered down the stairs. Panic coursed through Harry's body. "What can I do? I have done nothing but found a possible witness, only to lose him?"

The constable gave no immediate reply, speaking first to his son as they passed through the workshop, "I have to go out, and will be caught up in parish matters for the rest of the day." Then to Harry, while they stood on the pavement outside the shop, "It is nothing but a curse to be saddled with these duties for a year. It is enough to be bothered with drunkenness and wild dogs – but murder…" He allowed the rest of his thoughts to go unsaid. Both men paused for a moment, but it seemed Harry's last words had not gone unheard for finally Mr Woodall responded, "I don't know," he murmured. "Perhaps take a moment to pray? Sometimes it is the only thing to be done."

Chapter Six
Harry

On reaching the High Street the men parted, Harry feeling stunned to know his friend was to face the magistrates that afternoon. He crossed the street and turned into a short road fronted with modern red-brick buildings, including the elegant assembly rooms. In contrast, the Norman church was now before him, and the rector could be seen at the doorway set in the base of the tower. *What luck to find him and not have to go searching.* Harry raised his arm to attract attention. *Luck? I should not think of it in that way – if a man hadn't died, then I should have no need of Reverend Apps.*

"Can I help you?" the rector asked, as Harry approached. "Harry Farrers of Dymchurch, isn't it?"

"It is." Harry paused, noting the rector's ruddy complexion and stout frame. This man would not relish a trek across the sandhills of the Warren. One of his calves was visibly swollen, the skin red and peeling beneath the ties on the cuff of his breeches. "I come with sad news – a death. The rabbit keeper has been… There's no way to make this any prettier… murdered. It happened this morning."

"But who? Why?"

It was not for Harry to speak of the motives as he had with the constable, only to ask that the man's soul be attended to. "I don't know. The constable is on his way… and I thought you…"

"I shall pray for him and make the arrangements," the rector continued. "There is no need… no need for me to journey there?"

"No. Mr Edward Woodall is to arrange for the body to be brought back to the town."

The men spoke for a few minutes before parting – Reverend Apps retreating to the church, and Harry turning back to the High Street.

Town Hall House, a red-brick two-story building, was substantial yet dwarfed on either side. To the left was the medieval New Inn, hiding its history behind a newly created flat-fronted façade, and rows of matching sash windows. A wooden scaffold filled the pavement at one end and labourers completed the laborious task of pointing gaps between each one of the red bricks. To the other side, in an arcaded space, traders sold goods on market day. Now there was nothing but withered cabbage leaves, straw and stray feathers in the dusty corners. Pillars topped with sweeping curves of brickwork, supported the town's courtroom and offices above the market. Here the latest skills in carpentry and glazing were displayed – thin window bars holding squares of clear glass and each one of those upper windows being rounded on top. On the pediment above, the crest of the Cinque Ports was displayed, and a flag hung limp.

Four steps rose to the door of Town Hall House. When he stood at their summit, Harry glanced at a low window set against the pavement below and another the same level as him. They were barred. *Of course! This is where they are keeping him – the gaol.* He wanted to call out and make contact with Jesse, but it was pointless. *Even if he were to hear me, we could not speak with the noise from the street.* So, he lifted the iron knocker and rapped on the door.

A woman answered. Or at least she opened the door and gave Harry a look as if to say his being there was a bother.

"I'd like to speak with the keeper of the gaol," Harry began. "Tell him it is Harry Farrers, jurat from Dymchurch." It seemed prudent to use the esteemed title.

"I'm about to serve his dinner," came the reply.

"I'll not keep him long," Harry answered as he pressed forward, stepping into the hallway.

The response was a tut and the housekeeper turned away. A moment later, a man of perhaps fifty years appeared. *He looks tired with life,* Harry decided. *I'm sure there is no pleasure to be had in being the keeper of criminals… Or worse – an innocent man.*

"You wanted to see me?" the man said. "You're the prisoner's employer, aren't you? The one he was working for when the cup was taken."

"I am," Harry replied. "Can I see him? It's all a mistake and I am worried about him."

"He's in my cell, not a boarding house," came the abrupt response. "You can sit in on the court hearing at two o'clock. Now, if you'll excuse me, I would like to eat my dinner while it's hot."

"I've only just heard that Jesse is to stand before the magistrates this afternoon," Harry pushed for further information. "I understand about your dinner, sir, but a man's life is in the balance. Is there no way I can speak with him before the session?"

"Out of the question."

Harry knew when he had met a man who would stand firm whatever the reason. "I'll be in court at two," he said as he turned towards the open door.

"If you want to help your friend, then a man of your standing should have no issue with speaking to Sir Julian beforehand," the keeper of the gaol suggested. "I believe it is he who will lead proceedings."

"Thank you." Harry gave a nod and left.

The front door closed behind him, and Harry stood for a moment at the top of the four steps. *The town constable suggests that I pray for Jesse, and the gaol keeper says for me to speak with Sir Julian who can influence the matter. Which is the most powerful influence – God or a Lord of the Marsh Levels?* At this, a bell in St Nicholas church tower announced the hour. Harry almost grinned to hear his question answered. *If I were to disturb the gentleman at dinner, then he would not be best pleased. He may well feed me – but would not appreciate my disturbing the meal. I shall seek God's guidance first.*

In the heat of the late spring day, there was some pleasure to be had from stepping through the curved Norman doorway and into the square space at the base of the tower. Harry paused and breathed deeply, liking the musty smell of ancient stone and wood. As he did so, he felt some of the anxiety slip away from his young body.

It would have been easy for a stranger to see Harry as an older man: someone who had grown up learning the ways of Romney Marsh; someone to whom the draining of the land and the rhythm of the tides was a knowledge absorbed in childhood; someone who instinctively knew to turn his back when the traders were about and to ask no questions about his wife's lace shawl or the brandy her uncle plied upon him. Yet here he was – a relative newcomer with his own business, a fine house and holding the role of jurat –

only twenty-three years of age. He wore the air of a man who had more experience of life, who was born to the responsibilities he held, but this was not the case. Most of the time, Harry ran his life with ease, appreciating the support given by Phoebe, as well as Owen and Bess – the couple who were as adoptive parents to him – and Sir Rupert of the New Hall. It was rare his duties weighed heavy upon him, but this was one of those moments. He breathed again, allowing the still air to fill his lungs, feeling his arms and legs relax. For a moment, Harry let his gaze follow the lines of ancient stonework carved by those long-departed masons, then he stepped through to the main body of the church.

The vast space appeared empty. Perhaps the rector had gone for dinner, or parish business had led him elsewhere? Harry paused, taking in the columns leading to the chancel, the rows of matching pews, and the carved Caen stone which told the history of the church through the way it had been styled over the centuries. He appreciated the golden light cast on oak, stone and polished brass. Then, wanting to secrete himself in a private space, Harry lifted the latch on a box pew and sidled in until he could go no further, and was resting slightly on the base of an octagonal pillar. Comforted by the strength in the stone, he leaned forward, placing his forearms on his lap and linking his fingers as he prayed.

"Lord, I pray that you look down upon your son, my friend Jesse, and send your counsel upon him. Give him the strength to bear the coming days and let him hold onto the hope that justice will prevail. I pray the magistrates may have the judgement to seek… to seek the truth and that the jurors will be honourable men…"

At this Harry paused… *It will not be a case of a full court hearing today – surely not. Perhaps a decision will be made as to whether to try him for the theft or let him walk free? Sir Julian will know...*

"Lord give me the wisdom to guide my friend when he is freed, and to protect my family from those who wish us harm. Today I feel helpless and weary. Let me feel bold enough to continue my path with courage... and... I think that is all." Harry recalled the murdered man and continued, "No... there is more – Lord I pray for the soul of the man who was taken from us today, and for his killers to be found and made accountable. May this man, whose name I do not know, rest in peace, in your heavenly presence. Amen."

Harry remained hunched as if in prayer while his thoughts flitted about from matters of importance to irrelevant. When the clock chimed the half hour, he rose and slid out of the pew then retraced his steps, only pausing to look back at the altar. *Thank you for giving me some peace in this day.* He left St Nicholas, walking to the High Street and then to Fairfield Road, before crossing to Rolfe Lane and approaching a moated manor house on the outskirts of the town. He slowed as he approached, aware that he had arranged to meet Sir Rupert on the outskirts of the town rather than here with Sir Julian.

There was no need for Harry to consider his next move. The front door opened before he reached the house and the two men stepped onto a gravel path. "Ah Harry!" Sir Rupert boomed. "How fortuitous to meet you here! Have you heard – Jesse Alder is to appear in court this afternoon?"

"I have, but how can we prove his innocence?" Harry asked.

"I must make haste," Sir Julian Craythorne interjected. "If you don't mind, I will dash ahead and will see you in court."

61

Relieved that Sir Rupert was to accompany him to the courtroom, Harry waited to hear more.

"It is a matter of deciding if Jesse will stand trial," Sir Rupert explained. "I am afraid there is nothing to stop it. With the keeper dead, we have no evidence to help prove his innocence. What I have done is to ask that those hearing the trial be impartial – by that I mean they are not enemies of yours."

"Aaron Chapman."

"Exactly."

With little hope of Jesse being released that afternoon, Harry trailed behind Sir Rupert through the empty marketplace and upstairs to where much of the town's important business took place.

On entering the spacious courtroom, Harry noted that Sir Julian Craythorne was already seated on the raised dais at the far end. The bailiff, Jeremy Parris, was to his right, and jurat William Payne from St Mary in the Marsh, was to the left of Sir Julian. Each one of them acknowledged the arrival of the newcomers with the slightest nod.

Harry was not overly familiar with courtrooms, only knowing the one in Dymchurch's New Hall, but for some reason he expected there to be an excess of oak panelling and was not disappointed. The walls were clad to the height of a picture rail where, beyond this, plasterwork rose further before meeting a barrel-vaulted ceiling. Behind the magistrates' bench, the panels extended to the ceiling, wrapping themselves around the corners of the room, as if cocooning the most important figures assembled. Elsewhere the benches, tables, banisters and rails were all a rich brown oak. Framed within the same wood, he gazed at portraits, maps and, on aging paper, the records of town mayors spanning the centuries.

Seating himself on a bench at the side of the room, Harry looked high above Sir Julian's head to study the bold colours of the royal coat of arms. *I wonder what King George would think to see that in Romney Marsh we are six decades behind the times and still honouring Queen Anne,* Harry pondered. His thoughts were irrelevant but gave a welcome respite from the moment.

Movement from the staircase announced the arrival of three others: the parish constable, who murmured a greeting to Harry; Aaron Chapman, who seated himself on the opposite side of the room and fixed a knowing smirk on his face; and a third man, unknown to Harry. From a doorway behind the dais, the clerk emerged and sat at his desk in front of the magistrates.

Apart from a few quiet words passed between the three assembled under the outdated coat of arms, the courtroom was almost silent. The clerk moved his ledger into position, opened the inkwell, then checked the nib of his quill. Those on the benches shuffled a little, adjusted their clothes and Aaron tapped his feet.

"Are there many cases this afternoon?" Harry asked Sir Rupert.

"Just this one, and it will be over in minutes," came the reply.

They turned on hearing further footsteps. Jesse entered the courtroom, shackled at the wrists, and with the keeper of the gaol at his heels. He was escorted to the dock and his attendant stood to one side. It seemed as if Jesse fixed his gaze on the panelling surrounding the dais, and there he stood, motionless, while the proceedings began.

"We meet here today to decide if the man before us will remain in custody and stand trial for the theft of the Whitsun Gallop cup, stolen at the race held by the Corporation of New Romney yesterday." Sir Julian Craythorne stood, his voice ringing out loud and clear throughout the room. "We are not here to judge his innocence or guilt, merely to ascertain if there is enough evidence to hold him. Please tell the court your name," this last was directed at Jesse.

"Jesse Alder... Your Worship."

"Your address and occupation?"

"Dormers Cottages, Dymchurch. I'm an apprentice blacksmith working for Harry Farrers of Dymchurch." Jesse flashed a look at Harry.

"Thank you." Sir Julian's response was brief. "Mr Farrers, please come forward."

Harry stepped forward to stand before the magistrates and clerk. "Good afternoon, Your Worship."

"How long has this man been in your employ?" Sir Julian asked. "Can you vouch for his character?"

"A year, Your Worship." Harry straightened his back a little and continued, "and throughout that time Jesse Alder has proved to be reliable and trustworthy. He is of good temperament and has a commitment to learning the trade. I know he rarely frequents the inns and taverns and has plans to marry when his circumstances allow. By that I mean when the apprenticeship comes to an end, and he is earning a full wage. I fully intend to keep him in my employment."

"You may return to your seat," came the curt reply. "I was at the Whitsun Gallop, as were all of us in the room. We have no need to go over the events of the day. To summarise – the prize cup was on display in front of the stand which held many of the local dignitaries. It was stolen from the display and recovered at Mr Farrer's mobile blacksmith's cart. Mr Alder and his companion oversaw the cart. A witness claims that Mr Alder was seen looking at the cup and later running away with some sacking. The cup was found wrapped in sacking.

"If it were not for Mr Alder's previously good character, it would seem the outcome was inevitable." Sir Julian paused. "Also, there is a suggestion that Jesse Alder may be taking the blame for another. A fanciful suggestion, or the truth? Mr Chapman – please step forward."

Aaron Chapman swaggered the few steps before facing the magistrates.

"What did you see that day, Mr Chapman?"

"I was watching the race like everyone else," Aaron responded. "When word went around that the cup had been stolen, I put my pleasure aside to perform my duty. Going amongst the spectators, I was asking if anyone had witnessed the theft and that's when I came across a boy who said he had seen someone running off with it. He could name that man – there was no doubt at all – Jesse Alder!" The last words were expressed with relish.

Harry saw Jesse shake his head a little, but he gave no other response to the accusation, not even looking in Aaron's direction.

"You may be seated," Sir Julian said. "There are no further questions at this time. I will speak privately with Mr Parris and Mr Payne for a moment." They leaned in and murmured amongst themselves for a couple of minutes before Sir Julian stood. "It is rare that I take the place of head magistrate while Sir Rupert Bannerman, Leveller of the Marsh Scotts, sits aside. The accused is from his parish, while the crime took place in mine. We have decided that Sir Rupert will not be judge on this occasion or for the trial.

"Jesse Alder – you are to stand trial for the theft of the Whitsun Gallop cup. While your good name does not go unheard, I cannot release you before the trial. This will take place in nine days' time, allowing for more witnesses to come forward. There will be a call for further evidence during this time."

The proceedings had come to an end. Harry, risking the displeasure of both Sir Julian and Sir Rupert, stood and dashed towards Jesse. Reaching out, he placed a hand on his friend's forearm. "I won't let this rest. I'll prove your innocence."

Pushing between them, his expression showing a weariness in his role, the gaoler barked, "No speaking with the accused." Then, placing a hand on Jesse's upper arm, continued, "Down we go."

"He is innocent," Harry persisted. "And it will be proved."

Jesse raised his gaze to Harry's, and his lips twitched a little as he attempted to show his gratitude, then he turned away. Harry watched him leave, his posture awkward for his wrists were cuffed and chained together. He stumbled a little at the head of the stairs but managed to right himself. At this Aaron Chapman let out a loud guffaw. Harry did not allow him the pleasure of a response.

Chapter Seven
Phoebe

Phoebe and Janey hauled the sheet from the washing line then stretched and shook it, smoothing the creases as best they could. Having experienced a feeling of gloom settling upon her as the day progressed, Phoebe was finding the exertion energising.

"There we go," Janey exclaimed, as she did every time a piece of clean laundry dropped into the wide wicker basket.

They began on the undergarments, pulling at wooden pegs and gathering the linen vests, chemises and stockings. Delicate boned stays were the last to be released to the rising mound. Finally, they lifted the basket between them and side-stepped awkwardly towards the kitchen door before dumping it on the table.

"It's a warm day to be ironing," Janey began to bemoan the task ahead. She glanced towards the fire and the two hot-irons placed to the side of it. "Not much of a breeze coming through."

"I don't care!" Phoebe was defiant. "It will keep me busy." She began turning the latches and steadied the ironing board as it was lowered from its upright position against the wall. "Did I hear the hall clock chime three? Where's Harry with the news?"

Janey, unused to her employer being anything other than placid, attempted to soothe her, "He'll be back when he's done all he can for poor Jesse Alder. You can be sure of that."

"I didn't think it would take so long," Phoebe objected. "I can't think of anything else."

"Then best to keep busy, as you said." Janey moved the smalls aside and began to lug a sheet from the basket.

Phoebe pushed the two irons onto a tray above the fire, having first wiped their bases with a rag, then helped to arrange the sheet on the ironing board. As she did so, Phoebe noticed Janey's brow glistened and how red her cheeks had become. "I've been unkind to you!" the younger woman exclaimed. "I know we should be glad of this fair weather, and I know we must bring the sheets in to iron them while there is still some dampness in them, but you are weary and have not paused since you were up at first light."

"I put my feet up while you were out delivering the honey," Janey replied. She was blessed in her position as housekeeper to Mr and Mrs Farrers and did her utmost to ensure they were pleased with her work.

"That was hours ago," Phoebe declared. "There's cool fruit tea in the larder and honey cake in the tin over there." She indicated to the dresser. "Let's both have a drink and cake, but you will sit in your chair, and I will iron the sheets."

"It's easier with two…"

Phoebe shrugged. "But I want to work and the more awkward it is, the less I will be worrying."

A few minutes later and the women had settled into their positions: Phoebe with a scowl on her face and battling with the swathes of linen sheet; Janey with her eyelids drooping, and a cup of cool fruit tea balanced on her lap. They rested and worked in silence for some time before Janey roused herself and carried the first of the pressed linen upstairs to a spacious cupboard on the landing.

"Do you want Mary to stay on tomorrow and help with getting your dresses and Mr Harry's breeches washed and on the line?" Janey asked on Phoebe's return.

Mary, Janey's niece, worked alongside her aunt for a couple of hours every morning, mostly cleaning out the hearths, sweeping and dusting. She had stayed for longer that day – plunging the dolly into hot water, grating the lye soap, rubbing at stains and scuffs, and struggling with the mangle. Phoebe had toiled alongside the girl, as all hands were needed on a washday. She found Mary to be pleasant and eager to work. For the past year or more, there had been a suggestion that when Phoebe was blessed with a child, there would be a full-time position for Mary in Walker House and a room in the attic. *There is no child – at least not for me. Should we offer her permanent work anyway? It would be a shame to lose a good maid.* As she pressed the iron into the corners of a pillowcase, Phoebe decided to discuss the matter with Harry soon.

"The weather looks as if it's set to be fair for a few days, so best to get the washing done," Phoebe replied. "And the next day perhaps she could help with the ironing?"

"She'll be glad of the money," Janey confided. "Her ma can't continue going along to Cluny House – not in her condition."

Phoebe pondered on this for a moment. Janey's sister, Lizzie, was expecting a baby by the end of the summer. At forty-four years, this was her fifth child and an unexpected pregnancy, with her youngest son being twelve. *They will need the extra shillings if Lizzie can't work. I must ask Harry before we lose Mary to someone who can offer her a full day's work.*

"How is Lizzie keeping?" Phoebe asked while she folded a pillowcase.

"Weary and troubled by her veins, but you know Lizzie, she's a hard worker and will carry on as best she can," Janey answered. She had seen the pail of soiled linen pads and knew her employer's monthly bleed had arrived, as it did without fail, so changed the subject, "I'll do the shirts."

"Thank you." Phoebe placed the iron on the hot tray by the fire. "I'll finish the smalls this evening. That's enough for me for now." She picked up the pillowcases and turned towards the hallway.

For the households fortunate enough to afford a sizeable collection of undergarments, outer clothes, aprons and household linen, washday became an irregular event depending on the weather. They had no need to festoon the house with swathes of woollen and linen cloth, living amongst damp air while the laundry dried from ceiling racks and wherever else it could be draped. When the weather promised to be fair and the breeze warm, it was all hands to the copper, washboard and mangle, and not unusual for the lady of the house to work alongside the maids. Phoebe was no exception.

Once the pillowcases were placed in the linen cupboard, Phoebe moved to the front of the house to lift the sash window. She leaned out, gazing across the road to a flat piece of land with cottages, pens for chickens and vegetable plots haphazardly arranged towards the seawall. Figures moved on the wall, and a donkey ambled along pulling a cart. Turning to the left, Phoebe looked towards the New Hall, the gallows and church – all was quiet, other than an old man pushing a barrow. In the same direction, the back door of the Ship Inn opened, and the landlady stepped out, perhaps seeking a reprieve from ale slops and tobacco smoke. It was a sleepy scene.

Downstairs the grandfather clock in the hallway chimed four, its tones reverberating gently throughout the house. "He should be home by now," Phoebe muttered, the scowl returning to her face. "I'll go and check at the forge." At that moment there was the sound of horses' hooves on the village street, and she turned to the right. "At last!" There they were, Sir Rupert and Harry, heading for the New Hall no doubt. "I can't expect them to stop for me," she said to herself while descending the stairs. Then, raising her voice, Phoebe called to Janey, "Harry's just passed! On his way to the New Hall... I'll go and meet him."

Three years ago, Phoebe would have paced up and down the road outside the New Hall, not knowing if Harry would leave by the front or back door. When his wealth was new to him, their home being built and his business not yet purchased, Harry hadn't gained the quiet confidence that now sat so comfortably upon him. Today she perched upon the low churchyard wall with her gaze fixed firmly on the front door of the Bannermans' home. Her husband would never again leave by the servants' door.

Phoebe had great faith in Harry's ability to solve any problem thrown at him. He never acted rashly but considered his options carefully. However, today something had gone badly wrong. She felt it in her heart and in the heaviness which had descended upon her limbs as the day progressed. When the front door of the New Hall opened, Phoebe regretted that her intuition had been correct. The droop of Harry's shoulders and the weariness in his face were immediately visible.

Before any words passed between them, the couple walked a short way along the track leading to the lonely flatlands of the Marsh. They crossed a plank bridge and came to fields where the meandering dips in the landscape told of ancient sea creeks. The grass was ragged, thistles grew, and the fallen trunk of a willow tree made a welcome bench.

This was a place where Phoebe had once found refuge from her daily toil and the relentless nagging from Aunt Peggy and Uncle Giles. She could sit here facing the village church and think of her mother buried in the churchyard. Later, she had shown Harry this spot and, holding hands, they had found a place to be that was no distance from village life, but offered a retreat to sit and talk. Sometimes they faced Dymchurch, the church and seawall, and other times they turned towards the countryside, seeing no sign of human life other than the occasional shepherd or farm labourer.

Today they looked inland. "The rabbit keeper at the Warren was dead when we reached him," Harry began. "He couldn't tell us what he saw." With Phoebe asking very few questions he told of the journey to New Romney and having to deal with the matter of the murder – informing the constable and the rector – before he could even begin to consider what to do about Jesse. Harry spoke of the small, yet formal, meeting in the court room, and the way he felt sick to see a good man shackled with a chain and cuffs by his wrists. "Aaron was there, of course. There is no doubt he is involved. I wouldn't be surprised if he took the cup himself and passed it to someone else."

"Sir Rupert will not confront Aaron," Phoebe said. "He is a good man – fair to both those who work on the land and the seawall. But, as Leveller of the Marsh Scotts, will he challenge a landowner? No! He will turn his back and pretend that he knew nothing of these suspicions. Sir Rupert is a man who wants life to flow with ease." She paused, her gaze following the path of a turquoise-bodied dragonfly as it darted about then hovered above a marshy pool. "Sir Rupert is a man well-suited to Romney Marsh – he does enough to please everyone from the excisemen to the free traders. He sees it all, yet he sees nothing."

"I can't help but like him – he has been good to me," Harry admitted. "But in the case of Aaron, Sir Rupert will avoid confrontation."

Phoebe shrugged, "And we will continue to like him, regardless of Jesse's fate."

"What next?" Harry asked, before answering for himself, "I'll speak to everyone I can, and see if anyone saw anything that can either clear Jesse's name or discredit the witness provided by Aaron."

"Who persuaded Jesse to leave the cart?" Phoebe asked. "Who lured him saying there was a horse who needed tending, yet there was nothing wrong? Did anyone else, other than Lucy, witness him being taken from the blacksmith's cart for no reason?"

"For no reason other than to place him near the cup!" Harry scowled. "We can be sure that whoever led him away pocketed a coin or two from Aaron. Surely someone saw it."

They sat for a little longer, debating the matter, talking in circles, while still coming to the same conclusions. When they stood to make their way back along the track to the village street, it seemed to Phoebe that her husband's mood was a little lighter. Harry had plans for the next day – starting with walking the length of the seawall and speaking to the workers, many of whom had been at the race. As for Phoebe, a plan was forming in her mind...

While the dew still lay thick on the grass and the sun shone, bravely penetrating the early morning mists, Phoebe returned to the spot where she and Harry had spoken the previous afternoon. They had wandered no distance along the track, but if she followed it, she would eventually reach the small settlement of Burmarsh. The swirling mist suited her well, concealing her from view. If anyone were to walk the path or be working in the fields, then she would appear as a shrouded figure, soon disappearing. Phoebe wore a shawl over her head and shoulders, and plain walking boots, but her day dress was of good quality green linen, with lace at the neckline and the cuffs of her sleeves. Unable to look ahead and consider the undulations and turns in the track, she was forced to concentrate on each step, and this was a blessing to her. Every rabbit hole needed to be negotiated, every broken branch on the ground, every slippery plank crossing a dyke, took her full attention, so the task ahead could almost be pushed from her mind.

Eventually the track joined with the Burmarsh road, a trailing route leading to the depths of the lonely countryside, and outwardly with little purpose other than to connect the occasional farm and cottage. However, the soil in this area was a sticky clay-like substance and used for pressing amongst the bundles of blackthorn which created the core of the Dymchurch Wall. So, rather than the road being little used, it became the backbone of this eastern part of Romney Marsh, with a regular flow of carts to-ing and fro-ing for long hours of the day as donkeys pulled their load from the fields and trackways to the seawall. Now Phoebe felt exposed to whoever may see and recognise her on this busy stretch of road, so she pulled her shawl to allow it to fall partly across her face, and walked briskly, avoiding eye-contact with anyone who passed by.

It all seemed so easy when the plan developed in Phoebe's mind. Yet as she approached Burmarsh her pace faltered. Before her, Rothschild Farm faced outward from the centre of the village, as if it thought itself better than the rambling cottages, the humble village inn, and even the small ragstone church. There was a fashion for fronting older properties with a cladding of quality brickwork and evenly spaced sash windows, often with this wall rising high to partly shield the view of the roof. The Chapman residence, inherited by Aaron within the past two years, was to be no exception. It was said that his wife, whose family had grown wealthy by grazing sheep on the rich pasture of St Mary in the Marsh, had funded this extravagance.

Did I expect him to be standing there, with nothing better to do than strut about admiring his property? Phoebe scolded herself, although these thoughts would not have been entirely unfounded. Word amongst the tradespeople in Dymchurch was that the Chapmans had watched every step of the renovation process, critical of the smallest detail. *There will be a stable lad, or a maid or... someone who can fetch him for me. I know Aaron and he won't be far away – he likes to remain where he can be king of his empire. This house emphasises his position, for although there are other landowners, none of them have a property that shouts of their wealth such as this does.*

Forcing herself to continue, although in her head a voice screamed that she had made a terrible decision, Phoebe reached the wide track which swept past the house to the outbuildings beyond it. At that moment, a young housemaid opened the front door and shook out a cloth. She spotted the visitor and faltered. Raising her hand to beckon the maid, Phoebe held a penny between her fingers as the girl approached. "I'm looking for Mr Chapman," she said, pressing the coin into the small hand. "Is he at home?"

"He's due for his breakfast, so won't be far away," came the reply. "You don't want to come in and wait for him?"

"Can you ask him to come here?" Phoebe reached into her reticule and pulled out another coin. "And not a word to anyone. I'll wait in the lane."

"Or just here?" The maid nodded to an attractive arbour with wisteria trailing over the frame. "There's no windows overlooking."

"Thank you." Phoebe nodded her agreement. *This girl thinks I am his lover, but she has been paid for her silence, and would be foolish to displease her employer by gossiping.* She moved towards the arbour, her heart beating uncomfortably, and knowing she must harden herself to the task ahead. Once sheltered by the wooden framework, twisting stems and lush pointed leaves, Phoebe closed her eyes for a moment and attempted to steady herself. She breathed deeply, taking in the scent of the late blooms, and slowly exhaled.

There came the sound of footsteps on the gravel, then a soft padding over the grass. Phoebe turned to see Aaron approaching, and forced a smile, accepting a kiss on her cheek along with an overly familiar squeeze of her waist.

"This is an unexpected pleasure!" Aaron exclaimed, his voice light and playful. "What do you think of Rothschild Farm now? I seem to recall I brought you here once to meet my grandmother." He referred to a time when he courted Phoebe, although they had both known he was on the prowl for a match which would bring him fortune and breeding.

"It's very fine, Aaron," she replied. "It suits you well."

"As we speak, a stonemason is carving a house name more befitting – Rothschild Manor!"

"It has a grand sound to it – only right for the best house in the village and one of the finest on Romney Marsh." To flatter Aaron would help her cause and Phoebe knew how to please him. "You have chosen well – the slight rise in the land brings healthier air with it, and you are no distance from the coast if you should choose to go there. Yet if you wanted to mix with more fashionable society, the Roman road to Canterbury is within easy reach." Phoebe waved her hand towards the nearby hillside.

"Burmarsh is indeed healthy, unlike many of the Marsh villages, and it does me no harm to move within circles of more civilised people in the city," Aaron agreed, his eyes never leaving her face. "Perhaps you would care to come with me one day?"

Phoebe gave a small smile. "I think my husband would miss me, don't you? Mrs Chapman, your wife, would make a better companion."

"My wife is busy with the baby."

Now Phoebe used all her reserves of goodwill to compliment him further, "What a beautiful daughter you have, Aaron, and no doubt there will be sons and more daughters to follow! How good your life is!"

"Even better to have you come visiting me," he responded, stepping closer and reaching for her hand.

"Here you are Aaron, in Rothschild… Manor! Why worry yourself with a young man who works for my husband? Jesse is a fine, honest person who would never steal from anyone. He didn't take the gilded cup, as you know. Yet he may well be convicted of it."

"But there is a witness," Aaron declared, caressing the palm of her hand with his thumb, moving it in slow circular motions.

"A boy from Burmarsh," Phoebe stated. "How much did you pay him for his story, because that's all it is?"

At least Aaron had the decency not to deny it, but this was of no benefit to Phoebe. Instead, he resumed his flirting with the woman he had desired for years: "I declare that time has only enhanced your beauty. The girl of eighteen or nineteen was nothing compared to the woman before me. Not a week goes by when I do not regret letting you go. Tell me, Phoebe, what would you give for Jesse's freedom and to see his lovely Lucy smile again?"

Phoebe frowned, glancing towards the splendid Rothschild Farm – it had not yet been endowed with the name Manor - and knowing that his acres boasted prime pasture. She believed his wife came with her own riches, and it was well-known – if never spoken of – that the Chapmans were as busy working by night alongside those who traded with the French as they were working their land by day. What could she give him? Yet before she had voiced her thoughts, Phoebe knew what it was that Aaron wanted in return for Jesse's freedom. And then, as she snatched her hand away from his grasp, a terrible, sinful longing flashed through her mind – *What if he were to leave me with child?*

Chapter Eight
Harry

There was no need for Harry to ride the length of the seawall on horseback at speed, placing himself above those who toiled long hours on maintaining the great sea defence. Today he must take his time, moving amongst the workers, pausing to speak to every person who would spare him a minute or two. He joined the wall near Church Knocke, scrambling up the track to the top, and paused, momentarily surprised to see the number of workers had swelled in volume.

"Of course!" he exclaimed, recalling his past activities labouring there.

It was that time of year when the usual teams of eight to ten men trebled in size and, as the longest day of the year approached, they worked from dawn to dusk whilst the tides allowed. They took on tasks needing a greater number of men, usually labouring on the weaker parts of the seawall, often tearing out the heart of a section then renewing it with a framework of oak stakes and bundles of blackthorn. As Harry contemplated this, and the enormity of his mission to speak to each of these men, the first of the clay wagons pulled up at the landward base of the wall.

"I don't know about trade, sir, but he does a bit of digging out of the ditches and he keeps the hedges nice and tidy so there's plenty of wood for the seawall. And in the summer, he's busy fetching the clay for the wall."

The words of Toke Browne, that lad who pointed his grubby finger at Jesse, sprang to Harry's mind. *He'll be here in the thick of it – that boy and his father. And perhaps others... perhaps others will talk if they have a few pennies in their hands.*

The task ahead was far greater than Harry envisaged. There were not only the permanent wall-workers to speak with, which in isolation presented few difficulties for him, but now all the seasonal workers, and those who trekked to and fro with the donkeys and carts to consider.

However, there was one thing Harry was grateful for. The previous evening Frank Smith had approached him with an offer to look after the forge, and he knew it to be in good hands. Frank had owned the business and sold it to Harry two years previously. The men had then worked alongside each other for next year, with the older man gradually reducing his hours. Now he was back at the fire, with iron at the ready, leaving Harry to put all his time and concentration into seeking justice for Jesse.

Facing the sea, Harry took a deep breath, preparing himself for the mammoth undertaking he had set himself, knowing that this was not one day's work but two or even three days of talking to every man who would spare him the time. The tide was midway down the sands, retreating gradually and leaving pools of water forming around the knocks. As it receded further, the mudflats would be revealed, and men would go out digging for bait, or shrimping in the shallows beyond – all rather solitary figures, quite unrecognisable from a distance.

On turning again, focussing along the length of wall towards New Romney, Harry felt any tension leave his body and a smile spread over his face. "Owen! You've come to help me – thank you!"

There he was: Owen Bates, a man of about fifty years and the closest person Harry had to a father. "I couldn't leave you to do this on your own," Owen declared. "And Bess... she's going about the village, stopping and having a little chat with the women, to see if anyone knows anything..."

"Thank you!" Harry repeated. "I hadn't thought..." He paused, gesturing to the seasonal workers and the next cart trundling towards the seawall. "There's just so many to speak to and I was thinking that one of these... one of these lads shifting the clay about might be the person who claims to have seen Jesse take the cup, or perhaps has heard something about it."

"If I go about the carts, having a friendly word here and there, maybe I'll hear of someone who has been bragging about being given a coin or two, or telling a tall tale," Owen suggested. "A lad who is feeling like he's a bit special if Aaron Chapman has been giving him attention."

"That's a good idea, thanks. I'll stay here on the wall," Harry continued. "Asking around to see if anyone was at the Whitsun Gallop. Was there anyone who didn't speak up at the time?" He felt a positive surge throughout his body, energised by the project ahead. Straightening his back, he gazed along the length of the seawall as far as Everden Groyne, where manmade structure joined the shingle bank to the east. "I'll meet you down there."

"You will and by God – we'll do our best to free that young man," Owen gave a wide grin and bounded down the slope like a man twenty years his junior.

Harry worked his way amongst the men who were busy opening a section of wall between Church and Palmers Knockes. He knew there had been a couple of occasions last winter when emergency repairs had been carried out in that spot and he was glad the decision to replace this stretch had been unanimous amongst the jurats and Sir Rupert. As he spoke to the men, the core of the wall was being torn out – bundles of blackthorn branches, cut from trees many seasons ago, and the stakes which once held them in place. Clouds of dusty clay billowed out as the structure was disturbed, settling on his lips and tongue. The sensation felt familiar, and he longed for a swig of weak ale from the flask slung from the belt at his waist.

"I was there – what a drama, but I saw nothing. Nothing to help you."

"I hope they find the truth of it, Mr Farrers, but I can't help you."

"No, I wasn't there."

"There's all sorts of talk about it, but I was watching the race – I saw nothing."

Most of the men were happy to speak with Harry, but none had seen anything to help Jesse's cause. Harry thanked each one for their time and repeated the same words: "If you hear of anything, come and see me at Walker House. Leave a message with my wife or the housekeeper and I'll see you are rewarded for it – thank you. Pass the word around – there will be a reward,"

Moving along the seawall, Harry knew all the names of the knockes – Watch, Nethersoles, Beacon and more – and he knew the teams of villagers who were the regular workers on different sections. At times, he took a moment to reflect on the enduring cycle of work, and the fact that it was rare to hear of a serious breach in the great bank. Mostly he ploughed on, speaking to one man after the other, or to the small groups working together.

Occasionally, Harry scanned the ground by the landward base of the wall, looking for his friend Owen.

Further away, across the flats of Romney Marsh, he saw the trail of carts moving slowly along the tracks from the Burmarsh area and all heading towards him. It was in this area that the ground was a particularly sticky clay-like substance, well-suited to being packed into the wall to provide a protective skin. *He's down there somewhere,* Harry thought of young Toke Browne. *He's down there with a smile on his face and feeling like he's better than the rest of the lads. And he is – because I'm damned sure he's got a shilling or two tucked away, and the satisfaction of pleasing the local landowner, that wily Chapman. I wonder if Owen will find him, or anyone who has witnessed Toke bragging about his good fortune.*

Harry was passing the Willop Gut – an outlet for the water which gathered in the winding drainage ditches of the Marsh to be released at low tide onto the beach – when he noticed a chestnut horse in the distance approaching at speed. The rider appeared to be a young man, clearly confident in handling the beast, and seemingly looking out for someone. Harry watched his progress and was not surprised when the horse slowed to a halt just a couple of feet away. "Mr Farrers? Harry Farrers?" the rider asked.

"That's me!"

"I've a message from Sir Julian Craythorne!" This was announced in a manner almost warranting a fanfare of trumpets.

"A message?" Harry felt excitement ripple through him.

"You must attend the coroner's meeting in New Romney Town Hall at two o'clock this afternoon."

All hope crushed, Harry found himself repeating the words, "At two o'clock? I had planned to spend the whole day..."

But whatever Harry had planned was of no interest to the messenger. "Two o'clock," he confirmed. "New Romney."

By now the end of the seawall was in sight, and Harry picked up his pace, determined to reach the Everden Groyne. At this lonely spot, he met with a couple of men who had been to the race. One had not appreciated the way Aaron had pushed himself through the spectators in search of a witness. "That man is far too important for his own good," the wall-worker claimed. "He was out to cause trouble that day. I'm sure of it, but I saw nothing that can help you or Jesse." His friend nodded in agreement, and Harry thanked them for their support before starting on his trek back to Dymchurch.

Once more Harry passed the barred window of the town gaol and entered the arcaded area beneath the courtroom. Again, he ascended the staircase, taking him directly into the airy space with its abundance of wooden features and elegant windows to the front and rear. Yet, this time no one was to be judged. The men gathered as equals, or near enough, around a central table.

The coroner was a sombre faced fellow of advanced age, his wig of silver locks tied back with a ribbon of black velvet. Also seated were Edward Woodall, town constable, who gave a friendly smile of recognition to Harry; the cousins John and Bob Wright who found the body; the doctor, a young man with a head of glossy brown waves which no wig could better; and finally, Sir Julian Craythorne.

The business began on the strike of the church clock, immediately echoed by the chime of a clock within the room.

"Yesterday a man died on the land known as the Warren to the east of New Romney," the coroner began. "We know him to be Abraham Goode, keeper of rabbits. Does he have any family locally?"

The coroner scanned the faces seated at the table. *They say he had no living relatives,* Harry thought. *But it is not for me to say.*

"There's no family," Sir Julian confirmed. "The Corporation gave him the job because he was living in the workhouse. He was able-bodied and had a character well-suited to living and working on his own. His mother died in the workhouse, and his father... I know nothing of his father."

"Ask at the New Inn," John Wright suggested, "They'll remember him well enough. It was a sorry day for them when he fell drunk into a dyke. They were all the poorer for it!" He stopped and reddened. "Apologies, sir," he said to no one in particular. "No need to be disrespectful. No need at all."

"The father is dead?" the coroner asked for confirmation.

"He's dead." John Wright chose not to embellish the facts any further.

"Any other family? Uncles? Brothers?" Sir Julian asked.

This was followed by some discussion, and it was established that Abraham Goode had died with no known family.

"Doctor – can you tell me your findings?"

The doctor allowed his gaze to sweep around the table and finally he looked directly at the coroner as he responded, "Sir, I was called to inspect the body of Abraham Goode yesterday at approximately midday. I estimate that he had been dead for two hours."

Two hours, Harry reflected. *That puts John and Bob Wright in the clear. Had they killed him, they would not be waiting in the area for someone, such as Sir Rupert and myself, to happen to come along.*

"The cause of death was a blow to the back of the head," the doctor continued. "There were other injuries to his back and shoulders, but I would say the strike to the head was the cause. It would have been instant."

"Thank you," the coroner replied. "There seems to be no doubt at all."

"No doubt," the doctor confirmed.

"And it would be awkward, if not impossible for this man to injure himself in this way?"

"To fall and cause an injury is feasible. But a bloodied pole was cast upon the ground," the doctor informed.

"And did the blood match that of the victim? That is to say, was it likely to be his?"

"It was fresh, sir," the doctor answered. "Not yesterday's nor last week's but from that morning."

It seemed that the coroner was finished with his questioning as he now fell silent. No one liked to interrupt his thoughts, so they sat and waited. John Wright appeared subdued after his outpouring of gossip about the father of Abraham Goode, but Harry felt that the cousins would dissect the matter fully when they left the restrictions of the coroner's table behind them. Harry pondered on the tides: *By the time I am done here, the sea will be at its peak and the men will be resting. I've lost my chance to speak with those working on the stretch towards Wall End. Damn this inquest and being called here for no good reason. Where is Sir Rupert? He was with me when the body was found.* But he knew the Leveller of the Marsh Scotts had his own meetings to attend while overseeing the annual maintenance of the seawall.

Sir Julian cleared his throat, and the silver ringlets of his wig bounced. All eyes turned towards him. "Can I ask if those who found the body, or Mr Farrers of Dymchurch, saw anyone in the area who may have committed this heinous crime?"

The coroner turned his bloodshot eyes towards the younger man and replied, "With all due respect, sir, the coroner has not yet established this was a crime." He paused, as if for dramatic effect, then continued, "The deceased, Abraham Goode, was murdered by a person or persons unknown. The cause of death was injury to the back of the head by a pole." No emotion was expressed in these words, and there came a further hesitation before he resumed, "The body can be buried this afternoon. I believe a grave has been prepared at the expense of the Corporation and I now hand over the case to our town constable, Mr Woodall."

Edward Woodall, raised his eyes to the vaulted ceiling, gave an audible sigh and nodded his understanding. "I'll speak to you afterwards," he said to the Wright cousins. "Mr Farrers…"

Harry waited. *Am I to be constantly thwarted by the death of the rabbit keeper? I'd like to know what happened as much as the next man, but my time must be spent trying to help Jesse.*

"Mr Farrers," Edward Woodward continued, "spoke to me yesterday and I understand that he has pressing business to attend to. You may return to Dymchurch and if I have any questions, I'll send a messenger."

"Thank you!" Harry stood. "May I…?"

"You may go now," the coroner stated.

Harry, recalling Sir Julian's earlier question, responded, "Sir, I saw no one in the area other than the Wright cousins."

Released from his duty, Harry almost bounded down the stairs and through the marketplace. Once on the street he faltered, looking at the barred window then towards the front door of Town Hall House. *I'd be wasting my time. Perhaps making life more difficult for Jesse.* The glass of the windows was thick and the iron bars substantial. Leaves, straw and feathers were layered at each point where the bars crossed. *I wonder if he can see out through all this muck… if he can see me?* Harry sighed, glanced up at the sign for the New Inn, then strode on with purpose, pressing on the door and stepping into the tavern.

The shaft of light poured through the open doorway, catching on the millions of dust particles hanging in the air, highlighting the men with their tankards as they turned to see who entered. Sunlight glanced on the bottles of brandy, rum and wine that had found their way into the New Inn by dubious means. With a gentle thud, the door was closed, and the ancient building relaxed in the half-light.

There came a slight scraping of wooden stools on the stone floor, the whisper of clothing fabrics brushing against each other, and the intake of breath as lips drew on clay pipes. Then, as Harry was recognised, the murmur of conversation resumed, and all was well in the New Inn. He may not be from New Romney, but he was no stranger to the town, and respected locally.

"A tankard of ale, please," Harry pushed a coin across the bar.

"How's life along the coast in Dymchurch?" the landlord asked, as he placed the drink on the polished wood.

"I'm barely there since all this trouble at the Whitsun Gallop." Harry kept his voice casual, as if the words were no more than gossip. "But it seems like there's nothing I can do to help Jesse Alder who is next door in a cell, and then there was the murder…" He paused now, waiting for the reaction, and it came in the form of a silence falling over those sitting or standing nearby. "I've had to put a man in charge of the forge and I'm dashing between here and Dymchurch with no time to get any work done. The coroner called me to attend the inquest in the courtroom."

"And what did the coroner have to say?"

"There's no doubt it was murder," Harry replied. "It's in the hands of the town constable now."

"He was a strange person – there's no one who would say any different," a labourer at the bar gave his opinion, "but who would want him dead?"

Harry smiled to himself. This is what he came into the New Inn for – to encourage speculation and see what came of it. "I wondered if he had anything to do with the theft of the cup?" he attempted to lead the conversation.

"He wasn't a thief!"

"He didn't have the wits to try such a thing!"

"No… he wasn't. But did he see anything?" Harry expanded on his theory, "He was there watching from up on one of those sandhills – my wife and I both saw him. Did the thief know he'd been spotted and go back to deal with him?"

"The thief is in the town gaol!"

Harry looked to where this had come from and answered, "Jesse Alder is no thief. I'd vouch for that all day long. The cup was stashed at the farrier's cart for some reason, and now an innocent man is taking the blame." He paused, then raised his voice, "Were any of you there at the race? Did anyone see anything suspicious? Someone running away from the stands? Someone loitering near the cup?"

For a moment the bar hummed as the men digested this and spoke amongst themselves. Harry sipped on his ale, allowing them the time to consider this. For the first time that day he felt himself relax a little. Eventually, the men had to admit defeat. Each one of them wanted the glory of spotting something, but those at the race had been fully absorbed in the event.

"Why wouldn't we be watching the race?" Harry said. "It was what we went for, and there was quite a throng at the trackside. I was there and saw nothing but the horses and the others crowding around me." He returned to his drink, not wanting to appear that he was there to antagonise them. "And I saw Abraham up there on the sandhill because he was in front of me. I don't know who else would have been looking back towards the cup."

"It would have been them fancy folk, if you'll excuse me for saying so," an old man piped up. "They were the ones up on that stand with the cup sitting in front of them on a fancy table."

"Bloody fools they were if not one of them saw a thing!" someone let out a guffaw and sniggers ran about the place from those sitting beside the ancient brickwork of the vast fireplace, to others by the light of the newly glazed windows.

"It's a strange business," Harry admitted, "and if I'd been up there, I like to think I would have seen something." *Should I be questioning the wealthy and influential people of Romney Marsh, not the poor folk who gathered at the trackside? They wouldn't like that!*

He had aroused enough interest for now and any more prompting could lead to these men turning against him. Harry sipped his ale, savouring the flavour as it slipped down his throat, and the brief respite from his responsibilities.

Eventually one of the men stood, his stool clattering against the wall. "I'd heard that Abraham took an interest in our gentlemen traders and offered his snug little place as a hide. Who knows who he may have upset or what he might have been mixed up in?"

What a useful suggestion to have bandied about, Harry's response screamed in his head, but could not be voiced. *Blame the smugglers and that will be everything nicely wrapped up.* "Who says that?" he asked, keeping his tone even.

"I heard it in the Rome Tavern, or perhaps it was the Rose and Crown," the man replied. "It's nothing to me what he did, but I heard mention of it one place or the other."

"He certainly lived in a lonely spot and could have seen all manner of goings-on if he left his bed at night," Harry admitted. "Was there a run that night?" The beach between Dymchurch and New Romney was indeed a lonely spot, and the dunes offered a concealed path before the traders trailed the watercourses as they moved inland.

"A run?" someone echoed, his voice high.

"A run?" another repeated, "I'd know nothing about that."

"Nor me!" said a third.

Soon every man in the place had declared that he knew nothing of the smugglers' activities having slept soundly in their beds from nightfall to dawn. Harry smiled to himself, swallowed the last of his ale, and thanked the landlord. "Goodbye my friends, I must hasten to Dymchurch." He left by the back door, collecting his horse from the stable yard.

As rode away from New Romney, Warren House soon came into sight. "Ah," he murmured to himself. "We cannot know if the rabbit keeper saw the traders that night, and those good men in the New Inn slept soundly in their beds. But the nurses, here at the pest house, work through the night. No doubt they are wise to the ways of the Marsh. I shall ask Phoebe to pay them a visit."

Chapter Nine
Phoebe

"Nothing," Harry answered in response to Phoebe's raised eyebrows as he entered the parlour.

Seated by the window, she laid a tiny garment on her lap. A needle remained pressed through the material of the hem. It was a relief to be able to set it aside – this gift for Ellen on the birth of her baby had been sewn with longing and resentment rather than love.

"But surely someone…" Phoebe allowed her words to trail away. It was nothing that hadn't been talked about over and over at suppertime, before Harry had left yet again in search of someone who might help prove Jesse's innocence.

"I had to try." He slumped in a chair, clearly exhausted.

"And we will keep trying. There is a week before the trial." Phoebe felt determined to remain positive and kept her tone light. "There is such little evidence – how can any jury see him as guilty?"

"Little evidence against him, but nothing in his favour other than his good name," Harry reminded her.

"There is your word that the keeper saw the thief?"

"That's no more than a man of little intelligence running to and fro as if he were holding something. As if he were acting out a scene he witnessed. It could easily be said that it was Jesse he saw, although I am certain that isn't what he wanted to tell me."

With the light fading rapidly, the opportunity to complete the hem had passed. Phoebe folded the garment and placed it in a basket to her side. They tried to change the subject to other matters, but even their talk of the forthcoming trip to Wissant led to them returning to Jesse's predicament.

"How can we go a day after the trial?" Phoebe asked, her fears pouring from her. "They will be expecting us, and I … I was so looking forward to it. Grand-mère is becoming frail. This could be the last time. Think how they will worry if we don't arrive, and how can we expect Walter and Joshua to sail across the channel with only a message from us?"

"I've been thinking about it," Harry replied, when she finally paused. "You are right – whatever the outcome, I will be needed here. But you must go as arranged. I know how you miss your family and it's not fair to keep you from them."

"I'll see Walter tomorrow and tell him that I will be going." There was no pleasure felt in those words. To journey across the Channel would be a lonely time without her husband at her side to share the adventure.

"After you see him, can you go to Warren House?" Harry paced towards the window, standing with his back to the elegant room, furnished in shades of cream and sage green. "Something was said at the New Inn… there was a suggestion that Abraham was connected to the smugglers in some way. Perhaps they used his place as a hide when needed? When I wanted to know more, they claimed ignorance."

This raised a smile on Phoebe's face. "I'm sure they did! But what's this got to do with Warren House?"

"Oh – yes, sorry… Warren House – I was wondering if there was a run that night?" Harry swung around and his eyes met with Phoebe's. "The nurses there must see things when they are awake all hours. I was certain Abraham's murder related to Jesse. After all I'm sure he saw who stole the cup. But the men in the New Inn seemed to be linking it with those who trade by night."

"If they held a run that night, then it is more likely he was involved, or did something to upset them?" Phoebe began to understand. "If the murderer struck because he knew Abraham knew the truth behind the theft, then to blame the smugglers would be more than convenient!"

"It's confusing to say the least," Harry poured himself a brandy from the decanter and flopped into an armchair.

"I'll go to Warren House tomorrow," Phoebe confirmed. "I'm sure someone will know."

"Mary?" Phoebe called to the maid who she found pumping water from the well. "I need you to take this to Mr Chapman of Burmarsh." She handed a slim envelope to the girl.

"Mr Chapman? I know who he is." Mary immediately pushed it into the pocket of her apron.

"Can you do it when you have finished here? Straight away?" Phoebe offered a sixpence. "And not a word to anyone, not Janey nor your mother."

With the coin now settled within the folds of her cloth purse, Mary smiled her agreement. "But what if I can't find him?"

Phoebe considered this for a moment. "There is a girl working at Rothschild Farm, about your age with red hair. Ask her to hand him the note and give her this…" Phoebe reached into her reticule and produced a coin, "… give her this penny and tell her not to say a word to anyone."

"I'll do that Mrs Farrers and be happy to." Mary gave a final heave on the pump and water gushed into her bucket. "My ma can't work at the moment, and she needs every penny I can give her."

"I must speak to Mr Farrers about that," Phoebe replied, partly to herself. Her thoughts lingered on the letter now settled in Mary's pocket.

By mid-morning, Phoebe once more made her way to the hospital of infectious diseases. There was no precious honey to give to the sick, but Janey had made a fruit cake to be appreciated by the staff, if not the patients. She chose to walk along the seawall, knowing her thoughts could be lost amongst the views of both coast and countryside. If the wall became busy with labourers, and at times they clogged her path with tools or materials as well as themselves, then her mind would be compelled to focus on the walk, rather than drift to the unpleasant scenes tending to occupy it.

Towards Wall End, Phoebe came across a small group of wall-workers all known to her. Their numbers had not been swelled by the annual influx of labourers. This section of the great bank was holding strong and no part of it had been chosen to be rebuilt. With John Waller as leader of the men, they slouched on the wall, legs dangling over the beachside, their flasks of ale to hand. Each one of them straightened his back as Phoebe approached and they smiled or offered a greeting.

Amongst them was Albie Alder, father of Jesse, and a man well-liked amongst the team on the wall, as well as his neighbours in the village. He stood to speak to Phoebe. "I can't thank you enough for what you're doing to help Jesse," he began. "Not only is Mr Farrers going here and there trying to find someone to speak up for

Jesse, but now he's caught up in the death of that poor keeper at the Warren."

"There's no doubt in Harry's mind or mine – your son is no thief, and we'll do our best to prove it," Phoebe replied. "We are trying to judge if the murder is connected, and I'm going to Warren House to see if the nurses have seen anything out of place."

"We're all Jesse's family here." John Waller came to stand beside Albie. "He's Albie's son, and cousin to a couple of my men, but blood or not, we know a good man and he has our support. Your husband worked with us for just under a year, and he's part of the family too. Our days here are long, but if Harry needs help, then he can rely on us."

"Thank you." Phoebe smiled.

All these men worked from dawn to dusk on the seawall. Sometimes they took a break at high tide, but more often than not, they headed to Church Knocke, ready to help with rebuilding a section of that vulnerable part of the wall. Yet, despite those demands, she didn't doubt that if something could be done to help, every one of them would pitch in.

Amongst the men, Joshua, who occasionally crewed his brother's boat *Louisa-Ann,* placed his flask to one side and stood. "Will you still go to Wissant?" he asked. "I hear it's all arranged for next week."

"The day after the trial," Phoebe responded. "Harry says I should go, but he'll stay here." She pictured herself, hunched up in misery with seasickness sweeping over her, while *Louisa-Ann* rose and fell with the swell of the waves. The stickiness of the salty spray could almost be felt on her skin, and the stink of fish seemed to fill her nostrils. Phoebe pulled herself back to the present, "But if Harry must stay, then that is how it will be, and I am grateful to you and Walter. I went five years without seeing Papa and every day I thank God that I found my family."

"We were glad to be able to help you," Joshua replied, "and it's our pleasure to take you. Your family make us welcome, and we like to see your Pa. Jacques was a good man when he was fishing from here in Dymchurch, and it's a damned shame he wasn't treated as well as he should have been."

The story of Phoebe's mother, who lay in the churchyard, and her French father was a complicated one, bound up with Romney Marsh's long-established connections with the trading of goods across the Channel – and the avoidance of paying taxes to the Crown. Jacques Bernard had taken liberties in crossing the sea and remaining in Dymchurch, or so certain people thought.

"He is a good man," Phoebe agreed. "I miss him, but every year I get to spend time with my family, and I know he is happier there in Wissant." She gazed across the sea towards France, but the hills and cliffs never revealed themselves on a bright day – they would be there when the sky became overcast, or the sun lowered itself. "I'll see you soon Joshua and my thanks to you both." Then she turned to Jesse's father and said, "I'll pray for Jesse's release every day. There must be good news soon."

From the seawall, Phoebe continued towards New Romney, with Warren House soon coming into view. She noted a nun at an open window, then a stooped man at the log pile, and a maid pegging towels on the washing line. By the time she was nearing the back door, a nurse had appeared, swathed in an apron and carrying a bucket of slops. With a rueful grin towards Phoebe, she disappeared behind the outbuildings, calling out: "I'll be back in a minute."

Phoebe waited and wondered about the people who lived and worked within the solid brick walls of the pest house. She heard someone coughing, the hacking noise erupting through an open sash window, and watched the old man shift logs into a small cart. Then the nurse reappeared without the bucket, "Hello! Can I help you?"

"I'm sorry to disturb you," Phoebe began. "I came a few days ago..."

"With honey..."

"Yes, and I said to the nun that we had some trouble at the race – it was Jesse who works as an apprentice for my husband. He was accused of stealing the prize cup. It's not true – it can't be, but he is in gaol nonetheless."

"We heard about it," the nurse responded.

"It's hard to believe no one saw it happen," Phoebe enlarged. "At least no one who is still alive. Harry is sure the rabbit keeper witnessed the theft, but then he was found dead."

"Murdered?" the nurse asked.

"Yes." Phoebe paused for a moment. She was aware that words were tumbling from her, and time was needed to reflect on the events over the past few days.

"Are you wondering if we saw anything?"

"This sounds odd, but we need to know if there was anything going on that night after the race. If anyone witnessed horses or men or lights? You see... well, people are saying that the keeper was killed by smugglers, whereas Harry thinks it was to stop him revealing who really took the cup."

"That poor man." The nurse gazed towards the stretch of dunes and rough ground where the keeper had spent his days and, hidden amongst them, the home where he slept at night. "We often spotted him from upstairs, but our view is limited..." She pointed to the tiled catslide roof of the property. "We have no windows at the back."

"And I know you are all so busy…"

"We are, but it is late spring, and the windows are open. We nurses often lean out to take in the fresh air. I was awake that night and it all appeared quiet."

"Oh! No smugglers."

"I saw nothing," the nurse confirmed. "It's not to say that they were not about, but I saw nothing."

"Thank you. It's all such a mystery." Phoebe recalled the cake provided by Janey. She passed it to the nurse. "This is for you… For anyone who would enjoy it."

"If I hear anything then I'll let you know." The nurse smiled.

She looks weary, Phoebe thought. *There must be a satisfaction to be had in tending the sick, but sometimes she must wish to be free of it.* In her mind she pictured a long room under the eaves in the attic space, guessing it was where the nurses slept. Her imagination took her to a row of low beds, with a trunk at the end of each, and pegs on the wall for their aprons and plain dresses of hemp cloth. She saw a washstand, perhaps two, under the slope of the roof and a cracked mirror placed by the light of the small dormer windows. The nurses would creep about for there would often be one of them sleeping. A couple of the nurses were also nuns, so Phoebe added a small altar to the scene and a cushion for them to kneel on. Then she smiled to herself, knowing she would never see their rooms and wondering how accurate her images were.

"We don't speak of what we see… or if we spot anything untoward at night," the nurse continued, bringing Phoebe back to the present.

"Of course you don't," Phoebe agreed, knowing the ways of the Marsh. "I must return to Dymchurch. Thank you for your time."

They parted, the nurse to her duties after a short reprieve, and Phoebe to retrace her steps home. As she walked, Phoebe's thoughts flitted from Jesse in his cell to wondering if Harry had made any progress, and then to the imminent trip to France. The road was quiet, with the occasional cart, or rider on horseback. In time, she climbed the bank of the seawall, and at once the whole coastline was open to her. Where her path had been lonely, now men were dotted about everywhere. This time she didn't pause to speak with anyone, her midday meal beckoned, and she kept up a brisk pace.

"I was looking for you," Mary said, unnecessarily. She sat on the tattered grass bank of the seawall, her back to the coast, and facing a pool of water known as Marshland Gutt. The maid scrambled to her feet, and continued, "There's no note. But I saw him, and he gave me a message."

"Thank you." Phoebe waited, the knot of anxiety twisting in her stomach, yet outwardly needing to appear calm. She too gazed across the flat countryside from the elevated position of the wall.

"He said he'll meet you in the church," Mary told her. "He said something about having to do some praying."

"Today?" Phoebe could hear her voice sounded brusque as she ignored the comment about praying.

"Tomorrow, Mrs Farrers. At four o'clock."

Phoebe felt herself relax a little. That gave them another day to find some evidence which would clear Jesse's name and take the look of despair off the faces of his parents and Lucy.

Phoebe walked the field tracks to Burmarsh the following afternoon. The roads were at their busiest with the clay carts lumbering towards Dymchurch, and empty ones bouncing over the ruts. She wore a light shawl as well as her straw hat, hoping to conceal her distinctive dark hair, and her dress was a summery cream linen with darker stripes. A dusting of earth dulled her brown shoes, but these were her walking pair and easily cleaned.

There came a feeling that every maid peeped from the windows of Rothschild Farm as Phoebe passed by. She scowled a little and felt her body tense, almost as if she had placed a protective armour over herself. The cook, the maid and the boy, were all about their work, of course. Unknown to Phoebe, Mrs Chapman was visiting her mother, taking the baby with her. Only the bricklayer glimpsed Phoebe pass and he thought nothing of it – his attention was on the final rows of the parapet.

The pub slumbered, with a handful of old men sitting at its doorway on a low bench. Its walls were the same grey ragstone as the church and its land butted up to the churchyard. As she crossed a footbridge and looked along the length of the narrow waterway meandering through the village, Phoebe wondered which of the buildings – All Saints' Church or the Shepherd and Crook – was best attended by the people of this small village. It boasted no more than half a dozen houses at its centre, and a few farms dotted about the place.

Now, on entering the churchyard, Phoebe felt sheltered by the elms and ancient yew, and the upright church walls with their curiously castellated tops. The air became moist with a distinct earthy smell. A porch beckoned her and once she stepped within its shelter, a carved stone face offered a humorous grin from its place above the Norman doorway. *It's not funny.*

Phoebe scowled at the rounded face with its odd toothy grin and blank eyes. *Why are you there – do you judge everyone who walks through this doorway? Or do you laugh at us for the mistakes we make and those we are about to make?* She pushed on the door. There was no resistance and Phoebe stepped into the church.

It was cool inside, and the air a little musty. Sounds of the village and countryside were silenced, and now all Phoebe heard was her footsteps on the tiled floor, and her breathing – short and ragged. Shafts of light shone through plain glass windows, glancing upon the polished wood of the box pews and pulpit. She paused, poised to flee, thinking she was alone, but then noticed a movement from within the choir stalls, and with it came the creaking of wood and brushing of material on the smooth rails.

"You came!" Aaron announced. "I knew you would."

Hating his cockiness, Phoebe forced herself to reply, "I sent a message through my maid."

"You've missed me." Aaron now stood before her, placed his hand under her chin and forced a kiss upon Phoebe. His tongue pressed into her mouth before he released her.

"What are you going to do to help Jesse?"

Aaron smiled to himself. "Let's go somewhere a little more discrete," he suggested, placing a hand on the small of her back and guiding Phoebe to a private area at the base of the tower. Here he kissed her again, allowing his hands to delve into the bodice of her dress. "Errr… Jesse? Oh, I'll pass the boy, Toke Browne, a shilling or two, and suggest he forgets what he saw. Then I'll find a witness who has just recalled seeing someone else place the cup by the farrier's cart." Brushing back stray locks of hair, Aaron began to kiss Phoebe's neck, while murmuring, "Remind me how you are going to thank me."

Phoebe felt her body stiffen. She recalled her nineteen-year-old self who had allowed his demanding kisses and rough hands. She remembered how he would stroll about, seeing it as his right to squeeze her flesh or bite the fragile skin of her neck and breasts. He would tell her over and over how lucky she was to have his interest, something which was again repeated by her aunt and uncle. Yet now she knew the attention Aaron offered was worthless.

Not seeming to notice that she didn't respond, he began to lift her skirts, and as a hand grasped her thigh, Phoebe realised this was no way to save Jesse. If she was to succumb to Aaron's needs, then his power over her would be long-lasting and destroy all her happiness with Harry.

"No! No! Aaron – this isn't the way." She pulled back. "I can't do it, Aaron. Not even to save Jesse."

"Oh, come on… You can't say you won't enjoy it… I'll have a word with the witness by morning, and by then you'll be wanting to thank me again! It will still go to trial but there won't be enough evidence to convict him."

"I can't do it."

"This time next week, Jesse will be back in the forge and his pretty Lucy will be so thankful… Perhaps she'll be wanting to show how much she appreciates me?"

"But she wouldn't know, would she?" Phoebe snapped, her voice an angry whisper. "She wouldn't know how you paid that boy Toke to lie for you. Or how you arranged everything so there was no one to come forward and support Jesse. Leave her alone. Leave Lucy alone."

"I remember how you used to be a little fiery." Aaron gave a knowing smile. "I appreciate that in a woman."

"I'm leaving now," Phoebe responded, trying to keep the emotion from her words. "I'm leaving now and all I can do is pray that you have enough heart to spare a good man from the gallows."

Knowing that Aaron would not stoop to pressing himself upon her if it were against her will, Phoebe pushed her way past the curtain separating the tower from the aisle. Then she fled from the church, racing through the porch and shady churchyard and crossing the bridge before slowing to walk along the track which wound its way through the village. Once she had passed Rothschild Farm, the last property on the lane, Phoebe took to the fields and ran most of the way home to Dymchurch.

Chapter Ten
Harry

In New Romney's courtroom the atmosphere was tense, with anticipation growing as people assembled for the hearing. The first to fill the lofty space were those called upon as witnesses to the theft of the prize cup, and others who would speak of Jesse Alder's good character. Seated to one side, half a dozen men of education and standing in the parish took on the roles of jurors. On the dais, Sir Julian Craythorne, bewigged and splendid, prepared to lead the proceedings as judge. Jesse's family stood uncertain and self-conscious, with Lucy in their midst. A clerk, with quill and ink at the ready, readied himself close to the Sir Julian. The room hummed with whispers.

All of those who were necessary to the proceedings already crowded the room, and now onlookers poured in, eager for some entertainment. A good court hearing was as rewarding as a travelling show or indeed the Whitsun Gallop. The benches filled, and standing space became crammed. It was nothing for a bystander to receive a jab or a push as the best positions were secured. Those who had arrived in good time began to vent their displeasure to the latecomers who now obstructed their view, and the gentle hum of voices became punctuated with objections and bawdy comments.

Harry's spirits were low. He heard the courtroom scuffles but remained lost in his thoughts of recent events. Over the past days he had left Frank Smith working in the forge, then ridden and walked the Dymchurch Wall, before venturing onto the country lanes seeking someone who had either witnessed the theft or knew of the boy, Toke Browne, being paid for his lies. Without doubt they were lies, for all Harry heard was good words about Jesse and support for his cause.

Meanwhile, the death of Abraham Goode had undergone minimal investigation. There had been mutterings about him being in league with 'our men who trade with the French'. A search in the hovel which the dead man called home revealed a couple of hiding places where contraband could have been stashed. It seemed easier to dismiss his death as a skirmish or misunderstanding with smugglers, than to connect it with the theft of the Whitsun Gallop cup. The men who traded by night brought luxuries to all who were their friends, and a welcome additional income for those who would struggle to feed and clothe their families without the extra bonus. There were so many of them involved in this illicit side-line that it was barely worth the bother of trying to find any one individual to pin the blame on. The town constable and local jurats decided over a glass of fine French brandy that the case would be left unsolved, or so Harry believed for he had not been a part of the debate.

The sun blazed through the arched rear windows illuminating the courtroom. While the expectant audience whispered, squabbled and shuffled about, Harry pondered on his final worry. Phoebe had been preoccupied in the last week. Every small thing that went amiss within the home caused upset, and her manner to him was noticeably distant. Those small offerings of affection towards him were lacking, and their conversations unusually stilted. She would be sailing to France the following evening, and he feared she may leave without them being able to talk about whatever was upsetting her.

Silence fell upon the courtroom, and from outside the mocking cry of the gulls could be heard. Then from the stairs there came the heavy, lumbering footsteps of a man shackled by chains. All eyes turned, many of them eager to see the prisoner and delighting in their witnessing of his distress.

"All quiet in the court!" Sir Julian Craythorne bellowed, as the murmurings once more began in the room.

The ten days spent in gaol had taken its toll on Jesse. Already his frame was less upright, and his skin had lost the glow of youth. His eyes were dull, and he looked at no one as he shuffled along the corridor opening up as people allowed him to pass. He moved into a space to one side of the clerk, and stood, eyes lowered to the floor. Harry felt complete despair, knowing nothing more could be done to help him.

"Ladies and gentlemen, members of the jury and people of this parish," Sir Julian began, "on the day of the Whitsun Gallop the prize cup was stolen, then found secreted by the farrier's cart belonging to Mr Harry Farrers of Dymchurch. Mr Farrers was at the trackside with his wife, leaving a Mr Jesse Alder in charge of the cart. This man, Mr Alder, stands before us now, accused of stealing the cup. We are here to decide if he did indeed take it."

"Of course he did!" A call came from the back of the room.

"It was found with him," another cry came from a newcomer still midway up the stairs, but eager to throw himself into the fray.

From the side of the room someone threw a rotten cabbage towards Jesse. A cheer broke out and people started stamping their feet, causing the floorboards to vibrate.

"Enough!" Sir Julian rose to his feet. "The decision will be made by the jurors." He then proceeded to give the particulars of the day, leading up to the theft and the discovery of the prize cup. "You are accused of taking the cup," Sir Julian said to Jesse. "How do you plead?"

Jesse raised his head to look directly at the judge for the first time. "Not guilty. I didn't do it, Your Worship."

"Is there anyone who can speak for this man?" Sir Julian asked.

"I will – he did it!" came a reply from an onlooker. Once more a flurry of laughter erupted from the gathering.

With his face set in a frown, Harry stepped forward and answered, "I will speak for him, Your Worship." His voice commanded respect, and the room fell quiet. He took this opportunity to move to Jesse's side.

After noting Sir Julian's nod of approval, Harry began, "Jesse is my apprentice, learning the skills of a blacksmith under my guidance. He is good natured and hardworking, and I know him to be honest."

"How do you know him to be honest?" someone shouted.

"Please tell us – for the benefit of the jurors," Sir Julian asked.

"Because there has never been a discrepancy between the money taken and the money I count at the end of the day," Harry replied. "Because I have never had reason to think any item of mine has gone missing. I have worked alongside his father and cousins on the maintenance of the wall and know the whole family to be of good character."

"How do you account for the prize cup being found by your cart that day?"

"There is no doubt in my mind that the cup was taken and stashed there. Either until it was to be retrieved and hidden away until it could be sold, or it was meant to be found in order to tarnish my good name." At these words from Harry, there came some murmurings amongst those in the courtroom, but no heckling.

"Why would someone want to do that?" Sir Julian enquired.

"Sir, I have lived in Dymchurch for just five years, meaning I am a newcomer. If I were to live in Dymchurch for twenty years, I would remain a newcomer," Harry expanded on his theory. "I have a good house, my own business and have married a local girl. Some people feel resentment for that."

"It will be for the jury to decide if there is any truth in this," Sir Julian replied. "I know I have respect for you and your role as jurat."

He is Romney Marsh born and bred with land and wealth passed down through the generations. How old is Sir Julian? Perhaps fifty years of age. He appears to be fair and steady but knows nothing of being an outsider here. Harry knew his opinions had been dismissed and his chances to help Jesse were limited, so he spoke with an optimism he did not feel, hoping to influence the jury: "I personally guarantee to employ Jesse Alder, and to increase his wages by a shilling a week to enable him to save for the future. I maintain that I vouch for his good character not only with my words but in my actions in seeking to keep him in work with me."

Murmurings of approval spread through the crowd, a couple of people clapped, and someone let out a loud cheer. Now they were on the side of this good man, but the swaying opinions of those who had pressed into the courtroom that morning would make little difference. It would be Sir Julian and the witnesses who influenced the jury. Everyone awaited the judge's next words.

"Now we must hear from the two witnesses who claim to have seen Mr Alder steal the cup."

Two witnesses? Two? The words screamed and ricocheted about in Harry's mind. Before he could begin to question this new information, Aaron Chapman edged through the onlookers. Before him were two young ragamuffins, both wide-eyed and cowed by the attention which was soon to be upon them. One of these was Toke Browne, the boy who had revelled in Sir Rupert Bannerman's attention on the day of the Whitsun Gallop. The other was, as yet, unknown to Harry, but most likely he was also the son of a labourer from the Burmarsh area. These boys had, no doubt, been involved with the carting of clay from the Marsh to the coast recently. As they neared Harry, he saw their hands and faces had been scrubbed for this moment in court, and their clothes brushed. They wore clean shirts, but the tell-tale signs of clay clinging to the hems of their breeches and the backs of their waistcoats, and the murky colour of their skin at their wrists and necks, told a story of long days toiling on the land. Harry could not despise these boys if they had accepted a shilling or two for fabricating a story. He could and did despise the man who had offered them riches for their lies.

"Who are these boys?" Sir Julian asked as they were presented before him.

They looked back to Aaron who gave a nod. One spoke, "Toke Browne, sir... my lord...sir. From Burmarsh."

"Are you from a Burmarsh family?"

"I am, sir. We live in a cottage on Donkey Street. My Pa works on the land, and I work with him."

"You're missing out on your wages today – I assume you were needed to help with the shifting of clay?"

"I am, sir," Toke replied, his confidence growing. "But I can work this afternoon until nightfall and still earn tuppence."

"And the other one?"

The second boy opened and closed his mouth a few times before whispering his name. Aaron prodded him, and he repeated his words in a high squeak, "David Williams, sir. From Burmarsh, like Toke."

"And what does your father do?"

"He's a looker, and my uncle too. We live near Abbots Court."

"You know Mr Chapman then? Which is why you spoke to him about what you saw at the race?"

The boys exchanged glances and Toke spoke on their behalf, "Mr Chapman lives in our village and he's a good man, sir. He gives money to the church."

A snigger ran through the room, and someone took the opportunity to toss an egg towards the jury.

"I'll throw the lot of you out if there is any more disturbance in this room!" Sir Julian bellowed.

There was a ripple of laughter. Threats were all part of the entertainment! The onlookers fell quiet, not wanting to miss any part of what promised to be a good show.

"Toke Browne, think carefully before you answer this question: Did you see Mr Alder take the prize cup?"

The boy raised his eyes to the ceiling as if considering the matter and responded, "No sir, I didn't see him take it." Murmurs of frustration flowed through the room. But Toke was not finished. "I saw him looking at the cup in a sneaky way and then a few minutes later I looked around again, and there he was, running off with a sack of something under his arm."

111

"What did you think he was up to?"

"I didn't think anything, sir. I was watching the horse race. But then people came asking if anyone had seen anything, and I told Mr Chapman, and he took me to tell Sir Rupert Bannerman from the New Hall."

There were whispers of approval – those who had come to be amused were getting value from this boy!

"He was very respectful to me, Sir Rupert was," Toke added.

"You said you saw Mr Alder running, but then you told me that you were watching the race," Sir Julian queried. "Which was it? The track was one way and the cup the other."

Toke replied in a flash: "They are both true, sir. I was *mostly* watching the race, but I looked back to see who else was about."

"Thank you. That will be all." Sir Julian gestured towards the other boy and asked, "You – David Williams, what did you see on the day of the race?"

"I couldn't see much of the race, sir. I wasn't close enough, so I looked around a bit. I saw Mr Alder – him there… I saw him looking at the cup and standing about a bit."

"Did you see him take the cup?"

"Yes! Yes, I did. And running off… running off very fast."

Now the courtroom erupted and almost every person shared their views with those around them, while Jesse's family shouted out their disbelief.

"It's lies! Lies!" Albie Alder bellowed. "My son is no thief!"

"Silence!" yelled Sir Julian Craythorne.

"Is this true, boy? If our good rector came and placed a bible before you, would you rest your hand on it and swear it to be true?"

David glanced towards his protector, Aaron Chapman, and although his voice was a little shaky, he agreed that he would: "Yes, sir. If the rector cares to do that then I will!"

"Mr Alder..." Sir Julian turned his attention to the accused, "can you tell me why you were looking at the cup?"

"I was near the cup, Your Worship," Jesse said, his voice low but steady. "I can't say that I was looking at it. A boy came to the stall and said there was a gentleman needing assistance with his horse, and could I go to the stalls where the well-to-do folk sit."

"Did you know this boy?"

"I had never seen him before."

"But you went to the stalls?"

"I went to help as I was asked to," Jesse responded. "I looked around and there was no gentleman with a horse, so I went back to the farrier's cart. Not long after that everyone was saying the cup had been stolen."

"Did you see either of these boys who claim to have seen you running away from the stalls?"

"I didn't see them. I was looking for a gentleman and a horse."

Sir Julian allowed his eyes to roam around the room. "Has this boy who took Jesse Alder away from the cart come forward? Or the gentleman who needed assistance? Perhaps they are in this room now?"

There was a general murmuring, but no one spoke up. Finally, it was Harry who addressed him, "Sir, I have spent the last week searching for this boy or the gentleman he spoke of, or indeed anyone to speak in Jesse's favour. They are not to be found. I can send you a hundred men who will speak of Jesse's good name, but none who witnessed anything to help his cause."

"He done it then!" someone shouted from the back of the room.

"One more interruption and the court will be cleared of all spectators," Sir Julian shouted. No one dared to respond, and the jury were addressed, "Members of the jury, I leave it for you to now consider the case. We have the evidence from two boys who both saw the accused looking at the cup and one claims to have seen him take it. What would these boys have to gain by making these statements? Is there any reason for them to lie to the court? Then we have a well-liked and trusted man – the prize cup was found in his place of work not long after he was seen looking at it. I leave you to think carefully and make your judgement."

The jury left the court, retreating to a private office behind the dais. Harry pushed his way through the crowded room to stand with Jesse's family. No words were passed between them but being together gave some comfort. It had come as a shock to realise Aaron had produced two witnesses. *But will the jury believe their lies? Toke seems to be relishing the attention, and David seemed none too certain when asked if he would swear on the bible. Why could I find no one to speak for Jesse?* He considered the members of the jury – had any of them been influenced by Aaron beforehand?

Harry had not finished pondering upon each member of the jury when they filed back in. One spoke to Sir Julian, who had remained seated on the dais. The town constable and bailiff emerged from the swarm of locals and the three men conferred for a moment. The room was silent: everyone hoping to hear a word or two – wanting a hint of the verdict.

"Jesse Alder," Sir Julian Craythorne stood to deliver the verdict without preamble. "You have been accused of stealing and hiding the Whitsun Gallop cup during the day of the race. The jury find you… guilty!"

Chaos reigned within the room. First came the wails of despair and shouts of fury from Jesse's family. Then the cheers and the taunts from those who were there for no other reason than to enjoy the entertainment. A cabbage was thrown and hit the bailiff square on his back. Jesse said nothing – he merely stood with his shoulders slumped and looking at the floor.

"Your punishment…" Sir Julian began, and at once the disruption ceased, "is transportation to the American Colonies for a period of fourteen years." He looked to the gaoler, and ordered, "Take him away."

Chapter Eleven
Phoebe

"You're going this evening?" Phoebe reeled as if her body had taken a sharp slap. A sensation of nausea rose and settled in her throat. She turned away, but not before seeing the look of complete misery on her husband's face.

"I have to." Harry sounded defeated. He *was* defeated. Only the day before he had returned home with the devastating news that Jesse was to be transported. "Sir Rupert could not discuss the court case yesterday but was eager to learn what happened. He invited me to supper this evening, and you know how he expects everyone to do as he asks. We dine at eight."

It was a weak excuse, and Phoebe could not accept it. She gazed out of the parlour window and across the street. A clay cart rumbled by, and a delivery boy raced along with an empty barrow. There had been no rain for weeks, leaving a film of dust to settle on the window frames. "I must brush off these windows," she said, eager to be busy.

"We can send a message for Mary, asking her to help carry your luggage."

"I suppose we must." Phoebe pictured the case and bag, all packed and waiting in their bedroom. "I leave at nine."

"I know."

This distance between them was her fault, of that Phoebe had no doubt. Since the scene in Burmarsh church, she had been uneasy – fearing that mention of her liaison would have spread to Harry. Perhaps it would be Aaron himself who let it slip in the form of a knowing comment? The thought of it becoming known that she had considered... seriously considered being intimate with Aaron sickened Phoebe. Her behaviour towards Harry had been irritable... nervous... withdrawn... *I've not been fair to him. He works all hours and is wretched because he can't help Jesse. He worries, but I can't tell him what bothers me, so instead I leave him to dwell on it. Now Jesse has been found guilty and I am left realising that I could have saved him – but at what cost to my marriage?*

Turning back to face Harry, she said nothing. Not knowing how to apologise for the days of stilted conversation and her pulling away from any gestures of affection. *I know these past days have been difficult for both of us, but I am to sail to Wissant this evening and he... and he will dine with Sir Rupert, thinking nothing of me sitting in the boat for hour after hour. Have I been so intolerable that my husband refuses to walk to the boat with me and would prefer to sup brandy in the New Hall?*

So instead of offering any explanation or attempting to repair the rift between them – and it would only have taken a word or gesture of affection – Phoebe muttered something about the dirty windows and left the room. In the scullery she took an apron from a hook and a brush from a basket, then prepared to scour away her bad mood.

At seven o'clock, when the sun dropped low in the sky, and the palette of colours swathing the coastal village became a rich hue, Phoebe and Harry paused on the track between the church and New Hall. Desperately wanting to make peace with him, Phoebe had suggested that they walk together and say their goodbyes at the last possible moment. She would then go to visit her mother's grave, and he would leave to dine with Sir Rupert and the Bannerman family.

"I'm sorry I can't go with you. Please tell your father and everyone that it could not be helped." Harry reached for her hand.

"My family will be shocked by what happened but they'll understand," Phoebe replied. They had barely spoken during the short walk, and now their words seemed awkward. She paused, not knowing what else to say.

How can it be like this between us? He must think I am angry because he can't come to Wissant, and how he must hate me for it. And because I have been so... so distant since Aaron and I... Harry must think he is at fault, but the fault is all mine. How could I ever think of it? I should never have gone to Burmarsh... Now he goes to dine with Sir Rupert because he cannot bear to me with me for a moment longer than necessary. I am indeed a poor wife to him. As the words tumbled about in her mind. Phoebe allowed her hand to fall away from his. *But whatever my faults – how can he leave me like this? He chooses to be with Sir Rupert on the night I sail to Wissant.*

"I'm going to my mother's grave," she said, then stepped forward to rest her head on his chest for a moment. It was a desperate attempt to claw back some of their lost intimacy, but his body felt wooden.

Harry placed his arms around her and whispered something. His words were lost to Phoebe, and they parted. It seemed neither of them felt the urge to cling to the other despite the separation that lay ahead of them.

"I'll be looking out for Joshua or Walter, wanting to hear you are safe," Harry offered. "I'll be on the seawall, waiting for their return."

"You will be busy – Jesse's family are distraught, and Frank Smith cannot continue to work the forge without your help."

"I will be there," he insisted.

Phoebe moved away, and already she regretted her last words to him. As she stepped into the churchyard and looked towards him, Harry was at the front door of the New Hall. He didn't turn back.

Picking her way past gravestones and wooden markers, Phoebe reached her mother's final resting place on the edge of the holy ground. She chatted to her for a short time, recalling small details of her childhood and telling her that she was about to sail to Wissant. All the time she spoke of joyful things, Phoebe's body felt heavy as if resisting any happiness. She uttered not a word about her troubles with Harry or the guilt she would carry with her across the Channel.

It wasn't until Phoebe walked away that she whispered, "If he follows me to Wissant, then we can make our peace."

As the grandfather clock in the hallway chimed nine, Mary tapped on the back door and entered the kitchen of Walker House. Wearing a hooded cape. Phoebe had already gathered her case and bag. The left immediately, taking the track to the seawall, and exchanging few words. Phoebe was lost in her own thoughts, and the maid knew to be respectful to her mistress' quiet mood. By the time they reached Wall End, the sun had completed its flamboyant evening display and dipped below the horizon. The colours in the sky above the marshland to the west were now muted yellows and greys, while on the beach *Louisa-Ann* was a dark hulk with the water lapping at her hull.

"Let's get you onboard." Walter said, as he nodded a greeting to the two women. "Up the ladder you go, Phoebe, and Mary can pass the case and bag. Push them into the locker under the bow – you know the one."

"Where's Joshua?" Phoebe asked, feeling for the rope ladder at the stern.

"He'll be along soon enough."

The ladder was sticky beneath her hands, but Phoebe gripped tight and hauled herself up, almost toppling into the boat. She found an area of clear deck between the coils of rope and stacked crates, then reached for her case and bag. The exertion, and scents from the sea and boat, invigorated her for a moment. Then Mary's boots were crunching on the shingle bank, and she waved from the top. Her figure melded into the darkness now the last of the light from the sun had passed. Turning away from the beach, Phoebe grappled with the case first, then the bag, shuffling in a sideways movement, until they were deposited in the locker. As she pressed the lid into place, the *Louisa-Ann* lurched, and Phoebe sat down with a thud in her usual spot at the bow.

All at once, there came the sounds of misplaced shingle and the bump as someone threw themselves against the side of the boat, using all their strength to haul themselves up the ladder. Then the boat was afloat, and low voices coupled with the movement of heavy boots on the planks. Oars clunked in the oarlocks.

"Ready?" Walter called, his voice cutting through the chilly night air.

"Ready!" Joshua replied.

She didn't hear the oars slice through the water, but Phoebe felt the small boat begin to forge forwards. The cape she wore that night was thick, and she wrapped it tight around her, then tilting her chin, stared straight ahead into the night sky. Her jaw was tight, and a frown settled on her forehead. It would take at least six hours, probably longer, to cross the Channel and seasickness would soon begin to threaten. Here in the bow, Phoebe would not hinder the men as they changed from oars to sails and settled into their routines. When the nausea began, she was best in the fresh air and keeping herself to herself.

Before long, the oars were set aside and Phoebe turned to see Walter and Joshua setting up the sail, then one was at the tiller and the other remained by the sail as it caught the wind.

"Off she goes!" The satisfaction could be heard in Joshua's voice

"There's a decent breeze tonight," Walter responded.

They made good progress across the steely sea, *Louisa-Ann* rising and falling with the waves. Phoebe began to feel a little queasy. She took long, deep breaths, holding onto the salty air and releasing it slowly. Closing her eyes, she concentrated her thoughts on the dawn that would welcome them to the French coastline emerging before them. *This night will pass. This night will pass,* she told herself over and over.

An hour had gone by since leaving Dymchurch; Phoebe became accustomed to the creaking of the boat and the slap of the waves. She remained hunched in the bow, barely visible to the men who worked the tiller and adjusted the sails. Nausea rose within her, and a light sweat formed on her face until vomiting was the only thing she thought of, and she knew she should force her chilled body to stand. Yet the *Louisa-Ann* ploughed on and still Phoebe could not muster the

121

energy to move. Finally, she opened her eyes and pulled herself up to grasp the side of the boat. The sea breeze was refreshing, and the sickness eased slightly.

Footsteps sounded on the deck. *It will be Walter or Joshua come to see me.* Yet Phoebe didn't turn – she daren't stir up her supper which sloshed uneasily within her.

"Phoebe." Someone placed a hand on her shoulder.

The voice sounded familiar but was not that of the fisherman or his brother. *Who is this on the boat? I didn't realise…* Still holding onto the side, she turned a little.

"It's me – Jesse!"

Jesse? The boat lurched and Phoebe twisted back, pulling herself forward so the gunwale dug into her chest. Her vomit flowed, licking the side of *Louisa-Ann,* and even before it was over, she began to feel better.

"I'm sorry. I didn't mean to…"

There it was again – Jesse's voice. Phoebe fumbled, reaching for a flask of water. Swilling out her mouth, she spat into the sea, then wiped it with a hanky she kept tucked in her bodice. Finally, she was able to face him, unable to speak – unable to express her shock.

"You didn't know?" he asked.

"I didn't know… know about this… about you." Her mouth was sour. Phoebe gulped more water.

"I didn't know either… They just came – about a dozen of them. I know Joshua was one of them because he got on the boat with me, but the others – I don't know who they were."

"You… you were rescued," Phoebe stated. "Like my father was. Do you know about Papa?"

"Not really, but he'll be able to tell me." Jesse stood beside Phoebe and gazed ahead. "I'm going to stay there – that's what Joshua told me. They'll take me to

Wissant and ask your father to help. I'll be safe there. I don't know what I'll do... how I'll get by, but I'll be safe."

"You will!"

For a moment, they were quiet: scanning the sea, looking out for the tiny pinpricks of light emitted from the lamps on the fishing boats and watching the silvery crests of the breaking waves. It seemed they needed to reflect on Jesse being there, for it had come as a surprise to them both

"Harry wasn't there." Jesse broke the silence.

His words were unexpected, and Phoebe shivered. She rubbed her hands on her upper arms. "Harry was dining at the New Hall," she answered, not hiding the bitterness in her tone.

"Oh." Jesse considered this. "At first, I thought he would be here on the boat. I assumed you were both heading for Wissant, and then I realised that he was staying behind because of me. Because of what happened. But I thought he'd have come to see you off?"

"No. No, he didn't." Phoebe reached for a rough blanket Walter had left for her. She raised it, allowing it to unfold, then began to drape it around her shoulders.

"Of course he didn't!" The words erupted from Jesse as if he were triumphant.

Surprised, Phoebe turned to him and explained, "He didn't come because Sir Rupert asked him to dine."

"Yes! And all the while Harry was at the New Hall, no one could say he had any part in my rescue!"

Elation coursed through Phoebe's body. She looked upwards, to the stars shining brightly, winking back at her through the darkness. "I thought he... I thought..." But the words were left unsaid.

Yet Jesse understood. "Harry would always be beside you, unless he really couldn't. I'm sorry he didn't tell you the plan. He could have trusted you."

"It doesn't matter." Phoebe had said enough and changed the subject, "You will be like Papa, do you realise? He could never return to Dymchurch and never made contact. It was five years before I found him. But it will be different because your family will know where you are and even if they never speak of it, they will know you are safe."

"It's closer than the American Colonies," Jesse responded. "And I will arrive as a free man, not in chains. I'll have to learn to speak French..." His words tailed away, as if he was considering this.

"You will, but it will come easily when it is *la seule langue* you hear!" Phoebe laughed. "My family will help."

"I guess that you are saying I will learn soon enough."

Through the darkness Phoebe knew he was smiling, and she felt the anxiety of the last few days wash away. Back in Dymchurch, there would be repercussions for Jesse's disappearance and in Wissant he would have to make a new life, but with a freedom that wouldn't be afforded to him if he were to be transported to the American Colonies. Her thoughts drifted to Lucy, but Phoebe didn't like to mention the lovely young woman who was being left behind. *I hope she understands that Jesse had to leave in this way. When I am home, I can tell her all about Wissant and the people who live there. She could visit, as I do. Or perhaps... perhaps she will choose to go there?*

They spoke for a little longer about nothing of great importance. Phoebe still suffered from seasickness, and at times she could do nothing but face the open water and allow the breeze to sweep across her face while she attempted to breathe deeply and calm herself. She could only assume that Jesse was exhausted and while the elation of his escape had carried him through the past hours, soon the trauma of the last few days would catch up with him.

By the time the pre-dawn sky was showing pink behind the hills of France, and the cliffs and dunes were beginning to take shape, Jesse was fast asleep on the narrow bench in *Louisa-Ann's* cuddy, and Phoebe drowsed under her layers of shawl and blanket in the bow.

Chapter Twelve
Harry

The clock in the hallway of Walker House had just chimed half past eight when there came a brisk rapping on the front door. In the kitchen, Janey looked at Harry, her expression enquiring. He raised his eyebrows in response and pushed his near-empty porridge bowl aside.

"I suspect our visitor is the butler from the New Hall," Harry informed the housekeeper. "It could be that he as important news."

The relationship between Harry and the housekeeper was informal, going so far as him preferring to eat in the kitchen rather than the dining room, yet he had not divulged that he was expecting to be called upon at any moment. Later in the day, when Janey heard of Jesse's escape, she would only guess of her employer's involvement and would not presume to ask him about it.

"I'll answer the door," Janey replied, already moving into the hallway.

By the time she returned with Brown in tow, Harry had risen from the table.

"You're wanted at the New Hall," the butler told Harry. "By Sir Rupert's orders."

"I wonder what he could need from me when it was only last night we dined together," Harry responded, careful to keep his tone serious. "When does he want to see me?"

"Immediately!"

The reply came as a surprise, for it was well known that Sir Rupert rarely started his business of the day before half past ten. "Now?" Harry repeated. "Very well. I'll… I'll come straight away."

"Damn you, Farrers!" Sir Rupert exclaimed, as Harry entered the dining room. The Leveller of the Marsh Scotts was seated at the head of an elegant table with the remains of his eggs and bacon before him. His wig had not yet been tweaked to perfection and his face showed the signs of yesterday's hair growth. The shirt he wore was loose at the neck and without the adornment of a colourful cravat. "Damn you!" he repeated as he stood. "I'll swear that it was me who invited you to dine here last night, yet somehow you contrived it. And now you'll have me telling Sir Julian and the constable and whoever else cares to ask that you were in my company and innocent of any plot to free Jesse Alder!"

"And a delightful evening it was." Harry refrained from smiling. "Your daughter, Isabella, is growing into a true beauty – the very image of Lady Charlotte. Will she be in London for the next season? I swear every beau will be clamouring to marry her."

Sir Rupert, so easily side-tracked, beamed, "Indeed! They will stay in the Belsey-Knight's townhouse belonging to my Lady's brother. Eleanor is demanding to join her elder sister, but Isabella will have none of it!"

"And George shows a keen interest in local matters. I am sure all the jurats appreciate his growing knowledge. He is already quite the expert when discussing the seawall!"

"I am glad you see it!" Sir Rupert pushed the last of his egg onto the fork. "He is a little serious, but I believe within the next few years George will be seen as an authority on the structure and maintenance of our wall. He is speaking of journeying to Suffolk and Norfolk to study their sea defences, lest we may learn from them. I've told him that it is they who should travel here for there is no bigger and better structure than our own Dymchurch Wall!"

"I very much enjoyed hearing George speak of it over dinner," Harry replied, "and I would wholeheartedly support his plans. Although, without doubt, our wall is superior, it does no harm to see if we can learn from others."

Suddenly aware that Harry remained standing, Sir Rupert gestured for him to sit. "Don't clutter the place. Help yourself to breakfast if you like, and I am sure Brown will bring more coffee shortly." Then he looked at Harry as if seeing him for the first time and let out a guffaw. "You've had me over again! I had Brown fetch you at this ungodly hour so I could have a stern word with you. You were in on this scheme to release Jesse Alder – I'd swear on our good vicar's Bible. Not only where you up to your neck in it, but you fixed it that I was your alibi! Now we speak of my children, and you are about to eat breakfast at my table! I can't help but admire you, Harry Farrers!"

"Your words are most kind, Sir Rupert. I am honoured to eat at your table and hold the role of jurat."

Ignoring these words of flattery, the Leveller of the Marsh Scotts returned to the reason why Harry had been called upon at this early hour. "Young Jesse has gone. By God, there will be an uproar over this matter!"

"I won't insult you by pretending this is the first I heard of it," Harry responded.

"I knew it!" Sir Rupert was jubilant.

"It must have been past eleven last night when I left here and walked the short distance between our homes," Harry enlarged. "The night was peaceful, and I could hear the lapping of the tide against the wall. I didn't expect to see a soul, but there was a fellow resting against the trunk of the old oak tree – the one not far from the maypole. We exchanged a friendly greeting, and he told me that he had heard tales of a man being freed from the Romney gaol."

The account was truthful, with one important point omitted – although his features were obscured by a cap pulled low on his forehead and a scarf covering his chin, this man was known to Harry. Matthew Alder was cousin to Jesse and one of John Waller's team on the seawall. Their meeting was no fluke but planned. Few words had passed between the men, yet Harry had been told all he needed to know – the keeper of the town gaol had put up little resistance and Jesse had been freed from his cell without complication. Matthew had seen his cousin clamber onboard the *Louisa-Ann* and was sure that the plan had run without hitch.

"Did you think of returning to tell me, or hasten to New Romney to see if there was any truth in the matter? Or even seek to find Jesse Alder?"

"No, sir. Your fine brandy and the long day had made me quite sleepy. I can't pretend this was not good news to me, and I went to bed feeling quite unburdened."

"Unburdened!" Sir Rupert repeated. "Now that is a happy state to be in. No doubt I too should be unburdened if I had not been woken at some ungodly hour by Brown rapping on my bedroom door."

"I'm sorry to hear that sir, although I still can't help but be relieved that Jesse does not have to suffer transportation." He paused to thank Brown who silently slipped into the room and filled a coffee cup for Harry,

129

then replenished Sir Rupert's. "I wonder what will become of him?"

"I shall not breathe a word of this outside the room, not even to my Lady Charlotte," Sir Rupert paused to sip at his coffee, "But I do wonder at the coincidence that Jesse was freed on the very night your good wife set sail to Wissant."

"Phoebe's visit to her family was arranged months ago," Harry pointed out. "As you say, a mere coincidence. She will be there by now, God willing."

"With her father, Jacques Bernard, who displeased the people of Dymchurch by daring to marry a local woman and settle here. They are a funny lot, my people living in the shadows of our seawall. They will trade with the French all day long given half a chance, but to have one living amongst them – oh no! That will not do at all."

"Life in Wissant is pleasant for Jacques. I can only be grateful that Phoebe returned to be my wife."

With these words Harry felt a pang of guilt. *Whatever has been wrong between us for the past few days, I should never have let her leave me before it was settled. I should have spoken to her, but I was too caught up with trying to help Jesse. She knew that. She would have understood. It wasn't that Phoebe felt neglected. There was something else.*

"I hope I am freed from my duties here so I can go with Walter to collect Phoebe and spend a few hours with her family," Harry continued. "But who knows what the repercussions of Jesse's escape may be and, regardless of that, I am left without my apprentice, yet barely able to find the time to work in the forge myself. I must look for another assistant and hope that Frank Smith is able to offer a few more hours of his time. Will you excuse me now? Or was there anything you needed of me?"

Sir Rupert drained his cup and stood, giving Harry the permission he needed to leave the table. But when he spoke, the older man once more thwarted Harry's plans, "Good of you to offer – we are both busy men but of course it would serve you well to be seen to be fully engaged in the hunt for our escaped convict."

"Ah! So, I am wanted in New Romney?"

"I had the foresight to ask that my grey mare be made available for you. Your own horse is a reliable beast, but I thought you would appreciate..."

He is wily! I'll credit him with that! Now I am forced to thank him for his generosity and with the grey there is no excuse for me not making haste to New Romney.

"How kind of you! It will of course save me time if I don't have to prepare my own horse and I admit to being partial to yours." Harry forced a cheerful smile. *How will I ever begin to start on the duties of running my own business?*

By the time the church clock in New Romney was striking ten, Harry was dismounting the grey in the yard behind the New Inn. "I'll need her again shortly, but if you would rub her down and provide water, I'd appreciate it," he said to the young stablehand while passing him the reins. "I have some business to attend to."

"I'll wager you're here about that man who got out last night," the stablehand replied.

"No need to wager!" Harry replied. "What do you know about it?" The New Inn butted up against Town Hall House with its two cells, which in turn was beside the town hall.

"I've been courting Tilly who works for him over there," the stablehand nodded towards Town Hall House. "It was her who discovered them all locked up in the gaol when she got up to light the fire this morning."

"Them?" Harry asked, trying to picture the scene. "Locked up?" *I thought I knew what happened last night, but it seems I only heard part of it!*

"The town gaoler, his wife and the housekeeper," the stablehand told him. "Furious they were. In fact, Tilly didn't know who they were angriest with – whoever put them in there, or her for not hearing their cries for help. She sleeps sound, you see."

"They were left in the cell?" Harry found himself saying, despite it now being clear enough. "Blazes! What a thing to happen!"

"I can't help chuckling over it – each one of them is as dour as the next. They lead my Tilly a merry dance. Do this... do that... and never happy. She'll pay for sleeping all night, I'm telling you..." As he spoke, the stablehand pulled a rag from the pocket of his apron and began rubbing the ribbons of sweat from the mare's coat. His manner with the horse was gentle, and Harry couldn't help liking this lively fellow.

"Did you hear anything in the night?" Harry asked, curiosity getting the better of him.

"Oh yes! I've got my quarters up there in the loft and there's not much going on in these back yards that I don't hear." He waved the rag towards the cosy spaces above the stables. "But I keep my eyes shut and turn my back to any goings-on, if you know what I mean. I see nothing and then I don't get myself into trouble."

"You're a wise man," Harry assured him. "And I hope Tilly doesn't suffer for this."

"I'll look after your grey mare," the man assured him. "She's a beauty."

"Thank you. She is, but she belongs to Sir Rupert Bannerman of Dymchurch," Harry informed him. "I'll be back for her in no time at all."

He returned to Church Road, taking a few steps before approaching the town hall and covered marketplace from the rear. The market was in full swing with vendors peddling their wares from trestle tables, and housewives vying for attention. With the stalls tucked in below the courtroom, the air lingered thick with the combined odours of sweat, dried herbs, lavender, smoked cheese and cured meats – each one mixing with the next as Harry eased his way through.

"Fresh eggs!"

"Get your ham here!"

"Hot pies – no need to cook yer husband a dinner!"

Harry wound his way through the mêlée, suffering a jab in the hip from a wicker basket and almost tripping over a scrawny child who was dashing for discarded cabbage leaves. Brushing against the supporting pillars, then leaning down to flick straw from his breeches, he reached the relatively fresh air of the High Street.

"Ah! There you are!"

Before Harry had been given the chance to absorb his surroundings, someone approached him.

"I thought you would come," Edward Woodall, town constable, continued.

"Sir Rupert sent for me before I had finished breakfast," Harry told him. "We must see if the escapee can be found, of course."

Before Mr Woodall could even think of replying there came a clattering of hooves through the street. They turned to witness two horses being ridden with total disregard to the safety of the townsfolk of New Romney, nor to the magnificent beasts. A beautiful black steed, and the other a bay, were both sweating profusely, indicating they had been pushed at speed despite the gathering heat of the day. They came to a halt beside Harry and the constable, and the riders dismounted with ease, leaving the reins loose across their horses' withers. As Aaron Chapman and his brother, Daniel, stood there, Harry couldn't help noticing the riding crops in their hands and found their presence menacing.

"What do you have to say about this?" Aaron pointed his crop at Harry. "You had a hand in his release – I'm certain of it!"

"I had nothing to do with it," Harry kept his tone level as he responded. "I did everything I could to find someone who could prove Jesse innocent, but it couldn't be done."

"So, you resorted to breaking into a gaol!"

"How could I do that?"

"I'll find someone who saw you there," Aaron threatened. "Watch out Farrers!"

"Then you'll find someone who calls the Leveller of the Marsh Scotts a liar!" Harry retorted. "I dined at the New Hall last evening and stayed until late. Young George Bannerman is quite an authority on the maintenance of the wall. It was an interesting evening. But if you'll excuse me, I believe the constable wishes to speak with me."

Edward Woodall took the opportunity to continue their brief conversation. "Indeed, we must make a thorough search of the area. Men are going out in pairs but…" He shot a look towards the Chapman brothers, then continued. "…I suggest you wait for William Payne. He will be here in a moment.

"When he arrives, which direction should we take?" Harry asked.

"Take the road to Lydd and ride as far as the town, please. Look in any barns or likely hiding places as you go," Edward Woodall replied. "If there is no luck in finding our convict today, then we can assume he has gone further afield. I shall issue a warrant for his arrest should he return to Romney Marsh, but he is not a dangerous man and I see no reason to waste our time on this matter."

"No reason to waste our time?" Aaron repeated. "This man has not only been branded a thief but has escaped a fair and just punishment. Have him brought back to Romney and sent to the gallows!"

"Mr Chapman," the constable snapped. "Like you, I have my business and family to attend to. My role in keeping law and order is both voluntary and intended to fit around my other duties. With respect, I adhere to Sir Julian Craythorne's demands and am not here to suit the whims of every jurat on the Marsh."

Momentarily astounded by the force of these words, Aaron's response came with a shrug of his shoulders, "I will speak to Sir Julian myself then. In the meantime, has anyone set off along the Newchurch Road?"

"They haven't. If you were to ride to Newchurch and then Burmarsh, that would be helpful. I already have men scouring the lanes to St Mary in the Marsh and Ivychurch."

"Very well." Aaron glanced at his brother, and they turned to mount their horses.

Knowing that Jesse would not be found on Romney Marsh, or even within Kent or neighbouring Sussex, Harry felt relief to see Aaron tighten the reins and swing his horse around. However, there was to be no respite from his rival's poisonous tongue. His next words were to fester in Harry's mind for the following weeks, causing the rift between him and Phoebe to deepen…

Chapter Thirteen
Harry

"It was a pleasure to see your wife last week." Aaron twisted in the saddle and looking directly at Harry, he hurled his parting words towards him. "Just as seductive as I remembered her to be… Give her my regards when you get home."

Harry felt his body tense and a chill ran down his spine. Somehow he forced a reply, keeping his tone steady: "She is in Wissant."

"I shall look forward to her return then. Perhaps the maid could inform me of it. She seems obliging enough!" Turning away, he spoke to his brother, "Newchurch it is then…" In unison they pressed their heels against the flanks of their horses, commanding them to walk on.

"I'm glad to say I rarely have dealings with that man," Edward Woodall said after the men stood in silence for a moment watching the Chapman brothers depart. "There's some funny business surrounding the conviction of your apprentice, and I can't say I felt sorry to hear of his escape."

Harry barely heard his words. It took a moment for them to register and when they did his reply was vague, "Escape… I'm glad of it. He is a good man and didn't deserve this." He glanced towards the New Inn, feeling the need to stride in and demand a brandy. The tavern was not yet open, so instead he said, "I'll fetch my horse, then ride to Lydd as you suggested."

"There's William Payne now," Mr Woodall remarked as he looked along the High Street.

"I'll be no time at all," Harry replied. Already he was turning into the market, then weaving his way through stalls and pressing past women with their capacious baskets. He dashed past outbuildings and turned into the yard behind the New Inn.

"Back already!" the stablehand commented.

Harry gave him a couple of coins, then gathered the reins and prepared to mount the grey mare. "I've been asked to ride to Lydd. They want Jesse Alder found."

"I hope he's crossed the border to Sussex," the stablehand responded. "Those who freed him did a grand job."

I pray he's crossed the Channel by now, Harry thought, but as soon as he visualised Jesse walking across the beach at Wissant, another picture assaulted his mind. Now he saw Phoebe on those golden sands, her face tilted upwards and expression eager, but instead of its being her father or aunt waiting for her, Aaron stood eagerly watching her approach.

Harry had left the yard on the mare and was back in the High Street before realising that he had not answered the stablehand, nor thanked him for taking care of the horse. In those few minutes all he had seen was an image of Phoebe's radiant face and her eyes glowing as she greeted a love who was not her husband.

The present crashed through these improbable scenes, and Harry felt almost startled to hear William Payne greeting him. "Harry! I hear we are to ride to Lydd. It's as good a place as any to search for our missing man."

"If he's hiding out then it is..." came the automatic reply.

The men fell into place, walking the horses side by side. No other words were exchanged as they negotiated the busy High Street. Within minutes they were leaving New Romney behind them and taking the road to Lydd. Harry liked William Payne well enough. He was a man of about thirty years with a tendency to avoid the powdered wigs and ruffles which the men of fashion usually adorned themselves. If he was a little opinionated then he meant no harm, and he ran his farm with efficiency, treating his workers fairly.

The road swung to the south and with Lydd now directly ahead, Harry pressed his horse to canter for a few minutes. William stayed alongside, but eventually instructed his bay gelding to walk. "We won't spot anything amiss if we hasten to Lydd without pausing to search a barn or two."

"It's pointless." Harry slowed the mare. "*If* Jesse has gone this way, then he'll have journeyed further than Lydd by now. But you are right, we must be seen to have done our best."

"Your mind is on your wife and that weasel Chapman," William stated.

The words walloped Harry, and he felt vomit rise within him. He inhaled slowly and the sensation passed.

"The constable told me," William continued. "Said that there was some nastiness. Aaron likes to cause trouble and especially for you. He's jealous. Nothing more than that, but it still makes him dangerous."

"I've had difficulties with him since I arrived in Dymchurch," Harry replied. "But to have Jesse put in gaol for a crime he didn't commit, and to persuade people to lie for him... it's gone too far. Now Phoebe..."

"Phoebe is a lovely woman. My Marianne likes her a lot," William told him. "Whatever he suggested, it's nothing but malice. But it worked, didn't it? Aaron has got you thinking things you know aren't true." He looked directly at Harry, making sure his point was heard and understood, then continued, "We'll go to Lydd and back like we said we would. Perhaps we'll have a drink and a pie in the George and ask around. The constable will be happy enough, and you can go home and give your beautiful wife a bit of affection. You'll soon see where her fondness lies."

"She's in Wissant!" Harry responded, but he couldn't help smiling as he saw the dismay on William's face.

"Wissant! Well, there's not much to be done. I thought you usually went with her." There was a brief pause as William digested this news, before saying, "By God! You didn't stay behind because of that sewer rat Chapman?"

"No! I knew nothing of their apparent meeting until we met in the High Street just before you came along. Phoebe left last night."

"Last night?" William repeated.

They continued along the road to Lydd, walking the horses at a steady pace and both absorbed with their thoughts. Every so often Harry made a point of shading his eyes and gazing into the distance, as if looking for a likely hiding place, and his companion veered onto the grassy verge to study the drainage ditch, one of the likely places a fugitive might hide.

Finally, William voiced his thoughts, "Your wife left for Wissant at the same time as Jesse Alder escaped from his cell."

"It appears so," Harry replied, then added, "I was dining with Sir Rupert and his family."

"Good for you!" William let out a chortle. "I like you, Harry. I'll say no more of it. I like Phoebe too, so when you're free, go and join her."

Harry smiled. "I will. Thank you. I feel a lot better now."

Taking the lead by suddenly pressing his horse into a trot, William called out, "Pie and ale at the George?"

"Why not?"

From the dining parlour of the George Inn, the men could observe life passing along Lydd's busy High Street. The clatter of hooves, the rumble of a cart and snatches of conversation accompanied hearty pies filled with mutton, potato and onions. They drank red wine from the cellars of the inn, and each licked their fingers that dripped with gravy. Both the wine and company eased the last of Harry's troubled thoughts. On leaving the room, they came across a young man with a roll of posters, one of which he was displaying to the landlord.

"Imagine it! I'll wager the gentry will flock to Lydd. You and your lady wife will benefit – there's no doubt of it! If we were to put a poster here..."

"What's all this about?" William leaned across to read the poster. "Oh! Another race."

"You read in haste, my friend!" the young man protested. "I shall not have you going here and there talking of a race. It is a Match Against Time! What do you make of that?"

Neither Harry nor William could help but have their interest spiked by this. "A Match Against Time?" William queried.

"Indeed! A Mr Humphrey Fletcher, gentleman of Canterbury, is to ride twenty lengths of the Rype within the hour on his gelding, Whistlejacket!" At this the young man jabbed at both the name of the rider and that of his horse.

"Within an hour?" Harry tried to imagine the scene.

The Rype was an area of common ground, infertile, with a covering of tough grass. To the north-east, it tucked up against the cottages, windmills, taverns and shops of the town, making a handy area to tether goats, or create pens for chickens. The land, criss-crossed by tracks, stretched out towards the shingle headland of Dungeness, finally petering out where soil gave way to stones. Open and windswept, the few trees whose roots were bold enough to cling to and take what nutrients they could leech from the poor soil, bowed from years of being assaulted by the prevailing coastal winds.

"What brings a gentleman from Canterbury to Lydd?" William asked. "Why trek all this way to make a show of something, when it could be done just as well, if not better, nearer his home?"

"It's what he does!" the young man informed them. "And if the gentleman wants a stretch of firm ground to gallop without hindrance, then he could do no better than the Rype!"

"Or the beach?" William suggested.

But by now the landlord had caught up with the idea. "This gentleman – is he known amongst those who enjoy a flutter? Are we to bet on whether it can be done?"

"That's exactly what we shall do!" The young man beamed and smoothed the poster, preventing it from curling. "And I can assure you that he is known. Mr Humphrey Fletcher provokes interest wherever he and Whistlejacket go. He is both charming and daring. Full of plans for new challenges."

"It can't be done!" the landlord claimed. From one end to the other, turning around again and again. Twenty times in an hour, you say?"

"It says it here!"

"Then I shall indeed be wealthy on it!" the landlord exclaimed. "I shall produce my own poster offering hot dinners and stabling, as well as putting a pound against him winning this Match Against Time!"

"A pound?" William repeated. "Are you sure? Because you can be certain Mr Fletcher believes he can succeed."

"I am certain of it!" the landlord replied with bravado. "Can I have more than one poster? We are a large establishment here at the George."

"We must fetch our horses," Harry prompted William. "Let's leave these men to debate the matter. News of the challenge will soon spread if it goes ahead."

As they left by the door to the stable yard, a second poster was being unfurled and offered to the eager landlord.

Both Harry and William were in good spirits for the return journey to New Romney. Not a moment had passed recently when Harry had not been furiously trying to spare Jesse from being convicted. He had been thwarted at every turn and forced to leave his forge under the care of Frank Smith, only able to dash in to check that all was well. The ride to Lydd and the meal at the George had given him much-needed relief, despite being under the guise of searching for the escaped man.

"I'll find the constable or Sir Julian," William offered when they reached New Romney. "If anyone asks, then we searched every barn and hideaway, but now you must deal with your business in Dymchurch. After all, you have lost your apprentice, so must work twice as hard until you replace him."

"Thank you!" Harry grinned. "Thank you for your friendship and good advice. I'll miss Jesse but am grateful to Frank for stepping back into his old job."

New Romney was soon behind him, but without William's company Harry's thoughts soon returned to the rift between himself and Phoebe. Aaron's taunts had hit him hard and, much as he tried to ignore them, there was one which turned over and over in his mind: *'I shall look forward to her return then – perhaps the maid could inform me of it. She seems obliging enough!'* He encouraged the grey mare to canter for a short time but still the words pounded, almost in time with the beat of the horse's hooves.

Harry had planned to speak with Frank, but instead he pressed on past the forge, shops and taverns, not stopping at his own home and finally arriving at the stable yard of the New Hall. Here he handed the reins to a boy and gave the mare an affectionate pat before departing. Minutes later, he was entering Walker House and striding through to the kitchen.

"Janey?"

"Mr Farrers?" The housekeeper staggered to her feet, having been slumbering in an easy chair.

Harry felt a pang of guilt, knowing the long hours she worked. "I'm sorry! I didn't mean to… I was looking for Mary. I don't expect she's here?"

"Mary? No, she did the two hours as usual and went back home to help her ma."

"Of course she did." *We talked between ourselves about Mary coming to work here but never made her an offer. Why is there not enough time to deal with everything?* Harry walked through to the pantry and picked up a jug of small ale. He poured some into a glass and gulped it down without pausing, then placed the vessel in the scullery. "I'll be out for another couple of hours," he told Janey, retracing his steps to the front door.

After bounding across the road, Harry moved through a wedge of land with scattered homes, vegetable plots and animal pens. The grassy bank of the seawall rose before him, but this was not his destination. Instead, he paused near a low, two-roomed cottage, then spotted a woman on her knees gathering beans from trailing vines growing over a low frame. "Hello! I'm looking for Mary."

Lizzie turned and hauled herself up, placing one hand under the swell of her rounded stomach. "Mary? Oh! ...Mr Farrers... She's in the cottage preparing the cabbage and onions." Leaving the basket of beans on the ground, she toddled towards the open doorway. "Mary! It's Mr Farrers."

Mother and daughter exchanged a few words and Mary approached Harry, her hands nervously brushing at specks of dirt on her apron. "Is something wrong, Mr Farrers?"

"I hope not Mary, but I just needed to ask you something."

"Have I done something wrong?"

"Not at all, and as soon as Mrs Farrers is back then she'll be speaking to you about coming to work more hours for us, but that's not why I came." Harry paused, hardly knowing what to say next. "Do you know Mr Chapman from Burmarsh?"

Mary lowered her eyes while a pinkness bloomed on her cheeks and neck. "I know who he is, sir."

"Did my wife ask you to take him a message or... speak to him?" Harry felt his mouth dry. The residue from the ale tasted sour.

"She did... I took a note, and he said she was to meet him in the church."

Unable to bear the girl's discomfort, Harry smiled. "There must have been some business to attend to. She's gone to Wissant, as you know, and I can't ask her myself."

"Yes!" Mary clutched at the suggestion, "Church! She's very helpful, Mrs Farrers is. Always kind to me."

"And if you couldn't pass the note to Mr Chapman, would you give it to his wife or the housekeeper?"

Mary frowned as she considered this. "No. No, it was to go to a maid with red hair. But I saw him myself so there was no need."

"Of course not," Harry agreed. "I'll see you tomorrow then, Mary." He gave a nod to Lizzie who waited nearby, then turned away, walking briskly over the uneven ground.

Taking a steep path up the seawall, Harry soon had the whole bay before him. He took no notice of the view, walking briskly until he came to the City of London tavern which nestled beside the great bank. The door was open, and he entered, barely faltering despite its being so dim inside and the air thick with tobacco smoke. "A brandy please," Harry said. "Large."

Chapter Fourteen
Phoebe

"Que faire?" Grand-mère wondered.

"Il est si fatigué." Tante Marie placed a blanket over Jesse's knees as he slumbered in an armchair by the kitchen fire. She was already feeling maternal towards the young Englishman.

In the large kitchen with its whitewashed walls and soot-darkened paintings, the table had been extended with the addition of another from the garden, and both covered in linen cloths. Extra chairs came from the veranda and placed around, barely leaving enough space to squeeze past the pearwood dresser on one side, or into the scullery on the other. The aftermath of a generous feast was spread across the tables, from scattered breadcrumbs to the remains of a creamy cheese on a platter, slices of cured meat, now curling at the edges, and small jugs with dribbles of garlicky oil licking the spout.

There was an air of celebration and some confusion in the Bernard home. The conversation had flowed during their midday meal – a mixture of French and English, enhanced by gestures, and with voices raised in the hope of making the meaning clearer. Phoebe's French was almost fluent, while Walter and Joshua always made great efforts to join this family gathering on their annual trip to Wissant. Today a new

Englishman was unexpectedly amongst them, adding to the difficulties in communicating freely.

Jesse's story had been told, then repeated as Phoebe's two boy cousins arrived from the market. Every one of the family knew how her papa had been imprisoned in the Dymchurch gaol and accused of a crime he did not commit, so their instincts to shelter the young stranger were strong.

"These English from Dymchurch do not have the sense to see when a man is good and honest," Grand-mère complained. "We see it in his face, yet they do not."

"It is not all of Dymchurch," Phoebe objected, although it would make no difference. "It was one man wanting to cause trouble."

"The same man whose words almost sent me to the gallows," Jacques reminded her.

"Yes, the same man," Phoebe admitted. She could still feel Aaron's kisses on her lips and neck, and his hands squeezing at her breasts. She could still smell the damp of the ancient stone and musty embroidered cloth in the vestry of Burmarsh Church.

"He'll have to stay here," Grand-mère declared.

"Of course!" Tante Marie, Oncle Marc and Jacques agreed.

"But where?" Tante Marie asked, raising her palms upwards. "There is no room for another bed with the boys, and he cannot share with Grand-mère and our little Mireille."

"Maman, I am no longer little!" Phoebe's cousin proclaimed, "But we cannot have this man in our room!"

"You cannot have a man in your room!" Phoebe agreed. She wrapped an arm around the girl's waist. The affection between them was strong. "Jesse is a good man. He always has a smile, but there is no room for him here." She looked at Jacques, "Papa, is there room in your home?"

Jacques Bernard lived in a two-roomed cottage just a step away from the town square. It was one in a terrace of small, yet solid, homes, with a sizeable living room and a small bedroom in the loft space. The orange roof tiles, typical of the area, were cheerful and enhanced by the walls he whitewashed every now and then.

"I can offer him a bed downstairs," he said, "and be glad to help him."

"Can he handle a boat?" Oncle Marc asked the Dymchurch fishermen who followed the conversation the best they could.

"He can row or sail as well as any young man!" Walter replied.

"Then he will fish with us while he learns our language and decides if there is another trade he would rather follow," Marc concluded.

"But he won't stay?" Mireille asked. "He'll go home like Phoebe did, after the first time she came?"

"No, *ma chérie*, he won't go home. He can't ever go home," Phoebe replied. "Soon you will forget he came from Dymchurch, when he speaks French as well as you do, and he wears a beret and a smock!"

"And drinks wine not ale!" The girl laughed.

"But before that, he must have a wash!" Marie suggested. "The poor man has been imprisoned for ten days. Marc, do you have a pair of breeches and a shirt? He's about your size." She eyed her brother-in-law, Jacques. "You are too slim, but we only need one outfit. With Phoebe here as well, we can soon sew more garments, and the men can ask about in the market. He'll need a good coat if he is to go out to sea."

Those sat around the table pondering on this for a moment. The living from the sea was humble, and to give a man a thick coat would be an act of generosity beyond the means of most villagers.

"He can have mine from *Louisa-Ann*," Joshua suggested. "If I get a bit of a chill heading back, then we have a blanket. I'll be glad to tell Jesse's family that I could do something to help him."

"There's an idea," Walter agreed. "He has a decent pair of boots, and those clothes he is wearing will come clean."

"For now we need to let the man sleep," Jacques told them. "You cannot imagine the exhaustion he suffers."

The adults nodded their acceptance. Satisfied that her family were all in agreement with the plan to help the Dymchurch man who was to become a part of life in Wissant, a feeling of contentment settled upon Phoebe. She became increasingly drowsy and knew within the hour she would be compelled to sleep.

"The cherries!" the words burst from Mireille, and her young face beamed with expectation.

"The cherries?" her mother, Marie, dealt a swift slap. "*Sacrébleu!* You must wait for Grand-mère to decide when the cherries will be given. And we have our guest to consider."

In the centre of the table a wide-necked bottle held a clear, pure alcohol. Settled at the bottom, was a mound of fruit, infusing their flavour for the past year and in turn soaking up the liquor. In that time, whenever anyone had glanced at the bottle, usually stored on the top shelf in the scullery, they knew that it awaited the arrival of Phoebe. As dust gathered upon the thick glass, it marked the passing of time and the knowledge that she would visit again when the summer came, not long before the feast of *la Saint Jean-Baptiste* on June 24th.

They all looked at Jesse, slumped in the chair and oblivious to their chatter, then turned to Grand-mère who studied him the longest. Finally, she spoke. "Our visitor needs sleep more than he needs to celebrate his being here. We have *la belle* Phoebe in our home again, and he will not mind if we drink without him."

Mireille and her brothers let out muted cheers of approval, while eyeing *Maman* lest she should be too free with her slaps again.

Marie, giving a nod of approval, bustled towards the dresser, returning to the table with a tray holding numerous small glasses. First, she served Grand-mère, then Phoebe who took a tentative sip, enjoying the feeling of warmth flooding her mouth. Smiling, she raised the glass to her lips once more.

The children were each given four cherries from the bottle. They took each fruit with a pincer grip and bit into the flesh, sweet and potent with liquor. The stones were spat onto empty dinner plates and fingers licked clean.

Sleep beckoned the men, more so now the meal had left them pleasantly full, and the alcohol was dulling their senses. They had fished throughout the night, then accompanied the small boat as the donkeys hauled it from the beach and into the marketplace. As soon as the catch was displayed before the housewives, they had begun making purchases, while a cart was loaded to take fish inland. It was a hectic time for the fishermen and all this with the chaos and banter amongst the characters in the village square. Later that morning, the boat still needed swilling out, the nets cleaning and tools tidied away. Only then could they go to see Phoebe and learn more about the stranger who had arrived on their shore. Now they could sleep through the afternoon. Jacques dropped a kiss on Phoebe's head, and Oncle Marc patted her on the shoulder.

"*A bientôt*," she said, understanding that they must leave. "See you later." She reached for her glass of liquor and drained the last drop, while watching Tante Marie and Mireille gathering the dishes. *I must help,* Phoebe thought, yet she remained at the table listening to Grand-mère speaking. There was a sense of everything feeling not quite real, and Phoebe felt her head jerk. "Sorry. Sorry," she murmured to no one in particular.

"Go to bed." Marie was at her side, encouraging Phoebe to stand. "You must sleep."

"I must help you…" But Phoebe allowed herself to be led upstairs where she collapsed on the bed she would share with Mireille and fell asleep before the blanket had been draped across her.

"You are happy to be here, but what makes you feel so sad?" Tante Marie whispered. "We will talk about it soon."

It wasn't until the evening sun lent the sands at Wissant a golden glow and beamed through the open windows in the Barnard family home, settling on the face of the sleeping man, that he woke. Not long before, Phoebe had stumbled down the stairs, to the now peaceful kitchen and gulped at a cup of water freshly drawn from the well. Now she stood in the doorway between the scullery and kitchen, wondering what was to become of Jesse over the following months, and ready to go to him when he was fully roused.

The household slumbered. Phoebe's papa had gone home to rest, and Oncle Marc would be asleep in the downstairs bedroom. When she had glimpsed outside, there was no sign of the boys. Perhaps they had returned to the marketplace? Grand-mère and Mireille sat under the shade of the fruit trees, both sewing.

There was movement behind Phoebe, and Tante Marie came to stand next to her. "That poor man," she murmured. "He has left his family and home and comes to us knowing nothing of our ways."

"He is a good man and will be grateful," Phoebe whispered her reply. "Better to come to my family in Wissant than travel to the American Colonies to work as no more than a slave."

They spoke in French but stopped as Jesse's eyes focused on them, and he gave a smile. "I'm sorry I fell asleep." He eased himself out of the chair, his body still heavy and mind sluggish.

"I have only just woken," Phoebe stepped forward, wanting to reassure him. "And the men – my father, uncle, Walter and Joshua – they are all sleeping. My family here are fishermen, and they are used to resting all hours of the day."

"Come to the garden," Marie suggested. "Phoebe – perhaps he would like some water?"

"Merci," Jesse replied. "How do I say it? How do I thank them for welcoming me?"

"Merci de votre accueil chez vous," Phoebe spoke slowly.

"Merci de votre accueil chez vous," Jesse repeated looking at Marie.

Reaching out to touch his forearm, she replied, *"Nous sommes de la famille maintenant."*

"My family are your family now," Phoebe told him. "They are happy to help you."

They walked into the garden where Grand-mère and Mireille looked expectantly towards the newcomer.

"Merci de votre accueil chez vous," Jesse said, concentrating on each word.

"Bravo!" Mireille called out. "Very good!"

Jesse smiled at her enthusiasm, then turned to Phoebe his face serious and asked, "What am I to do?

I have been in these clothes for nearly two weeks, and I need to use the..."

"The closet?" Phoebe nodded towards a wooden shack. "Go – and then you will wash how we do it here in Wissant. Oncle Marc has left clean clothes in the kitchen, and yours will soon be laundered."

"*Merci.*" Jesse flashed a grin at her. "Teach me another word – the closet!"

"*Les toilettes!*" Phoebe called, as he scurried away. Mireille shrieked with laughter.

There were only the women at home to show Jesse how they washed behind a screen in the garden of the Bernard home. He was provided with a rough towel and a cloth, then shown a slab of soap in a dish. Three pitchers of water, full to the brim, had been placed by the screen. "They will have warmed a little," Marie suggested. "See how the sun has been shining on them?"

A fire was already burning under the copper in the scullery, and by the time Jesse was drying himself, his clothes were soaking in warm water. Before long, his hair was dry and Grand-mère was transfixed by the transformation from greasy matted locks to golden waves. The old woman provided him with a scarf to knot at his neck and a navy-blue beret, then proclaimed that he looked every bit a Frenchman.

Phoebe, on her return from agitating the clothes in the pan of soapy water, smiled to hear Grand-mère and Mireille teaching Jesse new words. The girl was pointing to things and naming them, while Grand-mère repeated the words at her slower pace. In turn, Jesse recited all he knew, and in no particular order, even recalling, *"Merci de votre accueil chez vous."*

It made a merry scene. *It will do him no harm to laugh for a moment,* Phoebe thought. *But I fear he will soon remember the troubles which brought him here.*

At this moment, he is having fun, but there is so much to learn and become used to. Their eyes met, and Phoebe was immediately saddened to see the smile fall from Jesse's face as he stepped towards her.

"You family are so kind," he said. "But I cannot live here. Where will I go with the dozen or so French words I know, and no money or anything of any value?"

"You can live with my Papa, Jacques," she replied.

"He lives here?" Jesse frowned.

"No. He lives alone in a cottage by the village square but eats here with the family. They are not fishing tomorrow so Papa will not sleep for long. I could take you there?"

"He doesn't mind?"

"Of course not." Phoebe smiled, attempting to reassure him. "You can see how they all want to help."

"And no one will come here from Dymchurch? Am I too close?"

"We do not trade with the people of Dymchurch. It is only Walter and Joshua who they trust because they bring me here. It's the same time every year, so my family know when to expect me."

"You are all so kind..." Jesse slumped onto a garden bench. "But... but I'll miss my home and... everyone." He turned to look at her, his eyes desperate and confused. Only two weeks ago, my life was good, then I was shut up in a cell for ten days... can you begin to imagine what that was like? Ten days – and after nine of those I was told I was to be transported. All this for a being at the race that day."

"And then you were taken from the cell and put on a fishing boat." Phoebe sat on the bench beside him and continued the story. "You may be amongst friends, but your life is changed forever."

"It is."

154

Phoebe did not reply. Instead, she left Jesse to his thoughts. She would stay in Wissant for a couple of weeks and sensed that they would return to this conversation many times before she had to leave. For the time being she must not press him to plan for the future but Phoebe knew that Jesse was young and strong, and would become used to new ways. Under the fruit trees Grand-mère and Mireille chatted, while at the well, Marie filled more pitchers. They understood the merriment from Jesse had passed and he was drawn into reliving the trauma inflicted on him over the past two weeks.

The sun, however, would not wait for Jesse to dwell. It began to touch upon the low-lying cloud on the horizon, and its warmth no longer wrapped around those in the garden. Grand-mère, already swathed in a new shawl made of Romney Marsh wool, ambled back to the house and the comfort of her armchair. Marie and Mireille worked together at the mangle and pegged Jesse's clothes on the line, in readiness for the return of the morning sun.

"Jesse?" Phoebe's tone was gentle. "We must go to Papa's cottage now. Before it gets dark."

The farewells were brief. With Jesse carrying a blanket and sheets donated by Marie, they left by the front gate and joined the rough track leading from the beach to the village square.

"Ah! Papa!" A familiar figure came striding towards them and Phoebe ran to him. They embraced and she beckoned Jesse. "Papa has come to meet us!"

"I have a bed for you," Jacques told him, "and you are welcome in my home. It is humble but comfortable."

"*Merci, Merci.*"

In Jacques Bernard, Jesse had found the best companion he could wish for in this foreign land. The older man's English was good, thanks to his fifteen years of marriage to Phoebe's mother from Dymchurch and having lived in the village with his wife and her family. Yet he too had suffered on account of Aaron Chapman's spite. When he was little more than a boy, Aaron had been instrumental in setting Jacques up as scapegoat for a smuggling tryst which went badly wrong, ending in the death of a customs officer.

After fleeing Dymchurch, Jacques had not seen his only child for five years, and she had been deprived of knowing if he was alive or dead. Now it was Jesse who had fled to Wissant, and he who would miss his family along with the woman he had planned to marry.

The three of them walked through the town square, and past a tavern where men gathered around roughly hewn tables. Plumes of strong-smelling tobacco surrounded them while they put the world around them to rights or became intent on a game of belote – wine in jugs already half devoured. The scene fascinated Jesse who slowed momentarily before entering the narrow street which would eventually lead back to the seafront. A row of cottages, with low, tiled roofs and small shuttered windows, lined the roadside. Their fronts were in shadow, and the street was desolate, other than a young woman squatting on the doorstep of a small wooden shack-like home, intent on her crocheting.

Jacques pushed on the front door of the second cottage in the terrace of four, and they followed him in. Jesse appeared to straighten a little, preparing himself for the space which was to become his sanctuary for as long as he needed it. Phoebe watched as he scanned the humble space, taking in the fire, the dresser and a small table with two chairs. He looked towards the back door, knowing it would lead to a scullery and the yard beyond. Then his eyes roamed to the open stairs leading to Jacques' bedroom under the eaves. Finally, he gazed at the wooden bedframe at the back of the living area, with its lumpy mattress, which Phoebe now began to cover with a sheet.

"There's a curtain," she said. "And a trunk for your belongings."

"I'll fix you up some pegs," Jacques said.

"Thank you," Jesse said. "*Merci.*"

"No need to say anything, my friend." Jacques placed a hand on his shoulder. "You are safe and now you can rest."

Phoebe looked at the two men and saw she was no longer needed. Tomorrow was Sunday and she could spend all day with her papa. At that moment, the men were best left to themselves, and she was very much at home in Grand-mère's cottage. She gave her papa a huge hug, and Jesse a quick pat on his arm. "*Bonne nuit. Dors bien. A demain.*"

Chapter Fifteen
Phoebe

"Mireille, go to *le marché*. How am I to cook for us with no flour or butter?" Marie tossed a purse of coins into the basket.

"I'll wait for Phoebe…"

"Wait for Phoebe?" Marie's voice rose. "She has only just started her breakfast while you are sitting here with nothing to do."

"*Oui, Maman.*"

"And I wish to see Véronique. Go with a message for her – ask if she can come here this afternoon – before the men are home."

"Véronique? *Oui, Maman.*" Mireille eyed her Romney Marsh woollen shawl, a gift from Phoebe.

"You'll need that in the winter," Phoebe told her. "Put it in the trunk and you can wear it and think of me when the weather is cooler." The girl left, leaving Phoebe with a feeling that Mireille was considered too innocent for the conversation which was to follow.

She was right, for as soon as the front door closed Grand-mère broached the subject: "I hoped this year you would be coming with a great-grandchild for me."

The bread lay dry in Phoebe's mouth, and she struggled to swallow it. "I know."

"But your monthly bleed still comes?" Marie asked.

"Without fail."

"What can be wrong?" Grand-mère asked. "Do you wish for a child? You and Harry?"

"*Bien sûr!*" Marie answered for her niece. "They are ready for a child – him so good and hardworking, and our *belle* Phoebe with her kind heart and a home ready to welcome a baby. She has a woman to help in her house, you know!"

"I know." Grand-mère rolled her eyes. "It is time they are blessed."

"It is high time," Marie agreed.

Phoebe listened to the exchange. She glanced towards Mireille's shawl, wanting to wrap it around herself and hide from this discussion. The room suddenly felt cold, and she wished Mireille had left the front door open, allowing the warmth of the day to enter.

"She needed to come home to her family so it could be resolved," Marie decided. "Isn't that right, Phoebe?"

"I hadn't thought…" Phoebe began. *I have spoken to Aunt Peggy and Bess about the emptiness, but neither of them were blessed with a child. Perhaps Marie is right. After all she is a mother to three.* "I hadn't thought of speaking about it. All I know is that I have disappointed you and Harry and Papa. People look at me and they wonder why we have no child, and sometimes they ask, but what can I tell them?"

"That a child will come when the time is right?" Marie suggested. "It is not for those people… those English from Dymchurch to say such a thing." She scowled, as she cleared the breakfast table, and dishes clattered against one another as they were placed on a tray.

159

"I am English and come from Dymchurch," Phoebe reminded her.

"Pah! You look like your French papa, and Oncle Marc, and *la petite* Mireille! You are a French woman who was born in England."

"*Mais oui*, her blood is French, with a little of her English *maman*," Grand-mère agreed.

"It's the Dymchurch air!" Marie stated. "Your *maman* waited three years to be blessed with you."

If she had not felt so utterly miserable to have her childless state discussed openly, then Phoebe could have smiled at her aunt's judgements. *They are expressed with love,* she told herself, for all that was none the easier to bear.

"There is no need to worry." Grand-mère reached out and placed her bony hand on Phoebe's arm. "Véronique is coming here later."

"Véronique?" Phoebe repeated. "I don't know...?"

"*Une sage-femme,*" Marie told her. She came for the birth of all my children. There is nothing she does not know about a woman's body."

"*Une sage-femme,*" Phoebe repeated. "A midwife. Perhaps... I don't know, but perhaps she will be able to help..."

"She will help," Grand-mère confirmed. Then she spoke to Marie, "This is enough for now. The worry does her no good."

"I'm going to see Papa come in with the boat," Phoebe replied, grasping at an opportunity to escape this talk of the midwife and the inevitable recurrence of her monthly courses. She needed the sea air and open skies, but a sense of duty forced her to ask, "Or shall I make the bread?"

"Go to see your papa, and I shall make the bread," Marie replied. "He will be pleased to see you."

Phoebe darted down the sandy track to the beach, almost gulping at the fresh air. At first, she was glad to be hemmed in by trees, but they soon became sparse, and the dunes rolled out to her right-hand side. To the left, the land opened as a flat wasteland, with tracks leading back to the village. She passed the dunes, almost cliff-like, and the whole of the bay stretched out before her. The tide had reached its highest point and was now retreating. It had left the Bernard family boat beached, and already the flat-bottomed vessel, known as a *flobart*, was being hauled up the sands by a pair of donkeys. Three men walked beside the strong beasts: brothers Jacques and Marc, with Jesse who was learning the ways of a Wissant fisherman.

"Papa!" Phoebe felt her spirits lift.

Jacques left the *flobart* and strode toward his daughter. He touched her lightly on the shoulder and planted a kiss on her forehead. "How have you been, *ma chérie*?"

"I am well, Papa," Phoebe responded, without her usual enthusiasm.

It was three days since she had arrived in Wissant, and her emotions had been mixed. At the forefront there came the pleasure of being with her family, but never far from her thoughts, those last awkward days with Harry lingered. Then there was her body which failed her each month, and in the village every year there were new babies to be admired, or the tell-tale swollen stomachs of young women. When she spent time with her papa or Jesse these subjects were not spoken of, so to meet them on the beach and walk with them to the marketplace offered Phoebe a reprieve. The women meant well, but their ways were different, more direct, than she was used to.

At first, they retraced her path past the dunes, then took the track to the village square. Phoebe's shoes brushed through thick sand and crunched on the stone the men of Wissant had hammered into the dips, attempting to smooth the route taken by the donkeys and *flobarts*. As they neared the square, humble cottages within small plots of land made way for taller buildings butting up against each other. Then they were in the liveliness of the marketplace, with the first two *flobarts* already unloading their catch and other stalls with sausages, cheese, fruit and vegetables vying for attention.

Phoebe watched, having been shooed away by the men, with comments about not spoiling her elegant English dress. Her gaze met Jesse's and they exchanged a grin. Only he knew that when she came to Wissant, Phoebe wore the dresses usually reserved for helping Janey in the house and garden. To dress in her finest linen and wool, would only set her apart from the women in her family.

"Would Lucy like it here?" The thought burst into Phoebe's mind, and she voiced it without thinking.

"Lucy?" he repeated.

They gazed around the marketplace, from the *flobarts* and stalls to the taverns, shops and homes lining three sides of the square. On the fourth side, the church of St Nicholas stood solid and plain, featuring a small bell tower, Norman doorway and creamy stonework. With the summer sun, the white sand swept along with the boats from the beach to square, and the exchange of words from one person to the next, Wissant was both lively and attractive.

In many ways, it offered a life not so unlike the one Jesse was used to: fishing and smuggling alongside all the other trades needed for a small community to thrive. While the dunes offered protection to nearby countryside, the village was open to the sea, and, like Dymchurch, there was a need to watch the tides and protect homes and businesses. Yet this was not Romney Marsh, and Jesse would have to rely on the kindness of the Bernard family.

"I hadn't thought before, but I wondered..." Phoebe began. *What do I wonder? It's not for me to suggest that Lucy leave her family for Wissant. She couldn't just come here with no place to stay, and Jesse far from settled. I couldn't expect my family to...* "Not yet," she voiced her understanding. "It's too soon."

Jesse didn't respond to the suggestion. Most likely he would ponder on it over the coming days, aware that a decision would have to be made before Phoebe left for Dymchurch. Instead, he said, "At least Lucy will know I'm free now. I hope she understands that I had no choice but to leave."

"I imagine she will be filled with joy to know you are free, and by now she will know you are here. Perhaps Joshua or Walter will have told her something about Wissant and she can picture you staying with Papa." Phoebe paused to consider the other woman's feelings, "But at the same time, her heart will be broken. The plans you had are changed forever."

"Jesse!" Marc called out from the boat. "*Le poisson!*"

Jesse turned back to the *flobart*, his arms outstretched for the crate. Already he was standing taller and the colour had returned to his skin. His young body had recovered from the ten days miserable days and nights spent in a cell, but Phoebe understood it would take months for his mind to recover since being ripped away from the life he knew so well.

"I must go…" It wasn't fair to leave Tante Marie at home with all the work. Feeling uplifted since her escape the probing questions at the breakfast table, Phoebe waved to the men, and walked away from the market. The inevitable visit from the midwife still hung over her, but in the meantime, she could keep herself busy and her thoughts full of baking, sweeping and chatting with her young cousin.

The afternoon was industrious for the women, while Oncle Marc slept, having been out fishing through the night. Tante Marie decided that despite the heat, she, Phoebe and Mireille would set about brushing away any cobwebs lurking in the kitchen and scullery then give the floor a thorough sweep. However, their most onerous task would be to take all the jars, bottles, boxes and pans off the scullery shelves and to wash each one of them. Grand-mère was dispatched to a garden chair, with her shawl to cover her knees.

Once Tante Marie has a plan, nothing will stop it. Phoebe had known her aunt long enough to understand this. *No one would dare suggest that we wait for a cooler day, or until Oncle Marc has woken.* So, she allowed herself to be swathed in an apron and stood on a stool, passing the contents of the shelves to Mireille, who in turn carried them to the basin of warm water in the garden.

A couple of hours later, Marie was satisfied with their efforts. Then there came a rush to drape a cloth over the tatty garden table and to place wine and savoury biscuits in the centre alongside small dishes with olives. "Véronique will not be late," she said several times, and with each repetition, Phoebe's nerves increased until she began to feel quite sick.

At exactly three o'clock, the much-anticipated midwife arrived. Phoebe paused in her task of setting glasses on the table to watch the petite woman weave her way around the side of the house, then past the chicken-pen and the well. Before Marie bustled in with her effusive greeting, Phoebe and Véronique had exchanged knowing looks and polite smiles.

"Ah! Véronique! Welcome to our home." Marie bounded forward to place her hands on the visitor's slim shoulders and kissed her lightly on each cheek.

"Marie, I have been looking forward to meeting *la petite nièce anglaise*, and here she is!" Véronique replied, her manner more restrained. She nodded to Phoebe, "Welcome back to Wissant."

"It is lovely to be here," Phoebe responded, offering a smile. Already she was finding that the midwife lacked the warmth of her French family. *Was Marie concerned that our guest might inspect the scullery? Is she anxious about her visit and this is why she kept us all so busy through the warmest hours of the day?* Phoebe glanced at Mireille. *As long as my cousin is with me, their questions about my childless state will be subtle.*

They drifted towards the shade of the fruit trees. Grand-mère had risen from her low chair in which she had been dozing and stepped forward to greet Véronique. She seemed at ease with this small, yet seemingly stern figure. "Good afternoon, my friend. Thank you for coming to meet my granddaughter. Do we have any new babies in Wissant?"

"There was one born to the *la famille* Moulin." Véronique gave an audible sniff as she seated herself. "I was not needed."

"Then all was well, and that is something to be grateful for." Marie neatly avoided the suggestion that the midwife had been slighted. "Some wine?"

They all sat at the table, with Phoebe deftly moving so she was between Grand-mère and Mireille. The next half an hour passed effortlessly, with some gossip about various characters living in Wissant, and enquiries about life in Dymchurch. Véronique downed two glasses of wine with ease while picking at the cheesy biscuits and olives. Phoebe began to relax.

"Mireille…" Marie gave her daughter a look full of meaning.

"*Oui, Maman.*" The girl rose from the table and scampered across the garden to the house.

"You have been married three years, yet have not been blessed with a child," Véronique cut straight to the point of her visit.

"I have no child," Phoebe agreed. Despite the warmth of the day, she longed to reach for Grand-mère's blanket and to wrap it around her shoulders.

"It is very sad," Grand-mère murmured. "Sad for Phoebe, and for her family who wish to welcome a little one into the family."

166

"Being sad will not produce a child," Véronique stated. "Why is there no child? That is what we must ask. Does your monthly bleed come when it should?"

"Every four weeks."

"Has there been a child lost, even one you knew nothing of – perhaps your courses were delayed by a few days?"

"There has been no delay," Phoebe told her.

"That is good!" Véronique flashed a smile. "Your body is ready to receive a child."

"*Et votre Harry: c'est un vrai homme?*" Marie probed.

"Harry?" Phoebe felt her mouth go dry. Memories of those last days in Dymchurch flooded her mind – from Aaron's lips on hers while his hands roamed her breasts and buttocks, to her guilt and the increasing awkwardness between her and Harry. "He is a good husband."

"Does he have enough fire in him to produce a child?" Véronique demanded more emphatically.

Phoebe felt her neck redden. Forcing thoughts of Aaron from her mind, she recalled her loving moments with her husband. "I think so," she replied.

"Pah! She is too English!" Véronique almost spat the insult across the table. "Too English!"

"What can be done about it?" Marie asked.

"If she refuses to make her home in Wissant, then nothing," Véronique declared. "As for the baby, she could take a lover or eat asparagus?"

"The asparagus season has almost ended!" Marie wailed.

"But it has not ended. There is hope." Véronique took a slug of wine, and Marie refilled her glass. "A French lover would be best," the midwife observed.

Chapter Sixteen
Harry

"Mr Farrers? ...Harry?"

With his hammer remained poised to hit the white-hot length of iron upon the anvil, Harry turned to the open doorway. "Just a moment," he responded before focussing once more on the task in hand.

Matthew Alder waited a respectful distance within the forge. He watched as Harry hammered then set the metal aside to cool.

"What can I do for you?"

"My cousin Jesse was a good man," Matthew began, "and a hard worker too. He was happy here, and you treated him well."

"Thank you. He'll be missed," Harry replied. "But at least we'll have a word from him occasionally."

"It's got me thinking that you'll be looking for someone else." Matthew smiled and Harry saw the family resemblance. Here was a man well-liked by John Waller's team with whom he laboured on the wall, as well as being part of a respected Dymchurch family.

"I'm desperate for help," Harry admitted. "Never been so busy since this incident at the Whitsun Gallop. It seems like I've been in New Romney more than Dymchurch recently, and if it wasn't for Frank Smith this

169

place would have been closed. Yes, I need someone, but I've not got the time to go looking." Harry paused, his eyes roaming to the ominously heavy sky to be seen through the doorway. It looked as if a summer storm was on its way from the direction of Wissant. "Are you interested in working here?" he asked.

"I'd be grateful for the opportunity," Matthew said immediately. "It seems wrong to be trying to jump into my cousin's shoes, and I wouldn't if I thought he would be back."

"No, you're right to come along," Harry reassured him. "Ideally, I need an experienced blacksmith, but more than that I need someone I can trust. Frank says he'll work for me in the mornings, so there will be someone here to train you if I'm elsewhere."

"You'd be happy to give me the job?" Matthew grinned, and once more Harry was reminded of Jesse.

"I'd be more than happy," Harry replied. "You understand it would be on an apprentice's wage for a year? But after that, there is plenty of work for the right person."

"I think you've found him!"

"I think I have!"

While the sky darkened to a steely purple, and a chill breeze began to gather speed, the men spoke more about the work and arranged for Matthew to start the following week. He left as the first heavy drops fell on the village, running back to the cottage on the High Street where he lived with his family.

Harry turned back to his labours. *Phoebe will be pleased to hear about this.* He pictured sharing the news while they ate their midday meal together. Then it came to him, as powerful as a punch in the stomach.

170

She's not here, and if she was, is it my company or Aaron's that she prefers?

Images of his wife and Aaron slammed into his mind. He recalled the other man's knowing looks and the way his eyes roamed over Phoebe as if still claiming some possession of her. Harry had never asked, but he was certain that they had once shared intimate moments, giving Aaron a secret knowledge, and Phoebe a cause for discomfort whenever they met.

It was a pleasure to see your wife last week. Just as seductive as I remembered her to be... How many times had those words repeated themselves in Harry's head over the past few days? How often had they led to him conjuring up pictures of private moments between his Phoebe and that dangerous man? *He knows what to say... how to get me wondering. There is nothing in it. Phoebe would never... she hates him just as much as I do... as much as half the village do.* Yet the images remained. As the raindrops fell on the windows, he watched as one began its inevitable slide downwards, taking others with it, growing and collecting the dust from past weeks. It raced, swollen and unhindered, just as Harry's fears grew and gathered pace. He found himself gazing into the street, watching the sand, earth and plant debris being washed away from the places they had lingered since the last rainfall. On the road, puddles formed, and rivulets of water scurried.

Janey busied herself in the scullery, while eyeing her employer with concern, noting that Harry ate in haste and seemingly without pleasure. He did the housekeeper the justice of finishing the meal, but afterwards he couldn't have said if it were mutton or beef, or even fish.

"I'm going back to work," Harry called out as he left by the back door.

Unseen to him, Janey nodded her approval. He may be master of the house but while dressed in his rough, working clothes it was only right that Harry showed some respect to the elegant frontage of his home.

Whatever his intention had been when he left the house, Harry immediately turned away from the village centre, then took the field tracks towards Burmarsh, with the intention of seeking out Aaron. Before long, his gait became increasingly shorter and more laboured as his boots were thickened with mud. His shoulders tensed as rain penetrated the coarse material of his shirt and waistcoat. He tramped on regardless, only pausing to peel off the layer of clay which attached itself as a second sole upon his boots. The rain eased, yet the pointed grasses, and resilient weeds with their fluffy seedheads clung onto the droplets and bowed with the heaviness. Harry immersed himself in the trek, conscious of the rhythmic thud of his boots on the ground and watching their progress. On the plank bridges, he clomped over, feeling the vibration in his calves.

It was only when the tracks met the road, that Harry became alert to his surroundings. This was the main route taken by the wagons loaded with clay and bound for the seawall. *If I see that young scoundrel, Toke Browne, then I swear I'll make him realise I know the truth. There is no doubt he lied in court and was paid well for doing so. It's too late for Jesse: he daren't risk returning to Dymchurch, and life in Wissant will be good for him, but Toke needs to hear that I have an eye on him.* As the cumbersome carts lumbered by, and the empty ones rattled along, Harry scanned the faces of the grubby boys, certain that the one he sought would still carry an air of cockiness. The recollection of his time in court and attention given by Aaron, along with the silver shillings, would, no doubt, be bolstering Toke's confidence over the weeks to come.

Each cart was accompanied by three or four boys. One to guide the donkey and the others to steady the load or to give it an extra heave through the ruts. Their clothes were not much more than rags, usually thick with clay dust, but today sodden and clinging to thin frames. Wide-eyed and looking for an opportunity to earn an extra penny, they glanced towards Harry but dismissed him as no more than a casual labourer, judging him by his dishevelled appearance and the attire he wore while working at the forge. In turn, Harry took in their features but recognised none of them. During the weeks when additional maintenance was carried out on the seawall, boys and men appeared from the far-flung corners of the Marsh, the coastal town of Hythe and from the surrounding hills. They bedded down in barns and lofts, gathered their shillings, spent them in the taverns, and then returned to their homes, or moved onto the next job.

Burmarsh was soon in sight and Harry picked up his pace. Rothschild Farmhouse, looking outward from the humble cottages, tavern and church, gleamed after the recent deluge, its new brickwork pristine. He could hear his boots slapping on the wet earth underfoot and attempted to focus on the rhythm, but now the sound of

Aaron's taunts returned to flood Harry's mind. It became impossible to think of anything else.

Then, seemingly with little thought, Harry turned abruptly, saying to himself, "What's the point?" and retraced his steps at an even greater speed. "Chapman can only gain more pleasure from my coming here to ask for the truth about him and Phoebe."

He continued without faltering until almost reaching the shortcut across the fields to Dymchurch. A cart was lumbering along behind him, and another rattling towards him, each accompanied by a motley collection of boys.

There he is! As Harry recognised the chestnut waves and freckled face of Toke Browne, he saw the look of recognition in the brown eyes. For a moment, the boy wavered as if about to back away, but then he lifted his chin and looked past the donkey's rump to the road ahead as if he felt no shame for the lies told in court.

"You! Toke Browne," Harry barked, "Come over here."

"I've got orders to fetch clay," the boy retorted.

"You've got orders to show respect to a jurat when he speaks to you," Harry responded, uncomfortable with the tone of his own voice. It wasn't the way he liked to communicate, but this boy riled him. "You can catch up quick enough. I'll not keep you long."

Toke glanced at the others working alongside him. They looked away, no doubt ill at ease and not wanting to be involved. "I didn't know you were a jurat," Toke excused himself. "I thought jurats dressed up fancy and rode about on horses, not walking about in all this muck."

"You know as well as I do, that a jurat works as hard as the next man," Harry responded. "I've got no time for wigs and fripperies. I work long hours and I expect the people around me to be honest and loyal. Are you honest, Toke Browne?"

"I'm a hard worker, Mr Farrers."

"Ah! So, you do know who I am!" Harry snapped at him.

"It just came to me," the boy countered.

"You are indeed a hard worker," Harry repeated. *I've heard those words before when he was telling Sir Rupert about himself. This is someone who is eager to please but has his mind on what he will gain from it.* "But, Toke Browne, I asked if you were honest? Were you honest when you stood in court and told Sir Julian Craythorne that you had seen Jesse Alder run off with a sack of something under his arm?"

Toke beamed, as if well-practised in his story. No doubt he still rode high on the attention given by the master of Rothschild Farm and perhaps the flow of coins into his pockets was not yet finished. "I've got respect for the Lords of the Levels, one who was also judge that day, and for the court."

"I'm sure you do," Harry conceded, "But you still don't answer my question. You're not stupid – I can see that – yet you cannot or will not vouch for your honesty. Let me tell you something: I know you didn't see Jesse Alder run off with the cup and that you are trying to please Mr Chapman. I have no doubt you have been paid well for your lies in court. If I offered you a guinea, I doubt you would betray your master. It wouldn't be wise to displease him, would it?"

175

For a moment, Toke's eyes widened as if he saw the guinea gleaming in the palm of his grubby hand.

"But I'll give you tuppence for some other information," Harry continued. "I can tell you're watching what goes on hereabouts. Have you seen a lady with dark hair walking along this road, or perhaps across the fields? Not a lady adorned with bows and lacy layers, but a lady nonetheless?"

"I've seen her twice!" Toke declared. "It was last week. Once I saw her walking and I thought to myself that she was too fine to be out in the fields so early."

"And the second time?"

"I was giving my pa a hand with clearing the ditch that runs through Burmarsh and I spied her going into the church."

"Did that seem odd to you?" Harry asked.

"Well..." Toke considered this. "Well... I don't get much time for church going. It doesn't get the clay carted to the wall, or the fences repaired, or the waterways cleared, but she was the sort that doesn't need to worry about that, so if she wants to go praying then it causes no bother to me."

"No, it doesn't." Harry now had his suspicions confirmed by this unlikely source. He reached for a tuppence, drawing it from a leather purse hanging from his belt. "You'd better catch up with the others," he said. The cart had ambled some distance and was turning into a lane known locally as Donkey Street.

Toke gave a nod and ran off, jumping over the ruts with ease. Harry watched him go. *I can't help liking him although I know I shouldn't!* Then he turned, left the main road, and took to the field tracks, his mind fully absorbed with the fact that Phoebe had indeed been to

Burmarsh. Both the housemaid, Mary, and now Toke had given him the proof that Aaron's taunts were not unfounded. As he walked, scenes of Aaron and Phoebe ran unhindered through Harry's mind, but every so often he was forced to admit that there was no doubting Phoebe's dislike of the man who had pursued her in the past. *Why would she go to meet him? And if there were nothing to hide, why did she not tell me about it? She's been so quiet… so cool towards me. Why?*

Once back in the village, Harry was struck with remorse. He had left Frank Smith to run the forge for no good reason and without telling him. "This has got to stop," he muttered to himself as he marched along the High Street. "All this running here, there and everywhere. I'll have no business left if I don't do any work."

The door to the forge was open and the chime of metal upon metal rang out. Pulling on his leather apron, Harry made his apology, "I'm sorry. I've been… never mind… There's good news though – Matthew Alder is going to start work here next week. And I'll be here to train him up. No more dashing about."

"That is good news," Frank replied. "He's a good lad, like his cousin was." Then he pondered on Harry's words for a moment before saying, "You're needed here, there's no doubt, but I thought you'd be off to Wissant now this business with Jesse is settled."

An image of Phoebe, lost in her thoughts and unresponsive to his gestures of affection, flashed into Harry's mind. "No! I've neglected this place for long enough. There will be no travelling to Wissant this summer."

Harry worked steadily through the afternoon and into the evening. Long after Frank had gone home to his wife, the fire in the forge burned bright, and a pair of wrought iron gates took shape under Harry's skilled hands. Later, as the charcoal burned away, the gates were put aside, and he swept the workshop from the cobwebs on the ceiling, to the dusty windows, the unseen crevices and finally the earth floor.

If Harry thought he could sweep away Aaron's taunts, and his fears of Phoebe's betrayal being confirmed by both Mary and Toke, then he was mistaken. He recalled her awkwardness around him during the days before her departure and allowed this to fester in his mind, blaming it solely on the likelihood that some intimate moments had passed between her and her former love.

It is because we have no child, Harry told himself. *She sees Aaron with his baby daughter, while Ellen has a son and is expecting her second child. Phoebe knows I have failed her. Now she looks at Aaron with fresh eyes – as someone who can father a child.*

If Harry had not been wearied by the struggle to clear Jesse's good name, or not felt the guilt of leaving his business in the hands of someone else, then perhaps the images building in his mind would have taken a different form. Had he thought to visit Owen and Bess and spend the evening in their company, allowing himself to relax and to listen to their calm reasoning, then perhaps he would have returned home and enjoyed a peaceful night's sleep.

Having locked and bolted the front door of the forge, then left his leather apron hanging on an ornate iron hook, Harry left by the back. The evening was fresh from the earlier downpour, and he walked briskly with the intention of returning home, and washing his body clean from the grime gathered through the hours of physical work. However, as he approached Walker House, the sight of the Ship Inn just a few steps along the road beckoned him. *I'll have a lonely time sitting at home with no one for company, whereas the inn will be full to bursting with those who have worked on the wall all day. And if I have a drink or two more than usual, then there's no one to answer to but myself.*

Without returning home to slosh cooling water over his face, or to change into a fresh shirt and waistcoat, Harry strode on. The Ship, not far from the gallows, church, and New Hall, was an elegant building, tall and long, with its front door in the centre and rows of matching sash windows. The roof was tiled, its chimney stacks upright, and the only decorative feature came in the form of an ornate portico. The outward signs of respectability may have fooled a passing traveller, but inside it was as rough as any tavern on the Marsh, with farmhands, tradesmen and wall-workers jostling amongst each other, their talk raucous. Keeping themselves to themselves, friendless and distrusted, the customs officers kept a close eye on these hardworking men of Dymchurch. They were wasting their time: not one word about smuggling activities was uttered in the bar however much alcohol had been consumed.

"A brandy, please." Harry gave the serving girl a brief smile.

"Of course, sir!" There was a cheeky tone to her voice and when she smiled, dimples appeared in both cheeks. She turned away, allowing her hips to sway a little, and reached for an ornamental glass bottle.

Harry watched her movements and asked, "Are you new here?"

"I've been here a week," she replied, again with a smile. "There's six of us at home in the cottage at Newchurch, so I had to go out to work." She passed the brandy, holding Harry's gaze as she did so. "Been working on the wall, have you?"

"Not me," Harry replied. "Although I won't deny it's a worthy job. No, I own a forge here in the village."

"Oh! Excuse me! I didn't know you were a man of business." Once again, her rosy cheeks creased into dimples.

"I'm a man who has been working long hours," Harry responded. He pushed a coin across the bar. "I hope you get to like Dymchurch."

"I'm liking it already, sir."

Harry couldn't help smiling as he weaved his way past the men to find a space amongst John Waller and his team of workers.

Lurking in an alcove near the fireplace, someone watched his progress. Then reaching into his pocket to feel for a shilling, he approached the comely serving girl.

Chapter Seventeen
Harry

"Another brandy, sir?" the serving girl reached for the bottle, allowing Harry to appreciate the curve of her breasts as she turned away from him. She turned to look over her shoulder, "I'll give you a little extra, but don't go telling anyone!" After pouring a generous amount, she kept hold of the glass. "You look as if you've had a hard day. There's no harm in relaxing for a while is there?" Her lips were full and glistened as she ran the tip of her tongue over them. "I'm Amelia, by the way."

"Nice to meet you, Amelia."

The name suited her. Harry had a feeling that even when she was clearing the ale spills, sweeping the floor or polishing the brass, there would still be a certain charm about this new serving girl. He imagined she modelled herself on the wealthier women in the area. *I wouldn't be surprised if she saves her pennies to buy face powder and scent.* Someone knocked over a stool nearby, causing it to clatter against the wall. Amelia turned her head a little as the noise drew her attention away from Harry. The light of the lamp momentarily flickered across the side of her face. *Ah! She has a beauty spot on her cheek.* He had an urge to reach out and touch it. *Just to see if it is real... but I am certain it is painted on.* He pictured her standing near the window of an attic room, turning her face this way and that, making the most of the light. There would be an aged mirror propped up, and in her hand a pencil with the softest of leads. In a box, perhaps painted or with a decorative inlay, he imagined she kept her powder, brushes and a small glass jar with scent. It would be secreted away, for this attic room was most to be likely shared. Amelia faced him again and pushed the brandy towards him. As she did so the swell of her fulsome breasts tipped towards Harry, and their eyes met.

"Nice to meet you…" She paused and raised her eyebrows a little, her expression enquiring.

"Harry. Harry Farrers."

She considered this for a moment and then replied, "I never took you for a gent, not even when you said you owned the forge, but am I right in thinking that you're one of the jurats? My apologies, sir. Fancy me thinking you'd come in after working on the seawall."

Harry shrugged and flashed a grin at her. "There's no shame in working on the wall. Where would we be without it? You're right, I am a jurat, but mostly I work in my forge."

"You're a hardworking gent then!" She gave a low burst of laughter.

"I am!" He reached in his pocket and added a further penny to the coins he had already placed on the bar. "Something for you, Amelia."

"Thank you. Very kind." She took the penny and slid it into the private space between her corset and chemise.

With reluctance, Harry moved away from the alluring Amelia and returned to his friends. They spoke with ease, their conversation flowing from local matters, spread by word of mouth, to news of politicians and royalty gleaned from news sheets.

A couple of hours passed, and dusk had fallen upon Dymchurch. The air in the Ship was thick with tobacco smoke, while clay dust carried in upon the workers clothes, settled on tables and stools. Men were either bathed in the pools of soft light emitted from the oil lamps or partially hidden in the darkened corners. Harry leaned against one of the inn's ancient beams and stayed within the shadows. He had been bought a tankard of ale by Matthew Alder, amidst some banter from the men who objected to Harry taking one of their most reliable workers for himself. By the time the ale was finished, he was feeling more relaxed than he had in weeks.

In the other parlour, Aaron Chapman drank wine with his brother and a couple of local men who pretended to like him. Harry hadn't noticed his adversary earlier, and until now Aaron had chosen to keep his distance. Now he strolled into the room and raised his hand to acknowledge John Waller. "How's the wall holding out at High Knocke? I heard there had been a crack on the landward side."

"It's all been dealt with," John replied.

"I said we could rely on you." The knowing expression on Aaron's face gave the impression that he was in sole charge of instructing the maintenance of the structure. "There was a suggestion that someone, young George Bannerman, I think, should come and monitor your progress. I said there was no need at all. John Waller and his team know exactly how to handle this, I told them."

"It's all in hand." John kept his response to a minimum. "But if George Bannerman cares to inspect our work, then he is more than welcome." Sir Rupert's son was well respected and liked within the village. Everyone knew he had a fascination with the building and repairs of the seawall, and a desire to learn from similar constructions.

"No doubt he'll be along in a day or so." Aaron paused and let his eyes roam over each man in the group. "There's a drink for all of you at the bar. A thank you for the long hours you're working at the moment." His gaze lingered on Harry. "And for you, of course. You must be missing your beautiful wife, but she'll be back in no time with tales of Wissant."

"Thank you," Harry forced a polite reply. To refuse a drink would cause more friction and place unwanted attention on himself.

"She's a lovely woman." Aaron gave his parting shot, "You're lucky I let you have her!"

Harry gave no reaction. How he would have loved to shout his response across the bar: *You didn't let me have her! Phoebe was free to make her own choice and she was done with you six months before we became close!* Yet now he wasn't so certain. Rather than look away, he watched as Aaron turned and re-joined his brother. A few minutes later they left, and Harry felt himself relax a little, but the evening had turned sour for him.

"He's a nasty one through and through," John Waller murmured as the door of the inn swung to close behind Aaron. "There's nothing that gives him more pleasure than other people's misfortune. It was a bad day for Dymchurch and Burmarsh when he inherited that fine house and land. Perhaps he would have remained a little humbler without it."

"I wonder how his wife fares?" Harry replied.

"She's gone to stay with her mother again!" John Waller grinned. "Perhaps that's your answer."

"Where's that?" Harry asked, but his thoughts were straying to darker matters.

"Appledore, I think. Or some place just off the Marsh."

"She was here for the Whitsun Gallop," Harry observed.

"Packed up just after that," John told him. "I saw her and the baby heading off the next day, or perhaps the one after that."

His wife is away. Not that her being here would stop Aaron from seeking his pleasure from anyone who took his fancy. But if Phoebe were to be his choice, then she would feel more at ease with his lady elsewhere.

"Don't let his taunts bother you," John said, as if he read Harry's mind.

"I don't." Harry shrugged. *I can't tell him. I can't tell anyone that I know there is some truth in it.* Where the brandy and ale had relaxed him, now Harry found his thoughts were rambling about in his head, turning this way and that without following through to any sensible conclusion.

"Go home and rest," John advised. "You've had a hell of a time over these past few weeks. Jesse is safe, and Phoebe will be home again soon. Get some sleep because this..." he gestured to the empty glasses and tankards, "is doing you no good at all."

"You're right." Harry stood and raised his hand in a gesture to indicate he was leaving. "Goodnight. God bless." He weaved his way past his companions, responding to their farewells and the obligatory banter. If his step was a little erratic due to the drink, then it was no wonder with all sorts of obstacles from men and dogs, to stools and benches. He lost his balance and reached out to steady himself on the bar.

"Look after yourself," Amelia called out. "There's many a pothole on the village street."

"Just a wobble." Harry grinned and pointed to the floor. "There's a damned dog getting in my way."

"I'll be seeing you soon then, darling?" Her voice became low, almost husky.

The smile dropped from Harry's face at this unexpected term of endearment. He frowned not knowing how to respond, part of him aware that flattery was part of her job but also acknowledging the strong attraction he felt for the buxom serving girl. "I expect so," he finally replied.

Turning to focus on the door, Harry set off, aiming for a straight line between the bar and his exit. The panelled door was ajar and swung open with ease before he closed it behind him.

The night air had a sharp chill to it and felt exceptionally fresh to Harry. In the Ship he had been enveloped in a heady mixture of tobacco smoke, alcohol fumes and dried sweat. The contrast was welcome, and he gulped at it, greedy for his lungs and mind to be cleansed.

From the side of the building there came a short rattle of stones being disturbed. Harry was immediately alert to someone or something moving towards him. *A fox, most likely.* Tucked close to the wall of the inn, a figure rounded the corner and beckoned him to her. Without asking, she tucked her arm through his and pulled him close, so now the richness of the scent she dabbed on her neck and breasts, and the sweet smell of her sweat, mingled with the cool air. She brought the odours of the bar on her dress and shawl, but now he welcomed their familiarity, where moments earlier he had been glad to rid himself of them.

"I can't let you walk home alone, not with all the dangers on the road," she purred.

Unable to know how to respond, Harry allowed himself to be led towards the village street by Amelia.

"Is this your forge?" she asked, looking towards a low building with a cottage butted up against it.

"My... my forge?" The words rattled about in his mind, until he was able to relate them to their previous conversation at the bar. "No. No, mine is at the other end of the village opposite the Ocean Inn."

They took a few more steps together, with Amelia clinging tightly to Harry's arm, so when she slipped on a loose stone, he was pulled with her. They righted themselves and she laughed, "I'm not doing a very good job of seeing you home, am I?"

He didn't respond. The words barely registered because she now stood in front of him, her shawl falling off her shoulders and the swell of her breasts tempting him. Some force took hold of Harry – later he would blame it on the brandy – and he ran his fingertip over her pale skin that shone in the light of the moon. Then he bent down and kissed the hollow between her curves, lingering within them.

"Aren't you a saucy one?" she murmured. "There's me trying to help you home and look at us!" She gave his buttock a squeeze.

He didn't reply but placed his hands on her waist and gazed at her full lips, seeing them part-open and inviting him to kiss her. She tasted of wine, and it pleased him. When her tongue flicked into his mouth, Harry forgot he was standing there in the village street, with the dark bulk of the parish church nearby and the sounds of chatter and laughter drifting through the windows of the Ship. When she led him to the shadowed area under the canopy of oak leaves from an ancient tree, his only thought was to let his fingers seek the soft flesh partially under the lacy frill of her bodice.

"Harry!" John Waller's voice cut through the darkness and the chill of the night.

Stepping back, Harry opened his eyes and the first thing he saw was the gallows. A stark structure, tall and upright, against the starlight sky. It was empty of any rotting carcass, but still the sight of it gave him an uncomfortable jolt.

"Harry!"

"See you soon, Mr Jurat with your forge!" Amelia leaned forward and pressed a quick kiss on his cheek, then ran a finger down his chest to his groin. "You know where to find me."

She moved away as the figure of John Waller bore down upon them, and Harry felt a hand on his shoulder. "Let's get you home. Thank God I saw that harlot slip away from the bar."

Shame crashed down upon Harry. It shattered all feelings of desire and the pleasure he felt in being sought by an attractive woman. *Harlot!* The word was harsh but now he saw the serving wench for what she was. *She intended for this to happen from the moment she saw me!*

No words passed between the men. John Waller had done his duty by his friend and there was no need to rake over the events of the evening. For this Harry was thankful. Without being invited, John walked into Harry's home, his instincts telling him where to find the kitchen and then the larder. On a slate shelf he found a jug of water, and on the dresser a clay mug. He filled the mug before handing it to his friend.

"Thanks," Harry said before guzzling the contents.

"There's a kettle beside the fire," John observed. "If you're lucky, it's got some warm water in it. If not, I expect Janey has a jug or bucket of cold in the scullery. Get yourself a towel... this will do..." He took a hand towel from a small pile the housekeeper had left on a stool, "...and no doubt there's a bar of soap in there. Wash away all the muck from the forge, and any trace of that strumpet." He looked towards the kettle again. "On second thoughts, you can make do with cold water, I'll use whatever is in here to make us a cup of tea."

Sobered by his foolishness, Harry sidled off to the scullery, with its stone sink and unforgiving pail of icy water. He didn't tell John that the towel was one Janey used for moving hot pans or mopping spills, or that he had never washed in the lean-to. Upstairs there was an elm washstand with a marble top, and a matching china bowl and jug on top. There were soft towels, neatly folded in the laundry cupboard and smelling of the lavender which nestled amongst them in carefully stitched sachets.

It was dark in the scullery. Harry daren't suggest that a lamp might be useful. Besides, he knew his way about the place, and his eyes would soon become accustomed. To wash in cold water, with his bare feet on the stone slabs, was part of his penance and he welcomed it. He stripped off his waistcoat and shirt, breeches and socks, then lathered a rag with the soap he found resting on a wooden slatted tray. Starting with his face, Harry swept away Amelia's kisses and the tobacco filled smog from the Ship, before he touched upon the grime and sweat from an afternoon spent in the forge.

By the time John was filling the teapot with boiling water, Harry had emerged from the scullery in his undergarments. "I'll just..." he muttered, passing through the kitchen. He crept up the stairs, conscious of Janey sleeping in her attic room and not wanting to disturb her, then entered his bedroom. From the closet, Harry pulled out fresh clothes and quickly pulled them on.

Back in the kitchen, John had poured the tea and produced a slab of bread pudding from the larder. "This will soak up the brandy," he said, looking thoroughly at home, sitting at the head of the pine table.

"Thank you." Harry broke off a piece and popped it in his mouth.

Up to this point, John had said very little. He had concentrated on the practical business of setting his friend back on the right path. Now he was ready to voice his opinions: "You've not got a father here, or an uncle or... well, you know how it is, coming from off the Marsh. But since you've been here, there's been me and Owen looking out for you. Him and Bess, they've been your family here in Dymchurch, haven't they?"

Harry nodded. "I don't know how I'd have managed without them in those first six months. And you... you kept an eye on me while I was working and knew who I should keep my distance from.

"My team on the wall, they're part of the family too," John said. "You've done well. Business, home, the respect of the local people, and your wife... I don't want to see you lose any of it. That Chapman, he's as slippery as a wet fish. Don't go listening to his stories, because you know Phoebe and she's not going to be toying with him or anyone else. There's things going on that I don't understand, but you can be certain he's at the heart of it."

"She's been to see him at Burmarsh," Harry stated.

"Well, if that's a fact then you'll need to ask her why, because you can be sure it's not for the reason he'll have you thinking about."

Harry sipped at his tea. "You're right," he admitted. "There's that lad, Toke, full of his stories, and no one able to stand up for Jesse... Then there's Aaron with his sneers and taunts. Two weeks ago we were going for a day at the race, then looking forward to seeing her family in Wissant. Now Jesse is in France, Matthew will be my apprentice and Phoebe... I went to dine with Sir Rupert rather than see her off from the beach."

"It's not quite like that," John reminded him. "It's those kinds of thoughts that took you to the Ship and set you up as fair prey for that brazen hussy at the bar."

"It was my fault." Harry thought of the fair Amelia with her dimples and tempting curves. He wasn't ready to cast her as a villain. "I was too friendly... at least I must have been..."

"I'm not saying that you're not handsome enough to turn the head of a pretty girl, but I'm going to suggest that someone slipped her a shilling to tempt you." John paused, allowing Harry to reflect on this.

The younger man felt the shame rise as an uncomfortable blush in his neck and suddenly the tea tasted sour.

"The best thing you can do now is to work full days in the forge and get Matthew trained. Then there's no reason why you can't sail to Wissant when they go to collect Phoebe. By the time you're back in Dymchurch, the pair of you can have everything settled. In the meantime, keep away from Chapman and the serving girl."

Appreciating John's blunt words, Harry went to bed feeling more at ease than he had over the past weeks. He woke with a throbbing head the next morning, but knew he only had himself to blame, and was determined to pay heed to John's wise words over the coming days.

Chapter Eighteen
Phoebe

Phoebe settled into a new routine with her father's family, and now Jesse became part of the extended group of relations. The rhythm of life flowed with the tides. Days would pass with the men sleeping to suit the times when they went to sea, and when they slept, the women spoke with hushed voices as they went about their tasks in the home.

The sun beat down upon the white sands on the beach, the orange tiled roofs of the cottages, and the hats of those who bartered and traded in the market. When the summer showers came, they were short and sharp, refreshing the town and offering new life to tired rows of leafy vegetables in their plots.

In the Bernard family, the women often worked at the long table set up under the shade of the fruit trees. Every morning, and again throughout the day, Grand-mère brushed it clean and here they would knead bread or prepare the fruit and vegetables. Later in the afternoon, the dry washing would be piled there and folded, or Marie and Phoebe would stitch and darn the never-ending loose hems, torn shirt sleeves, and worn heels of socks. Before mealtimes, the bread was collected from a communal oven in the village and butter lifted from its cool shelf built into the side of the well. Then the table became the place where everyone gathered to discuss their day and news from the village or further afield.

It was a humble life, with only the seasons and religious festivals changing the pattern of the days. Amongst the clothes to be repaired there was often an extra basket brought by families in the village who paid Marie to stitch and patch as necessary. Phoebe's male cousins, Vincent and Louis, earned money by scrubbing *flobarts* after their fishing trips, restoring nets and working on several allotments within the village. In the garden, amongst the wood store and the tool shed, there stood a tall, brick structure in which Vincent and Louis hung fish on long wires, preserving them with the smoke from a fire. The Bernard family were hardworking, taking any opportunity to earn a few more coins or to barter, offering labour in return for food, wood or materials.

"I'm back!" Mireille called as she came into view, running around the side of the house towards Phoebe who was arranging plates of cheese and salad on the table.

Inspired by tales of Aunt Peggy and Uncle Giles who ran a general store in Dymchurch, Mireille was keen to work in a shop as her cousin had done. A week had passed since Phoebe had arrived in Wissant, and Mireille had just experienced her first morning behind a counter.

"Did you like it?" Phoebe asked. "Was Madame Blanchett kind to you?"

"Yes, she was patient and said it will take me a few days to become used to it."

"That's what I told you!"

"I'd rather work for your Aunt Peggy – I wish I could come to Dymchurch and meet her!"

Images of Peggy perched on her stool and complaining about everything flashed through Phoebe's mind: From her swollen legs, to the dust around the open barrels of flour and oats; the ragamuffins who eyed the butterscotch twists, and the women who couldn't make up their minds quickly enough. Most of all she grumbled about Phoebe: she had been foolish to let Aaron Chapman go… she wasn't grateful enough to them for allowing her to live with them… she wasn't swift enough with her tasks about the home. *How did I ever make my life with Peggy and Giles sound appealing to my young cousin?*

"Did I tell you that I had to sleep in a room with the packets and sacks of food?" Phoebe asked. "And that Aunt Peggy grumbles all the time? Be thankful you work in Madame Blanchett's shop. Besides, you can come home afterwards, whereas I was always there on hand to be called day or night."

"Mireille!" Marie called from the back door. "Did you collect the bread?"

"*Oui, Maman,*" the girl placed it on the table. She glanced towards the house. "*She* is my Aunt Peggy!"

Phoebe couldn't help but let out a burst of laughter. She placed an arm around her cousin's shoulder and gave her an affectionate squeeze. "Don't say such things! I wish you could meet Aunt Peggy but…" This wasn't the first time Mireille had mentioned visiting Dymchurch. It seemed as if the arrival of Jesse made her all the more curious as to what life was like in the village across *La Manche*.

"Jesse will be here soon," Mireille said.

195

"Yes, the men have slept enough. They'll join us soon," Phoebe replied, but Mireille had moved away and was speaking to Grand-mère. *She is so lively... full of enthusiasm. But I wonder...* Phoebe recalled how her cousin frequently mentioned Jesse and how she liked to sit with him and help him learn her language. *She is fourteen, not too young to think of love, but too young to place her attention on an Englishman who is five years older than her and still thinks of his Lucy in Dymchurch. Marie will not be happy if she realises...* But Marie was all-seeing where her family were concerned and most likely she had noticed her daughter's passion for the young man who now lived amongst them. *I must speak to him about Lucy,* Phoebe realised. *If he wants her to join him here, then we must plan for it.*

The thoughts rattling about in Phoebe's mind were given no more time to develop as now Marie and Marc were joining them at the table, and at the same time Jacques and Jesse walked from the road and past the side of the house. The family busied themselves with the matter of settling at the table, but before Marie had placed a piece of brie or a slice of spiced sausage in her mouth, she recalled the asparagus simmering over the fire. "*Les kasperges!*"

Taking her plate with her, Phoebe dashed to the kitchen, knowing how Tante Marie made it her daily duty to source a small bundle of the green spears. It seemed that word had spread around the village – it was not unusual for someone to appear at the door with a handful of the vegetable, or even just a couple of pieces. The season was ending, but without fail the asparagus came. The women of Wissant were

208

196

determined to nurture her body to be receptive to pregnancy.

After lunch, and before the men slipped away to spend an hour or so at the tavern in the village square, Phoebe spoke to Jesse while he drew water from the well. "I've been here almost a week, and in another they'll come to take me home. Once I'm back in Dymchurch, I'll go to see Lucy…"

"I'll never see her again." Jesse put all his effort into hauling the bucket of water and avoided turning to face Phoebe. "Tell her I'm sorry that our lives didn't turn out as we expected, and I hope she meets a decent man who can look after her. Tell her I miss her but there is no point in thinking I could go back to Dymchurch." He took the bucket in both hands and poured the water into a pail. "I've been lucky – more than lucky – to find myself here with your family."

"Do you think Lucy should come here?"

"No!" Jesse's response came swiftly, catching Phoebe by surprise.

The relationship between Jesse and Phoebe was one they were forging with some caution. In Dymchurch, their roles were clear, with Jesse showing his employer's wife the respect she deserved, and Phoebe in turn taking a polite interest in his work, family, and, more recently, his affection for Lucy. In Wissant, Phoebe lived a humbler life, and they now met several times a day, with him swiftly becoming adopted as a member of her family. They were not yet at the stage where confidences could be shared freely.

"I wondered…" Phoebe began. "But I don't know how…" Jesse was living with Jacques and working with

197

him and Marc on the boat. There was only one family boat and already Vincent was learning to fish alongside his father and uncle. In a couple of years, Louis would follow him. There was no call for another member of the crew. She was aware, through conversations with her father, that Jesse hoped to be accepted as an apprentice and to learn a trade. He had ten months experience as a blacksmith but would happily turn his hand to barrel-making, carpentry, leatherwork, or wherever there was an opportunity. *It will take time – months or years – to become accepted as part of our community. And until he has a regular income and can provide a home for himself and Lucy, then there is no hope of her joining him.*

"I am here as a free man, but dependent on your family." Jesse began to lift the second bucket of water. "I have nothing to offer her."

"I understand." Phoebe knew that Jesse would not appreciate suggestions of a better life to come when, at this moment, he was on the brink of his journey. So instead, she said, "Of course we have no idea if Lucy would be prepared to leave Dymchurch, but we can be sure that she and your family will be relieved to know you are safe."

The second bucket had its contents emptied into a couple of large jugs. "Thanks to you and Harry," Jesse said as he straightened himself and ran a hand through his blond hair. He gave her a grin and looked once more like the man she had known back in Dymchurch.

"I didn't know about the plans to free you," Phoebe reminded him.

"But thankfully you had a family who have been more welcoming than I could have hoped for." He

210

198

picked up the pail. "When Harry comes in a week's time, then at least I'll be able to thank him."

"I don't know if he'll come..." Phoebe replied, instantly regretting her words.

"He will!" Jesse responded. "He's got Frank Smith to help out if needed, and it's only a trip across the Channel and back."

Phoebe said no more. She had no intention of voicing her concerns that her husband may not choose to journey to Wissant. As the days passed, the images of her assignation with Aaron grew more vivid in her mind, and the fear Harry had heard rumour of her betrayal taunted her day and night. She often saw Tante Marie studying her with concern etched on her face, and knew she was drawing close to the time when her aunt would demand a frank conversation. Phoebe hoped when that moment came, the act of sharing her fears and admitting her wrongdoing would bring her some peace.

On the second Sunday of her time in Wissant, Phoebe donned a lacy coiffe, and attended Mass with her family. She welcomed the cool interior of the parish church, immediately following the lead of others before her and blessing herself with holy water before kneeling beside Mireille in a pew. When the holy procession entered, she gazed at the priest and altar servers, finding comfort in the heady aroma from the censer as it was swung around the altar. There was a familiarity in the Latin, born from Phoebe's time spent in France over the past few years, and she felt soothed by it.

"Come with me." Marie took Phoebe's arm as they left the church and passed through the congregation, now fanning out across the village square where the market was held. In contrast to the villagers who meandered while exchanging the news of the day, Marie's step was purposeful.

Glancing towards Mireille, Phoebe noticed her cousin was hanging back. *She has been told to allow her mother some time alone with me.* Marie's hand almost clamped upon Phoebe's arm, only loosening its claw-like grip as they left the congregation in their wake and set off along the dirt road leading to the countryside. Soon a stream, flowing in the direction of the coast, met with the track. In the winter the waters would have raced and tumbled over the rocks and fallen branches; now it was sluggish, sometimes forming stagnant pools. A path ran alongside the ribbon of water, and they followed it, entering a glade and slowing their pace, appreciating the shade.

"Are we going to the cemetery?" Phoebe asked.

"It's the best place to find both peace and answers to our troubles." Marie's voice softened. Once more she placed her hand on Phoebe's arm, this time as a gesture of comfort and affection.

An image of the churchyard in Dymchurch flashed into Phoebe's mind. She found it a comforting place to be and could almost hide away amongst the trees and ancient stone walls. "It is," she agreed. "Sometimes I go to speak to my mother."

"I'm sorry I never met your mother," Marie said. "Now Grand-mère is becoming frail, I must be the one who speaks to you about the matters I can see are weighing heavy on you."

"My life is good," Phoebe protested. "I cannot complain."

"You do not complain, but those who know and love you can see the sorrow you carry," Marie answered. "But we will not talk about it yet."

They left the seclusion of the trees, both lifting their hands to shield their eyes from the bright sunlight. The path joined the country lane again, and they were flanked either side by trees. Their walk led them steadily upwards, and the cemetery took shape as a rectangular piece of land, encased by low stone walls, surrounded by open fields. At the gateway, the women turned to gaze across the countryside to the rooftops of Wissant and beyond to the sparkling sea. For a moment they were silent, both appreciating the view, then they turned and stepped into the hallowed grounds where their ancestors rested.

Beneath their shoes, the gravel path was freshly raked of weeds and, in formal lines, the tomb slabs, crosses, pillars and headstones stretched across and up the hillside. They were all neatly contained within the boundaries of the walls with no additional burial areas spreading out from the original confines. Phoebe noted a formality to this rural scene which was rarely, if ever, found in its Romney Marsh counterpart.

She studied it for a moment, then said, "I come here every year, and each time I am surprised by how formal it is. In Dymchurch we have grass around the graves, and there seems to be no order at all, other than families being put in the groups together. There are trees, so in the autumn leaves drop everywhere."

"And there are sheep!" Marie commented. This was not the first time she had heard the differences described.

"Sometimes!" Phoebe smiled. "But you welcome their wool in this region of France."

"We do, but we are not here to talk about sheep," Marie reminded her. She led the way past the graves, occasionally pausing as if paying her silent respects to someone she remembered. When they reached the far side, where Phoebe's relations rested near the stone walls, it was time to pause.

Once more gazing across the open fields and towards the coast, Marie broached the subject which was worrying her. "I know you are sad that you don't have a son or daughter to bring with you to meet your family in Wissant, but last year you had no child, nor the year before… is this the reason why you appear to carry such a burden?"

"It gets no easier, but there is still time," Phoebe replied. "My friend Ellen will soon have another baby and even the housekeeper's sister is to be blessed, twelve years after her last. Yet without fail my monthly courses come."

"Maybe the asparagus…?"

"Maybe…"

"Perhaps it would do no harm for Harry to speak with a wise person, or someone who could advise him, if such a person exists on Romney Marsh?"

"I… I don't know about that…" Phoebe pictured the men who had shown unfailing support for Harry over the past years. Owen Bates had no child of his own, meaning he could offer understanding but no practical advice, and John Waller was father to six children. No doubt this brood came with ease, and he sought no remedies or advice. Then there was Sir Rupert… a man of education who had a broader experience of life, but

214

who bumbled along showing no deep compassion or sensitivity. "There is no one I can think of."

"Soon we will celebrate the feast day of Saint Jean-Baptiste! Harry will join us as always. You must miss him."

At this everything became too much for Phoebe and she fought to hold back her tears. The distress of Jesse being imprisoned, coupled with her guilt about meeting with Aaron, and the fear of Harry finding out about the meeting was at the forefront of her mind. In the background, the images of her bloodstained rags, taunted her as each month she suffered her emotions swinging from hope to despair.

"He may not want to come," she told her aunt, her voice dull. "I've done a terrible thing."

"You cannot have done anything so bad that Harry wouldn't want to see you," Marie responded, her tone uncharacteristically gentle. "Tell me and you'll see it's not so bad."

With tears slowly falling down her cheeks, Phoebe told the tale of how she had hoped to save Jesse by pleasing Aaron. When she was finished, there was nothing more Marie could say to soothe her niece. They were in Wissant and could only guess if rumour of Phoebe's meeting with Aaron had reached Harry.

"And if he has heard of it, surely he has the sense to know you would never betray him?" Marie questioned.

"I don't know," Phoebe replied. "You don't know Aaron. You don't know how he mocks people."

"I know I'd like to have a word with his mother!" Marie declared.

"His mother?" Phoebe couldn't help smiling as she pictured Mrs Chapman in her elegant drawing room.

"She should never have allowed this behaviour. She nurtured it when he was a child and had she been sharper with him, he would have become an honourable man."

"Perhaps you are right."

The women took one last look at the family graves and retraced their steps along the gravel paths, through the gateway and back onto the country lane. In a week's time Harry was due to be in Wissant for the feast day of Saint Jean-Baptiste, until he arrived, they could only hope of him treating Phoebe with understanding. They didn't know that Harry carried his own guilt, and that while Phoebe confided to her aunt, the serving wench Amelia was meeting with Aaron at the back door of the Ship Inn.

Chapter Nineteen
Harry

"It's not very friendly… I thought you would have come to see me again…"

Harry blanched and a chill ran through him, despite the warmth of the day and the heat radiating from the fire in the forge. Standing at his workbench overlooking the street, all his attention had been on the intricate metalwork before him. He had failed to notice the attractive young woman passing by before entering the open doorway. His eyes darted unnecessarily around the workshop. Frank and Matthew had just left for their midday meals. Most likely, Amelia had seen them leave and planned her arrival to coincide with that.

"I'm busy with my work," Harry replied. "I don't have time to go drinking."

There was some truth in his response. Ten days had passed since Jesse had been freed and *Louisa-Ann* had left for Wissant. Harry had been making up for lost time and was determined to spend every hour possible at work. With Matthew now learning the trade, there was no excuse for Harry not to be there and doing the best he could to ease him through the first weeks of his apprenticeship.

"That's a shame." Amelia stepped closer to him, allowing her light shawl to fall away from her shoulders, exposing the lacy trim of her bodice and the swell of her breasts.

Harry moved back. "I'm sorry if I encouraged you. Too much brandy... I have a wife."

"Your wife's not here, is she?"

"She'll be back in a few days." Harry turned and plunged his hands in a bowl of water. He was aware of his dinner being ready and could picture Janey's scowl if he were to be late. "And I'm looking forward to seeing her," he said with more confidence than he felt.

"I heard rumour that she had been a little free with her affections." Amelia smiled sweetly, "I can't imagine how that must make you feel. Perhaps in need of a little comfort yourself? That's how I thought it might be."

"Free with her affections?" Harry repeated. "You've only just arrived in the village, what do you know of it?"

"Someone mentioned it – I can't think who," Amelia lied.

"There's no truth in it," Harry asserted. Yet all the time he tidied the workbench and checked the fire, a nervous energy raced through his limbs. "I've got to go home now," he said, standing at the open door, hoping she would understand their conversation was over.

"Of course." She swept through the doorway with a sway of her hips. "You wouldn't want her... your wife... to hear of your little indiscretion, would you?"

"Hear of it?" Harry heard his voice was high, and it embarrassed him as he closed the door. "I don't have time for this. I'm a busy man." He began to stride out along the High Street, past shops and cottages.

"Sixpence a week would help me hold my tongue!" Amelia suggested, as she caught up with him. "I'm not greedy!"

Harry nodded to Phoebe's Uncle Giles who stood at the entrance to his shop. "Good afternoon!"

218

"You wouldn't want me causing a scene, would you?"

Giles had already seen Harry being pursued by a comely wench and, most likely, he would hasten to spread the news to his wife, Peggy.

"No. I want to be left to face the scowls from my housekeeper, eat my cold meal, and get back to work." Harry loosened the leather ties on his money pouch and pressed his fingers into the opening, pulling out a small collection of coins. Without pausing to check the value, he thrust them towards Amelia. "There. I'm not having you following me about for sixpence a week. Take this and leave me alone. It was only a kiss."

"Thank you, kindly!" Amelia's words were followed by a chirp of laughter. "You know where I am if you'd like me to oblige again." She crossed the road and ran up the slope known as Seawall Road.

The last few days had been kind to Harry. Finally, he had been able to run his business without having to deal with more pressing matters, or pander to the whims of Sir Rupert. Matthew Alder was proving himself to be keen to learn and cheerful company in the forge, just as his cousin had been.

There was talk in the village about Humphrey Fletcher and his horse Whistlejacket who were to journey to Lydd in early July, a couple of days before their Match Against Time. It lent an air of anticipation to the people as they discussed a day trip to the town and what entertainment might be on offer alongside the race across the Rype.

Harry looked forward to sharing the news of Mr Fletcher and Whistlejacket with Phoebe. The thought of their discussing the day and planning for it, encouraged him to look upon her return with optimism. He had already arranged for Owen and Bess to ride in a cart with them alongside Phoebe's Aunt Peggy and Uncle Giles.

This day, and the expectation of enjoyment, would mark an end to any awkwardness between them. At least, this is how Harry chose to see it until Amelia had once more entered his life. Now, as he strode along, nodding at friends and acquaintances, all he could envisage was the seductive serving wench making her presence known at every opportunity. Before long, no doubt, Phoebe would be given cause to wonder if Harry had dallied with the young woman from the Ship Inn, and all his good intentions to repair the rift between them would be cast aside.

Entering through the back door of his home, Harry sensed disapproval radiating from Janey as she clattered about in the scullery.

"I'm late – sorry," he said, hastily sitting down and taking a swig of cool ale.

"It's a cold meal, so nothing spoiled," Janey responded as she placed ham, cheese and pickled vegetables before him. The bread followed, with its wooden board making a definite thud and the knife falling upon the scrubbed pine tabletop.

She returned to the scullery and Harry ate in silence, left to his concerns that a handful of coins would not satisfy the young woman who had interrupted his day with her suggestions and demands. The food was good, but he tasted none of it and refused a piece of fruit cake, instead accepting Janey's offer to take some back to the forge to share with Matthew and Frank that afternoon.

"A girl – pretty young thing with red hair – came with a note for Mrs Farrers," Janey told him when she cleared his plate. "I put it on the dresser."

'Pretty young thing with red hair'. Harry pondered on the words. There was something familiar about

them. *Red hair… where have I heard that recently?* "Did you know her, Janey?" he asked. "Was she from the New Hall?"

"The New Hall? No, she wasn't a Dymchurch girl. I'd say she came from one of the villages."

"Phoebe will see it soon enough. I'll put it on her dressing table so it can't be missed." Harry pushed his chair back, and turned as he stood, reaching for the note. There was no weight to the envelope, as if the contents were a scrap of paper. He turned it to examine the wax seal, but it was no more than an irregular spill on the paper, with no stamp to give any clues as to the sender. The handwriting on the front was neat, without any additional flourishes to give a hint as to whether the writer was male or female. "I'll be off to work in a minute," he told the housekeeper as he left the kitchen with the paper in his hand.

Once in the bedroom, and about to place the note on the dressing table, Harry realised that the seal was poorly placed and barely holding the folds of paper. As the envelope dropped onto the polished wood, it sprang open, leaving the contents vulnerable to Harry's eyes. He gazed at it, almost in horror, for now there was a choice to be made: should he leave it for Phoebe to read on her return, or take a discreet peek? *After all, the sender may be unaware of Phoebe being away and will be expecting a response…* Harry touched the paper with his fingertips. *It was not intended for me and is not my business to be looking at it.* He extracted the note from its envelope.

'There was no need to run away. Looking forward to resuming our talk. Send a note with your maid. A xx'

Dropping the note as if it burned in his hands, Harry watched it fall onto the dressing table and brush against the envelope. Without pausing to consider the words sprawling across the paper, he left the room, running down the stairs and calling out to Janey, "I'm off to work."

Two days later, *Louisa-Ann*, crewed by Walter and Joshua, left Dymchurch for Wissant. While they rowed away from the shore, Harry remained in his forge working on an ornate garden gate for Lady Bannerman. An hour later, John Waller passed by and frowned to see Harry there. He turned about and went directly to the home of Owen and Bess Bates.

"Harry! what have you done?" Owen wasted no time on a polite greeting. "I hoped John had got it wrong…"

"Got it wrong?" Harry asked, carefully placing a wrought iron bar on the workbench.

"He says *Louisa-Ann* has left for Wissant and you… you're still here."

"I thought it was for the best."

"You'd better come along to the cottage," Owen offered. "Bess is making tea, and we need to hear what's troubling you. We've been worried, and whatever is wrong, it has gone too far now."

"The fire…"

"When is Matthew due back?"

"Any moment now," Harry admitted.

Owen would hear of no other objections. He had watched Harry over the past few days, curious as to why he had not joined Phoebe in Wissant within a week of the trial and Jesse's subsequent escape, but assuming the pressure of work had not allowed for time away. The occasional passing comment had come to his ears: reports of Aaron taunting Harry; tales of Phoebe hurrying to Burmarsh under the cover of a misty morning; then, and most concerning, a rumour of Harry flirting with the new serving girl from the Ship. As isolated incidents, none of these overly concerned

210

Owen or his wife, Bess. There was likely to be little truth in any story which passed from one mouth to the next within the village. Yet when he combined these snippets of information, they spoke of troubles between Harry and Phoebe. Worse than that – troubles which could not be resolved all the time she was in France. But for Harry to remain in Dymchurch, not to go and see the Bernard family and to miss the feast of Saint Jean-Baptiste – it was unforgivable. If Owen had been unable to imagine the humiliation Phoebe would feel when Walter and Joshua walked up the white sands without Harry, then Bess was quick to point it out as her heart filled with sorrow for the young woman whom she loved as if she were her own daughter.

No more words were exchanged while the men walked past village shops and turned onto a small patch of land with scattered one-storey cottages, sheds, animal pens and vegetable plots between the High Street and seawall.

"I hoped it wasn't true!" Bess' first words spoke of her disappointment in him, yet she opened her arms to Harry, showing her unfailing support for him.

In the cottage which Harry had made his home for the first two years of his time in Dymchurch and where he had brought Phoebe as his bride before their own house was built, he began to explain the rift which had opened between the pair.

Bess delved deeper into the story, relying on her intuition as she stirred the tea and pressed ginger cake upon Harry. "This Amelia…" she began.

"Let's not talk about her anymore," Harry suggested. To admit to this wrongdoing made him feel sick. The details of Phoebe's meeting with Aaron were unknown and unproven, yet there was no denying his dalliance with the shapely wench.

"No, Harry, this has to be said," Bess insisted. "It smacks of funny business. I'm not saying you're not a handsome man, and you hold a position of authority in this village that will always make you attractive to women, but it seems as though she's taken it a bit too far. This Amelia is new to Dymchurch and she wouldn't want to be sent back to Newchurch when her family need her to be earning. There's a large family over there to feed and clothe, or so I hear. We all know there's someone who wants to make trouble for you, and I'm wondering if he slipped her a coin or two that night."

"She was paid to? Harry pushed the ginger cake away.

"I wouldn't be surprised."

"Aaron was in the Ship that evening," Harry stated. There was no need for him to say any more on the matter.

"It's my sister's husband's cousin who owns the Ship," Bess announced, seeming to have changed the subject.

"Does he?" Sometimes Harry struggled to understand the intricate web connecting one villager to the next.

"I'll have a word, because no one wants that sort of carry-on, and it seems like that young woman needs a talking to."

Now Harry realised the significance in her words. If the landlord of the Ship became aware of his serving girl accepting payments to cause trouble, then his displeasure would, no doubt, lead to stern words. Amelia faced losing her cosy room in the attic of the inn, and the humiliation of being sent home to Newchurch unless she showed remorse and promised to be more respectful to the patrons. "Thank you." His response was simple but the gratitude in his words was clear.

For the first time in days, Harry began to relax while seated at the table crafted by Owen, the cosy atmosphere of the cottage enveloping him. Much as he appreciated his modern home with the high ceilings and elegant joinery, there was something more homely about the place which had sheltered him when he arrived in Dymchurch four years beforehand. He loved the beams he could reach up to and touch, the depth of the huge fireplace, and the small windows, often shuttered to keep out the harsh winds. Most of all he cherished the couple who had nurtured him and continued in the role of parents after he married and bought his own business.

"There's nothing to be done about Aaron until you speak to Phoebe, but I am certain her distaste for him has not changed," Owen said. "The man is still the same sewer rat that he always was. There's a story to all this... something that gives him reason to taunt you, but it won't be as he makes it seem. Be sure you are waiting for your wife when she returns, and that nothing stops you both from speaking truthfully about what has happened over the past weeks."

Harry, knowing full well that he had made a grave mistake in not boarding the little fishing boat bound to France, agreed, "I'll be there on the beach. If I'd spoken to you before, then I would be in Wissant with her now. I have been a fool and I can only pray that Phoebe will forgive me."

Two days passed and Harry's resolve to make amends had not weakened. At mid-afternoon on a Saturday, he walked to Wall End, just beyond High Knocke, and waited for the first glimpse of *Louisa-Ann*. The boat was one of four fishing smacks returning to shore and had lowered her nets, so she too brought in a catch. Gulls screamed, flying close to the water, and the sea crashed upon the beach.

At first, the sun shone too bright, and the boats remained too distant for any one of them to be distinguished from the others. No clouds softened the azure sky, and a curious haze lingered above both land and sea. Later, when Harry was certain *Louisa-Ann* was the second to close in on the beach, the individual figures could still not be recognised. His eyes were fixed on the prow, and an awareness grew of there being two figures leaning over the front, as well as the two working the boat.

Who else is there? Surely, they would not risk bringing Jesse back? Nothing has changed. All sorts of scenarios raced about in Harry's mind, each one erratically bouncing off the next, with not one of them making any sense. Then, as the rising tide brought *Louisa-Ann* nudging against the shingle bank at the top of the sand, he saw that the person standing beside Phoebe was a woman.

Chapter Twenty
Phoebe

Phoebe's emotions had been washed away with her vomit earlier that morning, when the sun beat down upon the little boat, and the voyage from Wissant to Dymchurch had seemed like an eternity. For the past days she had flitted from one state of anxiety to the next: first the anticipation of seeing Harry again, only to be crushed by him not arriving with the Dymchurch fishermen; then the fear of what could have led to her husband deciding not to join her, coupled with the certainty that somehow Aaron would be involved; finally, the nervousness rising as the hours came closer to her leaving her family and facing Harry. Then, somewhere at the midway point across the Channel, something in Phoebe died and she felt nothing.

He has come to meet me, Phoebe realised. It was merely a thought, a recognition of the fact. No joy, fear or anticipation erupted in her body. *I am exhausted by it all.*

The men went about their business of preparing the boat to nudge against the beach. Then Joshua joined the women at the bow, readying himself to jump into the shallows, before securing the boat to the winch rope. There came the crunch of wood upon the pebbles and, without faltering, he bounded over the side to battle against the shingle which fell back with every step he took upon it.

Harry looked at Phoebe, his expression both confused and, she hoped, pleased. In return, she attempted to smile but knew the result was feeble. Then the moment was lost because he ran to take the handle of the winch and prepared to haul *Louisa-Ann* free of the high tide mark.

What happened next shook the dulled sensation from Phoebe, startling both her and Harry, forcing them to face their difficulties there and then. Tante Marie, who had shown an unnaturally subdued character throughout the voyage, vaulted, without warning, over the gunwale and into the shallow water.

Still ankle deep in water and struggling with the stones, she raised her voice and begun her tirade upon Harry in her own tongue, "Here you are! For two weeks your wife has been left in Wissant thinking you would come to her. Two weeks! What excuse do you have, Harry? What excuse can there be to neglect my niece? None that I can think of. I am forced to leave my family to hear your reasons for myself. How will any of us settle if we cannot be sure of Phoebe being content here in Dymchurch. I'm telling you, that if I cannot be assured of her being happy here, I will take her back to Wissant, where we can be certain of her being loved and respected."

Standing with his hand on the worn handle of the winch, Harry could only listen to the outpouring and barely grasp the gist of her meaning. That she felt furious, there could be no doubt. In turn, his reply was steady, "Hello Marie, I'm sorry I couldn't come to Wissant, but now you are here, and I'm pleased you can visit."

Phoebe watched, knowing that neither fully understood the other, but in Harry's measured response, she saw the man she loved and felt hope that their differences could be resolved.

216

"Pleased?" Marie continued her rant, *"Peut-être bien que vous êtes content, vous, mais moi, je ne serai satisfaite que quand je verrai ma Phoebe en train de sourire de nouveau, avec un enfant dans le ventre."*

With this surge of fury from her aunt, the last of Phoebe's lethargy was released. In its place there came a feeling of pride in her forthright aunt and horror that such words could be screamed upon the beach at Dymchurch. *I thank God she speaks mostly in French!*

Seeing the need for Phoebe to scramble from the boat, Joshua left the winch and ran to hold the ladder that had been lowered over the side. Phoebe landed on the stony bank with ease and took a few steps closer to her aunt before she too raised her voice, "Tante Marie! We do not say such things in Dymchurch – in England!"

"Pah! These words must be said if you are to be happy. What does he have to say for himself?"

"He will speak when we are at home."

"No, Phoebe! We have waited two weeks. I will hear him speak now…"

Harry, with his hand on the winch handle, was not about to shirk his duties to the Dymchurch fishermen and so he began to turn it, slowly and steadily. However, rather than look to the sea, he faced the women. "She is right, Phoebe. My apology should not wait until we are home, and Janey has presented us with a pot of tea in the parlour. I am here now to say I am sorry… more than sorry that I didn't come to Wissant. There have been rumours and difficulties that we *will* speak of in private, but none of them give me any excuse for remaining here rather than being with my wife."

"We are both at fault, and if there are rumours then I fear you know I have made some foolish choices," Phoebe responded.

For those minutes while *Louisa-Ann* was hauled slowly up the bank, Phoebe had only been aware of the outburst from Marie, followed by Harry's measured response. Her world had shrunk to the three of them, the shingle at her feet and the winch. Now she became aware of the other boat nearby, and a third one about to grind to a halt on the shore. Despite the fishing fleet being some way from the village centre, boys had emerged, as they always did, to help with the catch and pocket a Dymchurch token for their efforts, as well as some fish to take home for supper.

"Let the lads bring the boat in," Walter called. "Get yourself home, Harry." He lowered Phoebe's case over the prow.

Harry looked towards the fisherman, and it seemed for a moment that he was not going to react to Phoebe's last words. She felt the anxiety rise. *'Rumours,' he said. What has he heard? It can only be about Aaron and there can be no denying that there is truth in them.*

Rather than persisting with the talk of their rift, Harry merely said, "I'm glad you're home," and placed a kiss on Phoebe's cheek as he stepped away from the winch. He then picked up the case and both bags before joining the women.

"I'm glad I'm home," Phoebe replied, reassured for the moment. There was no need to say any more. She knew explanations must be made and the whole story to be told, but for now they were on the right path towards returning their marriage to its usual happy state. "Tante Marie, we must walk to Dymchurch now. Do you see it over there? It's no distance at all."

They strolled along the seawall track to the village. "It is so flat – I cannot see where Romney Marsh ends and England begins," Marie attempted to express her surprise at the endless low-lying land.

Phoebe couldn't help smiling. "It's still England!"

"Not as I imagined it."

The fury directed at Harry as soon as the Frenchwoman had vaulted into the shallows had now abated. Phoebe believed her aunt was satisfied to see Harry suitably repentant and had noted that the easy rapport between the couple was fast returning. "I'm glad you came to meet us," she said to Harry. "I wonder what Tante Marie will think of Dymchurch."

"I am sure she will tell us." The smile he offered was warm. Phoebe liked the way his freckled nose crinkled, and grey eyes sparkled.

"Is this your forge?" Marie asked. They looked across at the first of the properties on the road stretching through the village from their elevated position atop the wall. At that moment, a man appeared at the door. He was clad in a heavy blacksmith's apron and raised his hand in greeting.

It can't be! Phoebe felt a shock run through her, yet before it dispersed, she knew this wasn't Jesse, but his cousin, Matthew. *What a good idea. I wonder how that happened – did Harry ask him or...*

Her thoughts were halted by Marie's questioning, "Jesse? How can it be?"

"It's his cousin," Phoebe explained. "Come and meet him," and then to Harry, "I hadn't thought until now that Jesse's family will want to meet Tante Marie and to see who has been taking care of him."

"I am sure it would help," Harry said. They hadn't yet spoken about what had happened that night when Phoebe left for Wissant, only to then have Jesse bundled on the boat. Neither had they discussed his future in Wissant.

As they crossed the street to introduce Marie, Phoebe said, "Jesse is staying with Papa. It seemed like the best idea, and Papa wants to help."

There was no need to say any more at that moment. Harry understood that in living with Jacques, Jesse would be very much a part of the extended family, and already Marie would have taken him under her wing.

While Marie and Matthew spoke in broken English and the occasional French word, Harry lowered his voice and asked Phoebe, "Why is she here?"

Already their comfortable relationship had returned, and Phoebe felt at ease with her husband. She flashed a grin and replied, "She's here to ensure that all is well with our marriage."

"We can talk about that in private, I hope." Pausing for a moment, perhaps considering his next words, Harry then continued, "I like your aunt a lot but can't help wondering when she's leaving!" It had never been suggested that any member of Phoebe's family might visit Dymchurch. "They will miss her... need her..."

"She'll stay for ten days," Phoebe told him. "We can only hope she warms to Dymchurch in that time, but I fear her prejudices run deep."

Laughter burst from Harry, and he leaned over to place an arm around Phoebe's shoulders. Tante Marie looked and smiled her approval.

"Let's show Marie our home," Harry said. "Janey will be waiting."

Having left the forge, they meandered along the High Street. indicating to the general store where Phoebe had lived with her aunt and uncle, and the cottage where she and Harry had stayed as a newly married couple. The village slumbered, it being that lull at the end of the afternoon when the shops were due to close, but the men were not yet gathering at the taverns. The sun cast a soft light upon the hotchpotch of roofs in slate, tile or thatch, and on walls of brick, stone or wood. It was a straggly street, not widening to a central marketplace as Marie was accustomed too.

She observed the surroundings without her usual patter of comments, no doubt tiring both from the voyage and her growing anxiety for Phoebe over the past days.

When the properties no longer butted up against each other, Walker House came into view. The sun shone upon its red brick façade and reflected from the square panes of glass between narrow glazing bars. Having been completed two years before, the walls retained their sharp lines, the chimneys had not yet considered bowing, and the planting alongside the front path remained youthful with slender branches.

Pausing and glancing at Marie, Harry's tone was almost apologetic, "This is our home."

In that moment while they watched Marie observe the splendour, Phoebe imagined all sorts of conflicting thoughts bounding about in her aunt's mind. When she spoke, the Frenchwoman expressed her joy and horror as best she could. "Phoebe! We put you to sleep in a bed with your cousin, and yet here you live as if... as if you are rich! Sacrébleu! This is a fine life you have in Dymchurch with your English husband, and we did not know... Jacques has not told us."

"Tante Marie, Papa did not know. How could he? Tomorrow you will meet Aunt Peggy and Uncle Giles, and Owen and Bess, and you will see our family here live humble lives."

Marie's mind returned to a person Harry had mentioned not long before – a person whose role she had not queried at the time. "This Janey you spoke of... she is the housekeeper who works here?"

Placing a hand on her aunt's arm, Phoebe replied, "She is, but we treat her as part of our family here. We do not act as if we are wealthy."

"We are neither poor nor rich!" Harry found his voice. "I am the son of a blacksmith and I own the forge here in Dymchurch. Phoebe is the daughter of a fisherman, and here on the High Street her family have a shop. Marie, come into our home and enjoy your stay, but don't think of us as anything but a hardworking ordinary family!"

Phoebe smiled, again proud of her husband's confidence and pleased that he remembered the people who were important to them both. He may well be at ease dining at the New Hall, but Harry was equally, if not more, comfortable with the wall-workers and tradespeople in the village.

"I will remember that!" Marie declared. "But do not forget, Harry, I am here for a reason and shall not return to Wissant until I am satisfied."

The following morning, Phoebe faltered at her closet. They had planned to go to church where Marie would be introduced to Dymchurch society, and most likely feel cowed by Sir Rupert and Lady Charlotte. Neither the Lord of the Marsh Scotts nor his good wife skimped on their finery, despite the church being modest and most of the congregation being uncomplicated folk who worked the land, laboured on the seawall or fished from small vessels.

With her slim figure, Marie could fit into one of Phoebe's outfits. *There is some give around the waist and bust if it were not to be fastened as tightly. But will it suit her?* Marie typically wore long dresses of linen which had none of the frivolous layers of fancy trimmings at the elbows or neckline that adorned Phoebe's garments. *What would be the best for my aunt?* Phoebe looked down at her own summer dress in primrose linen with lace frills. *This is modest compared to those worn by the Bannerman ladies, but for my aunt it would be far too... too extravagant. What is the best for her?*

Faced with indecision, Phoebe lingered. Her gaze ran over a second summer dress of pale blue which she decided was equally unsuitable. On the next shelf, carefully folded there was her beige outfit with a subtle stripe running through the material and only one layer of trimming, and another of a similar style but in a soft green. *She would feel more comfortable in the beige…*

Or would she rather…? Lower down, the dress Phoebe wore about the house when helping Janey with the chores or tending the garden caught her eye. It was from this shelf that she also selected her clothes to wear in Wissant. *These are not unlike those that Marie already wears and can be embellished with a decorative shawl. How will she feel if she attends church wearing something I wear to sweep the front path or tend the chickens? No, it's not good enough. Not at all.*

In the end, having decided upon the striped beige dress from the shelf and paired it with a light lace shawl, Phoebe left her bedroom and tentatively knocked on the door of her aunt's bedroom.

A couple of hours later, Marie, accompanied Harry and Phoebe to the village church of St Peter and St Paul. Phoebe noted her aunt relax as they neared the plain Norman church. The building sat with dappled sunlight upon its stone walls, a testament to the skilled masons who created it when Dymchurch was no more than a scattered collection of cottages behind a natural shingle bank. It invited the humble folk to worship within its solid walls, the interior bathed in the soft light filtered through plain glass leaded windows and shouted no pretences of grandeur or extravagance.

Here Marie Bernard had her first introductions to the people of Dymchurch, although, of course, the villagers knew of her being there and each one of them was curious to witness the stranger in their midst. They noted a dark-eyed, upright woman of almost forty years of age, her long brown hair severely tied in a bun and glistening with streaks of silver. Her smile was friendly, yet tentative, and Phoebe encouraged no more than a swift greeting as they walked along the short path to the porch and passed under a carved Norman archway before entering the church. With a lace shawl pulled tight around her shoulders, Marie was ushered into a pew not far from the front, and instinctively knelt to pray.

Smiling at Harry, Phoebe linked her fingers with his for a moment. The evening before she had been exhausted from the hours spent upon *Louisa-Ann,* coupled with the trepidation of the return to Dymchurch. They had agreed to delay any talk of the rift between them and had fallen asleep with their bodies close. It had become clear that whatever would be revealed when they did speak, was nothing that could not be resolved.

In the comfort of the church, with the gentle patina on the oak pews, and the aroma of ancient stone mingling with sweet scents from displays of summer flowers, Phoebe followed the familiar rhythm of the service. She found the parson's words to be soothing, and the hymns uplifting.

Afterwards they lingered in the churchyard, making arrangements to visit Giles and Peggy, and then Owen and Bess that afternoon. "First we must go to see Lucy," Phoebe said, "I know Harry has told her about Wissant, but she will want to see us."

"Will she want to come to be with Jesse?" Marie asked, while lifting the skirt of the beige stripped dress to avoid it brushing on the gravestones leaning towards the narrow path.

"I don't know," Phoebe replied. "But he is adamant she must stay here."

The women walked ahead, leaving Harry to return home on his own. Soon they were passing Walker House and nearing the village centre. Lucy lived at the end cottage in a terrace, one of which, Rose Cottage, opened its front parlour for the sale of ale. It had no such thing as a bar, being a humble establishment, but offered good ale and a place for men to chew over the events of the day. Six mornings a week, Lucy's mother swept the floor of the alehouse, and wiped the tables and chairs. She then returned to her family home and repeated the chores.

On a Sunday, peace reigned in the terrace, with only the landlord supping ale in his chair by the front window. Phoebe spotted him there before rapping on the door of Lucy's home, suddenly feeling nervous of what confidences would be shared within its walls. She glanced at Marie, "Will Lucy understand? Will she be angry at us for taking him to Wissant? Will she be upset that no one told her before he went?"

Before Marie could even think of responding, the door opened, and Lucy stood there. She fixed a welcoming smile on her pale face and invited them in. "You've heard!" she said, before any other greetings were exchanged. "I'm glad you came."

Chapter Twenty-One
Phoebe

Phoebe and Marie exchanged glances, both unsure of the meaning behind Lucy's words. "This is my aunt, Marie," Phoebe said, then added, "She's come from Wissant to Dymchurch."

"Welcome to Dymchurch," Lucy replied. She gestured for them to sit down. "We don't usually have visitors… only my sister, or grandmother. Or Matthew, of course…"

Not understanding the reference to Matthew, or indeed which Matthew she referred to, Phoebe smiled and nodded as if she knew. "I'm sorry I couldn't tell you before I left for Wissant. No one told me – I didn't know there was a plan to release Jesse. I didn't even know he was on the boat until we were some distance from the shore."

"It was a shock." Lucy perched herself on the edge of a chair. "But I couldn't be angry. I didn't know what to think at first. One minute we were planning our future together, the next he was in gaol. Then he was going to be transported, and the following morning there were men here wanting to search for him. It was the first we knew of him being released."

"They came here?" Phoebe pictured the cottage being searched. She felt sick to think of furniture being pushed aside and the home being ransacked for any likely hiding places. This was a home to a decent, honest family, and they deserved to feel safe in it.

"It was over almost before we understood what was happening," Lucy admitted. "I think they knew he wouldn't be here. Then later in the afternoon Harry came and he told us, but we couldn't say a word about it, and I didn't. I couldn't risk it being my fault if they went after him."

"He is staying with my father," Phoebe told Lucy. "Tante Marie, and the rest of the family live nearby and the men, Papa and Jesse, go to eat with them. They have made him welcome." She paused. There was something odd about Lucy. The young woman looked tired. It appeared as if the bloom of youth had left her skin, and her blonde hair hung rather than bounced. Yet there was a sparkle to her eyes contradicting her manner and appearance. Phoebe considered the words uttered as Lucy opened the door: *'You've heard'. What did she mean? What am I meant to have heard?*

"You've been very kind to him," Lucy spoke to Marie. "Thank you."

"He will earn his keep by fishing with my father and uncle," Phoebe told her. "Then, in time, he can decide how he wants to earn a living. Perhaps when his French improves?"

"I can't imagine Jesse speaking French!" Lucy laughed – a girlish tinkle bursting from her.

She is nervous, Phoebe realised. *Why?*

"He is learning quickly," Marie told her. "We are happy to welcome him into our family." There was a protectiveness in her manner, and a hint of maternal pride.

"You must miss him," Phoebe said.

Two spots of pink appeared high in Lucy's cheeks. "Of course!" she replied, her voice high and rushed.

"I didn't know…" Phoebe began. "I wasn't sure if you expected to join him. In Wissant. You see, he has nothing to offer you now…"

"No! I mean I hadn't thought it would be possible," Lucy answered immediately. "I never considered… which is why… why I agreed to marry Matthew. I thought you knew?"

Silence fell upon the small front parlour. Outside, on the street a pair of horses trotted past the window, offering a welcome distraction. In the kitchen at the back of the house, pans clattered.

Phoebe, who now saw Jesse as part of her Wissant family, recalled his torment as he made the decision not to ask Lucy to join him. She felt his pain and loss all the more now she understood there had been no need for him to agonise over his choice. Lucy had already planned a future without him. "Marry?" she repeated at last, her response inadequate.

"Who is Matthew?" Marie was unable to keep the scowl from her face. "The cousin?"

"Yes. He is older than Jesse by four years and has money saved for us to set up a home. I have three younger brothers living here and they all sleep in the one bed. All of us are sharing a room, and me a grown woman," Lucy explained. "Jesse and I had plans, but now I must make others."

Phoebe softened towards the desperate young woman. "I understand," she said. "Matthew is a good man, like Jesse is, and you will be happy with him." She looked at Marie, "There will be no need to speak of this when you return to Wissant. Not yet anyway."

"Not yet," Marie agreed. "But in time I will. Jesse needs to know he is free from any commitment. Then…" she darted a knowing look towards Lucy, "he will find a good French wife."

"I hope he does," Lucy responded, her voice weary.

"Let me know when the wedding is," Phoebe said, as she stood to indicate it was time to leave. "I know Harry will want to help you both. Matthew is proving himself a good worker."

Aunt and niece strolled along in silence, each one of them glad the meeting was over, both absorbing the latest turn of events. As they approached Walker House, Phoebe remarked, "It is better this way. If Lucy were to come to Wissant then there would be no doubt of where Jesse is, and that Harry was involved."

"I find it hard to like that young woman," Marie replied.

That afternoon, Marie was introduced first to Giles and Peggy in their small living room behind the shop. Peggy, the sister of Phoebe's late mother, eyed Marie with suspicion. She had a liking for the French lace that adorned her plump shoulders on a Sunday but preferred it if the people of France remained on their side of the Channel! In turn, Marie had formed her own opinion of the English woman four years before this meeting. On her first visit to Wissant, Phoebe had told of a life where she slept amongst the boxes in her bedroom-cum-storeroom, always at the beck and call of her petulant and demanding aunt.

Despite their seemingly mutual dislike of each other, by the time the first cup of tea had been drained, the women appeared to have come to an uneasy truce. Both approved of the other's outspoken ways, as the news of Lucy's forthcoming marriage and her casual abandonment of Jesse was aired. Condemnation for the young woman emanated from them both – to replace Jesse so quickly showed a callous nature, and a heart which could not be dependable.

"Aunt, didn't you suggest that Jesse was guilty and that his eyes flitted about like a man who couldn't be trusted?" Phoebe said, part in jest, but knowing this to be a true account of Peggy's response when news of the theft and arrest came to her ears.

"Not at all! I never met a better young man, apart from your Harry, of course!" Peggy responded, having noted the swift scowl passing over Marie's face.

"Ah! That was it!" Phoebe replied, a glint in her eyes as she tried not to smile.

Afterwards, Phoebe and Marie crossed the road to Bess and Owen's cottage, to spend a pleasant hour in their company. While sitting outside. where the ground was scattered with shavings and sawdust trailing from Owen's shed, Marie showed a keen interest in the cottage he had built a couple of decades before.

"Come and see the room he added for Harry," Bess offered, leading her guest into the cottage and through to the extension.

Phoebe smiled and felt herself relax. She knew Marie had nothing but warm feelings towards the couple who had gladly taken on the roles of parents to Harry and Phoebe.

"That friend of yours, Ellen, I heard she had the baby last night," Owen told Phoebe, his voice low and steady.

"I didn't know." Phoebe felt her body chill. Yet at the same time she was glad to have heard the news from someone who would pass it on without embellishment nor reference to Phoebe's own childlessness. A woman would have pointed out that there was less than a year between the two babies and recalled every snippet of information that circulated amongst the villagers.

"I don't know what it is – another boy I believe," Owen continued. "Bess will know."

"We will find out soon enough," Phoebe responded, then almost to herself. "I was hemming some nightgowns before... before I went away. I'd better finish them."

"Good to hear Matthew Alder is proving himself to be a good worker," Owen changed the subject.

In the evening, Phoebe and Harry took the opportunity to talk without Marie's company. Having walked past the Ship, they took a track to the seawall and, with unspoken consent, turned in the direction of Hythe. The tide flowed high, idly rolling towards the lower reaches of the seawall. With the sun low in the sky behind them, and not another soul about, it made a peaceful scene.

There were mistakes to be admitted to and apologies to be heard, but with the last of the day's summer sunshine on their limbs and the gentle sound of the push and pull of the sea, Phoebe felt relaxed and ready to talk. They sat on the edge of the wall, with their feet dangling above the curve of the bank and linked their fingers.

"I was never angry about you trying to help Jesse," she began. "That wasn't why I became so... why things weren't the same. I came up with a plan to try to help..."

"A plan?" Harry's tone was curious.

"It was a terrible plan. It might have worked, but I couldn't do it," Phoebe began. "I let you down and I'll understand if you can never forgive me."

"It's got something to do with Aaron, hasn't it?"

Knowing that giving her former love an opportunity to press himself into their lives could only bring discord within their marriage, Phoebe nodded. The waves continued their leisurely journey, breaking without fuss or fury. *I think it would be better if they raged,* she reflected. *And Harry too – he should be angry with me, but I have a feeling that he won't be, and I wonder why.* "It has everything to do with Aaron," she admitted.

"You went to see him," Harry prompted.

"How do you know?" her response came quickly.

"He hinted at it, and Mary admitted that she'd taken a note."

"Poor Mary." Phoebe hadn't thought about Janey's niece, and her involvement. "I shouldn't have asked her."

"She wasn't to know what the note was about," Harry reminded her. "And I did nothing to make her feel uncomfortable about it. At least I tried not to."

"We must offer her some more work," Phoebe reminded him, aware of the conversation shifting to a safer topic. "I meant to before I went to France. Her mother is expecting, and it will be difficult for them to manage."

"Ask her tomorrow," Harry suggested. "I know we spoke of taking on extra help when…"

When our baby came, the voice in Phoebe's head screamed. *But it won't. Not now.* They sat in silence for a moment before she forced herself to say, "Yes, I'll ask Mary. It's not fair to keep her waiting."

"What happened when you went to see Aaron?" Harry prompted.

Phoebe removed her hand from his. "I asked if he would reconsider. I said that I knew he had paid the boy, Toke, to say he had seen Jesse with the cup, and it wasn't fair. Aaron has a wife and a daughter, and I don't know why he still wants to cause trouble for you." She paused for a moment, gathering the courage to admit to what happened next. The tide rolled on, and a gull flew low, screaming and breaking the calm of the evening. "Aaron said that he could get the witness to change his story, but I would have to pay for that… Pay by pleasing him. And I wondered if I should – for Jesse and Lucy. Because it is my fault that he hates you and he arranged all this to cause trouble for you. It's all because of me."

"But you didn't because Jesse was convicted?" Harry queried.

"I didn't, but I did go to meet him again," Phoebe admitted. Now she was back there in the church with Aaron's lips on hers and his hands roaming about her bodice. "And I did let him kiss me. It was awful, but I thought I had to. Then I stopped it, but the worst of it was... sometimes I wish I hadn't because... because perhaps he could give me a child."

Phoebe wrapped her arms around her body and looked at her feet hanging over the edge of the wall, swaying above the water. *I've said it now. It was the worst thing I could ever say to him. I have the finest husband in Dymchurch, in Romney Marsh, but he is still not good enough.*

"I'm glad you didn't... you know," Harry began. "And I'm sorry. Sorry there is no child. But there still might be. In time...

"There might be," Phoebe admitted. "Marie brought a *sage-femme*, a midwife, to see me. They fed me asparagus!"

"Do you think it might help?"

"I don't know."

"I understand about Aaron," Harry told her. "I don't like it, but I understand. He can't hurt me now with his taunts because I know what happened and why. Now I have to tell you something and there is no excuse for it. This is about my foolish pride and not knowing better, not trusting you..."

Phoebe reached out and placed her hand on his knee, hoping to reassure him that all would be well.

"I saw him – Aaron – on the day after you left. Sir Rupert told me to go to New Romney and then the constable said we were to search for Jesse. Aaron was there and sending his best wishes to you and making it clear he had seen you recently. He mentioned Mary and a note. It wasn't hard to ask Mary, so I soon knew it to be true. I tried not to think about it, but I went to Burmarsh to speak to him." He paused for a moment, staring unseeingly into the distance, then continued, "I mean I planned to go to Burmarsh, but there was no point. He would only derive pleasure from my fears. I saw Toke though, and I asked him about Jesse and about you. Not that he can be trusted – he is paid to do as Aaron says. He said he saw you though, and there was no reason to think it wasn't true. He saw you going to Burmarsh."

"What happened next?" Phoebe asked.

"I went to the Ship. I've been drinking too much brandy since all this trouble with Jesse. Not any more though – not since that night. There was a serving girl... she was new, and she kept... She gave me attention. But it's worse than that because Aaron was there as well, and I think... I am sure... he persuaded her to flirt with me. It felt good at the time. Just for that moment."

"Because you thought I had betrayed you," Phoebe said. She wanted to move her hand and to edge away but knew that if they were to survive that moment then she must give him the love and support that he had shown her.

"Yes. I left and it felt good to be admired. Appreciated. But I thought that was all until she followed me..."

"Followed you?" Phoebe felt sick and it took all her willpower to remain close to him. She tried to tell herself that this was the end of the story – there would be no more to reveal.

"She followed me, and we kissed," he admitted. "There is no excuse for it. You had a reason and you hated yourself for it. I had no reason but my own stupid pride. Then John Waller came."

Relief flooded Phoebe's body.

"When she saw him, she ran off. John came back to the house and made me sober up, and we spoke about everything. It helped. He made me see sense about Aaron."

"But you didn't come to Wissant." For a moment, Phoebe was back on the beach when *Louisa-Ann* arrived and reliving the humiliation when she realised that Harry had not come to be with her.

"No. She came to the forge and tried to extract money from me for her silence, but there was no more… no more, well, you know… I told Owen and he said he would have a word, or Bess would, with the landlord at the Ship and make sure this was the end of it. I was going to come to Wissant, and then the note came… It was from Aaron and sent to you at the house. I went to put it on your dressing table and the seal broke, so I looked…"

"I understand," Phoebe assured him. "There should be no secrets."

"It was short. Just a note about looking forward to seeing you again. But it was enough for me not to come to Wissant. Of course, Owen and Bess found out and they gave me a good talking to. So, I came to meet you from the boat, and there you were – you and Tante Marie!"

"At least you came to meet me in the end," Phoebe said. "I think we should go home now. We can talk about our baby another time."

They pulled themselves up from their seat on the edge of the wall and brushed the clay dust and sand from their clothes. Then Harry wrapped his arms around Phoebe and held her for a moment. She felt the warmth and love radiate from him and knew there was nothing that had been said that could harm them. Tilting her head, she reached upwards, and they kissed gently, before turning towards home. The sun was truly setting now – a sensational blaze of colour in the sky above Romney Marsh as the flaming ball dipped below the horizon.

Over the next couple of days, Marie saw that Phoebe became very much involved with the domestic side of running the household when needed. Also, that her niece was never too proud to pause for a cup of tea with Janey and Mary, or to eat a meal at the kitchen table. On the Monday, two days after Marie's arrival, they set about the mammoth task of washing, drying and pressing the laundry. Phoebe noted that her aunt appeared to relax, comfortable in the knowledge that these tasks would take several days and, despite the surroundings being grander than the Wissant cottage, these were chores she could become engaged with.

Although keeping herself busy, thoughts of those who suffered within the walls of Warren House were never far from Phoebe's mind. By Wednesday afternoon, satisfied with the sheets pegged out on the washing line, she and Marie set off along the Dymchurch Wall with a gift of honey. Once the village was left behind them, and the sweep of the seawall track marking their path ahead, the women fell into speaking in French. The sea glittered to one side, and to the other Marie was able to appreciate the vast flatness of the countryside.

Before long, the pest house and racecourse could be seen, and the conversation naturally moved to Jesse and the day of the Whitsun Gallop. This led to their wondering about the event which was to be held on the following Saturday: Humphrey Fletcher's Match Against Time and the trip to Lydd which Marie would be a part of.

In the grounds of Warren House both women were welcomed by the nun they came across tending vegetable plots, and the honey given while they exchanged a few words. Two new cases of smallpox had been admitted only that morning. "The air is too still," the nun told them. "Where is the fresh sea breeze we need to drive the disease out of our rooms?"

Phoebe gazed up to the open windows, then across the road to the line of trees, where not a breath of air ruffled the leaves. "Here on Romney Marsh, the wind is never far away," she replied with optimism.

"Mary says her ma is ill with a fever," the housekeeper commented when Phoebe and Marie returned. "She told me when she came back from her dinner. It's a worry in her condition, especially as she'll be forty-four this summer." She referred to her sister who was pregnant with her fifth child after a break of twelve years.

"A fever?" Phoebe replied. "Didn't her husband's brother have the pox recently?"

"He did," Janey confirmed, "Got off lightly, he did, and is back working on the wall already. And his son, he's in the pest house now, but Christopher – that's her husband – he never got it even though they all work together down Slodden way."

Phoebe glanced out of the back window to where she could see Mary removing smalls from the washing line. Her mother, Lizzie, was expecting a baby within a week or so, and although the smallpox was not in her home, it lingered nearby amongst the wall-workers and family members who her husband worked with. *Could it travel... the infection... could it travel by touch... unseen... could it move from one person to another and into Mary's home? What fanciful thoughts you have, Phoebe!*

"Could it be..." Phoebe couldn't bring herself to say the word.

"No!" Janey's reply came in a rush. "It's nothing more than a pregnancy twenty years after it should be, and the weather being far too warm for her liking. It's a summer cold, that's all."

"Of course it is," Phoebe responded, but the doubt remained. She folded a neatly pressed pillowcase.

"I'll do the sheets," Janey offered.

"Thank you." Phoebe placed the pillowcase on the pile of smooth linen squares. "I'll finish the smalls this evening. That's enough for now. I'm going to speak to Mary."

In the garden, the ground was dusty and air sweet. Phoebe reached for a chemise and brushed away creases before placing it in the capacious wicker basket. Mary was pulling the wrinkles from stockings.

"I'm sorry to hear your ma is ill," Phoebe began. "You must be worried."

"I am, but it's no wonder with this heat and Ma being past her youth," Mary replied. "At least there are no little ones running about and she can rest. She was grateful for the honey you sent, and said it was like you knew she was ill."

"I wish I could do more," Phoebe replied. "What I can do is give you permanent work here, so you can pass on a few shillings to help your family, and there's a room for you if you'd like it."

"I'd like that very much," Mary gave a broad smile. "It would be a relief to my parents, and they'd be grateful for the space. I'll be a good worker, you know that."

"You can go home now and see if Lizzie needs anything." Phoebe picked up the basket and continued, "Tomorrow we'll make some extra broth for your ma, and a pie for your pa. It will take some of the burdens away."

She'll go home happy, but the beam on Mary's face and skip to her step as she left, did nothing to lift

Phoebe's concerns. *It feels as if the pox is only a step away from our home. I must be wary and pray that Janey and Mary are right in saying this is no more than a summer cold and the weariness of pregnancy in a woman who should have put her childbearing years behind her.*

Chapter Twenty-Two
Harry

There was a sensation of being part of a parade as the throng descended upon Lydd, nearing the outskirts of the small town. The road was crowded with all manner of characters, many of them walking, several travelling by cart, and others on horseback. While most were respectful, for they had not yet taken their fill of ale or wine at this early hour, some rode without care or thought to the safety of others. Children and small dogs felt the excitement and became reckless, darting about, dangerously close to the wheels of carts, while the occasional gentleman hollered his demands for order and decorum. Haphazard lines from popular songs burst through the air, and melodies flowed from wooden pipes. There was an air of anticipation, of its being a day when everyone could set their concerns aside to enjoy the sport on offer.

Harry led his horse and cart, negotiating the undulations on the road. His diverse family group travelled with him, both on foot and seated in the cart. Walking at his side, Giles Woods offered guidance as to the best path for the sturdy horse to take. In turn, Harry murmured his thanks and continued, perfectly capable of choosing the best course.

Riding in the cart, her ample backside spread across a cushion, Peggy Woods sat as if she were royalty in a gilded coach, even extending a condescending wave to those whom she considered to be beneath her in society. She voiced her complaints loudly, with no thought for all that her niece and Harry had provided for her comfort: the cart was too small; the ragamuffins should keep to the side of the road; they must be wary of those with shifty eyes who were, no doubt, pickpockets. Beside her, Tante Marie rolled her eyes at this tirade and exclaimed at new sights as they presented themselves. She voiced her curiosity at the flatness of the Marsh and wondered what entertainment the people of Lydd would offer.

What opposites this pair of aunts were: one who had not walked a step of the journey and was vocal in her opinions and fault-finding, the other who had trekked for much of the time and uttered nothing but her thanks, taking an interest in her surroundings.

The final couple amongst them was Owen and Bess, always a reliable and steady influence. Also in the cart, Bess soothed Peggy and offered Marie snippets of local news and history. Her husband attempted to divert Giles' simpering attention from Harry. "It will do us all good to have some entertainment, and no one having to think of tending the farrier's cart," Owen said. "Today it's Lydd's business to look after us."

"Think of us having a table reserved at the George Inn!" Peggy preened, moving her head this way and that so her blonde coils, twisted in rags until the final moments before leaving home, bobbed about. Then she fanned herself, despite the day being pleasantly warm, unlike the intense heat of recent weeks.

The George had taken full advantage of this day with flyers being pasted up as far as Hythe, or so it was said. Two sittings of a roast lamb dinner were on offer, and Harry had sent a message in good time to reserve their table. The chestnut horse was to be stabled at the George as well. Nothing had been left to chance – if anything was to go amiss on this day, then it would not be for Harry's lack of planning. He glanced at the sky, grateful for the scattered clouds, but with them carrying no threat of rain.

Phoebe saw him looking, "It will be better for everyone if we are spared the full heat of the sun," she said.

"Better for that poor horse what's got to gallop back and forth for no good reason!" Giles, an expert in everything, commented.

"You're right." Phoebe had gained years of experience in trying to please her uncle. "To think of him having to race with no respite from the sun would spoil the day for me."

They passed the first cottages, sprawling places with their own areas of land, then a short, terraced row with a much-patched roof of reed thatch. Narrow roads began to spring up, offering a direct path to the Rype, but Harry continued to lead his horse along the main road. A fine steed trotted by, causing Peggy to exclaim, "Lord above! Look at him! He's a superior gent and doesn't he know it?"

"That's Sir Edward Wingwood from Warehorne," Harry told her.

"He looks like he don't lift a finger for himself. Probably even got someone to feed him with his silver spoons!" Peggy let out a guffaw, and her companions couldn't help smiling to themselves.

The gentleman in question, his back straight, neck raised by a stiff, silk covered, stock, and not deeming to gaze upon those he would leave in his wake, moved out of sight. The next time Harry saw him was in the stable yard, when the chestnut had been unharnessed from the cart. Now dismounted, Sir Edward was demanding that a soft brush be brought to sweep away the dust on his shoes, and strands of hay caught upon the silver buckles.

The history of Lydd stretched back to Roman times, when it was no more than an island emerging as the sea levels dropped. It boasted the longest church, coupled with the tallest tower, on the whole of the Romney Marsh, yet it was a small place inhabited, in most part, by humble folk.

The town's wealth came largely from the lucrative movement of smuggled goods, and those who traded illegally with the French benefitted from there being too few riding officers to disrupt their plans. There may well have been kegs of brandy secreted within All Saints parish church, a network of secret passages along the High Street, and woolpacks piled high in the lonely ruins of nearby Midley Church, but to an outsider Lydd was no more than a sleepy backwater.

Until this day, never in the history of the town had so many people descended upon it, tripling, perhaps quadrupling the population. The townspeople would never have expected Humphrey Fletcher's Match Against Time to attract such attention when they first heard of it. Yet, it seemed that the gentleman rider was endowed with the ability to promote himself and drew a crowd of followers from across the county. These well-to-do visitors had booked accommodation in local inns, while their entourage was hastily provided with makeshift mattresses in the tithe barn, stable lofts and several cottages.

Standing on the edge of the Rype, Harry and his family group fell silent as they soaked up the scene. On the opposite side, some distance from the townsfolk, a pen and shelter had been erected for the safety and comfort of Whistlejacket, the bay gelding. He could be seen standing tall while his already gleaming coat was brushed. Simultaneously, a gentleman checked the horse's legs.

"He's brought his own vet and trainer, I hear." William Payne and his wife, Marianne, approached with their three offspring in tow. The necessary greetings took place before he continued, "I just met a gentleman from Rochester and one from Bromley – can you believe it!"

"I can't!" Harry responded. "What a long way to travel for an hour's sport."

"They must know of his reputation and believe it to be worthwhile," William concluded. "Come, let's sit together. Our good wives will enjoy each other's company. Do you have a meal booked at the George?"

"We do – for one o'clock," Harry answered. He knew Phoebe would be happy in the company of Marianne Payne, and so they moved as a group along the edge of the Rype to where benches could be hired for a penny.

Although they walked no distance, their path was impeded by the sheer volume of people who meandered back and forth, greeting friends or choosing the best place to settle. Some carried rugs or their own kitchen chairs, while the more affluent already had seats reserved on the wooden staging. Mingling amongst the racegoers, peddlers touted their wares from baskets or barrows. Many of these vendors seemed be able to smell an opportunity and travelled from one town to the next to scrape a meagre living.

Seated behind a long table bedecked with green and yellow bunting, the bookkeepers were already gathering funds. They wore ribbons of the same colours on their tweed waistcoats, and each had a ledger before him. "All very professional," Giles remarked. "No one wants a chancer taking their money and pocketing it."

On the far north of the open land, food stalls had been erected, and already tantalising aromas drifted across the green. "It's a long time until dinner!" Peggy raised her pert nose to sniff at the air.

"We've got almost an hour before the race," Phoebe reminded her. "Let's choose our seats first, and then have a look around."

"Well, all right, but you're having me walk down there for a bench, then back there for the food, and with all these people getting in the way..."

"How would you feel if we were to have nowhere to sit, but on the ground?" Over the years, Phoebe had become bolder in her handling of Aunt Peggy.

"Oh, Harry and his fine friend here wouldn't allow that!" Peggy asserted. Then as if to get the better of Phoebe, "Remember, my girl, it's not a race. He calls it a Match Against Time, that Mr Fletcher does."

Harry smiled to hear the exchange. "Look at these ribbons." He steered Peggy towards a stall. "Summer hats too!"

The vendor gave a cheeky smile while her eyes assessed Harry's worth. "Latest fashion these hats are. My cousin's been up to London town and seen for herself what the ladies are wearing this summer. Suit you nicely, it would, madam."

Peggy, not inclined to fall for this type of patter, began to turn away. "Perhaps later, thank you. We need to find some seats first."

William Payne had already staked a claim to four long benches, not far from the one hurdle Whistlejacket would jump on each length of the Rype. Pennies for the hire of the seating were paid, and cushions placed for the women. "Look at this – the best view of the race," he declared.

The next hour was spent wandering amongst the stalls and placing their bets on the chance of Humphrey Fletcher being successful in his challenge. As eleven o'clock neared, the beautiful gelding was led from his stall by a groom who began to walk him proudly in front of the eager crowds. The calls of the peddlers, food sellers and bookies ceased, and people made haste to their seats or the edge of the roped-off area. All attention was on Whistlejacket, and no one was to be disappointed as they craned their necks to see the moment when the gentleman jockey from Canterbury placed his foot in the stirrup and swung himself up with ease. The groom stepped back, and the horse walked in a stately manner towards the start line.

Almost the whole length of the Rype had been roped off to create a wide track, measuring exactly a mile. Attendants stood at intervals, wearing Mr Fletcher's signature colours of yellow and green. Yet the great man did not clad himself in garish colours, his breeches were ivory – some swore they were silk – and his shirt ruffled, but not overly so. His jacket was a dark brown, matching his steed's coat to perfection. He looked every part the gentleman, and whispers of admiration flew about, from the stalls where the gentry were seated, to the ragamuffin children who slipped through the crowds, hoping something might fall from a purse and into their safekeeping.

As the minute hand on the church tower clock inched towards the hour, silence fell upon the spectators. Craning their necks, they witnessed the town's mayor lift a flag attached to a mahogany staff. Mr Humphrey Fletcher raised his knees, tightened the reins and crouched low over Whistlejacket's neck. Within the tower a hammer struck upon a bell eleven times. On that final chime, the flag dropped and

246

Whistlejacket sped away from the start line, soon gathering pace and approaching the hurdle.

Soaring over the jump, both horse and rider appeared at ease. Soon they were galloping to that distant end of the Rype with markers indicating the point where a mile had been covered. Whistlejacket circled and began his return run towards the crowds and flags at the start. Settling into a steady rhythm, the miles soon passed and with each length completed a flag was raised not far from the jump, on the far side of the Rype where they were clear for all to see.

Cheers were raised at every two miles accomplished, on each time the gelding leapt the hurdle with inches to spare, and when Mr Fletcher was generous enough to give a wave or a nod to his appreciative audience. Those who were fortunate enough to own a pocket watch referred to them constantly, and then to their companions.

"He's making good time. Halfway now, and three minutes before the half-hour has passed!"

"Zounds! I wagered against him – what a fool!"

"The horse will tire – you can be certain of it."

"I swear Mr Fletcher never pushes the gelding beyond his limits. I've not seen him use the whip or spur, and you can be sure I've kept a sharp eye on him."

"Is my pocket watch right? Does yours say five minutes to the hour?"

"It does, and look he's turned for the last time!"

To a deafening applause, Whistlejacket and the gentleman jockey thundered along the final stretch and the Match Against Time ended a full two-and-a-half minutes before the church clock struck the hour. With a wave to the admiring onlookers, Humphrey Fletcher swung himself to the ground, and proceeded to walk the gelding up and down enabling him to cool down slowly before handing him over to one of two vets attending.

As the cheers and clapping died down, the air was filled with a joyous peal from the church bells. Harry looked at Phoebe. "What a day! I thought he'd do it. He had such confidence."

She leaned towards him, tucking her arm through his. "I thought so too! Let's mark this day as an end to our troubles. I feel certain good things are coming to us."

"What sort of good things?" Harry asked. Was there some secret she wasn't yet ready to reveal? *A baby... No, not a baby – she has only been home a week. It's not possible.*

"I don't know," Phoebe admitted. "It is just a feeling that something momentous is going to happen."

Nothing could spoil their enjoyment on that day of Mr Humphrey Fletcher's Match Against Time. Harry and Owen queued to collect their winnings, while Giles berated them and everyone else for the fact that he had bet against Whistlejacket and her owner succeeding. Yet all this was said in good humour – there was a sit-down meal at the George to look forward to and not one, but two, jurats accompanying Giles and his good wife.

The local roast lamb was flavoursome, and service efficient. If Peggy was inclined to scold a rushed serving girl, then Phoebe and Marianne Payne were generous in their thanks. Feeling pleasantly full after the meal, the group of family and friends, wandered about the Rype, drawn to the fripperies on sale and to the pen where Whistlejacket was carefully guarded by two grooms.

A couple of times, they spotted Lucy in the distance, her hand tucked into the arm of her betrothed. It brought back a sharp reminder of the Whitsun Gallop and the anxieties suffered that day.

"Pah! I shall find Jesse a good French wife." Marie scowled to see the young woman.

Phoebe who knew her better, saw a sadness in Lucy's eyes, despite the smile fixed on her face. "It is for the best," she replied.

They prepared to leave Lydd before the church clock struck three. Peggy hauled herself up into the cart at the first opportunity. With a new straw hat perched on her head, and a satisfied smile on her face, she instructed Harry to set off towards home.

The roads were crowded, as they had been that morning, although the mood was calmer. Upon nearing Romney, it became apparent that the light was changing – above the hills to the north, the sky had become ominously purple as the cloud thickened. They now travelled through a land where the colours of the countryside and buildings became curiously enhanced. With three miles to journey, it was clear that a break in the fine weather was imminent. In anticipation of heavy rainfall, Harry picked up his pace, feeling the responsibility for getting everyone home safely. He saw that Phoebe had wrapped her shawl snug against her shoulders and upper arms. "Do you still feel something momentous is about to happen?" he asked, recalling their earlier conversation.

"I do," she replied. "I don't know what, but somehow it only feels right that it is heralded by this storm."

Harry smiled, not understanding, but curious as to what the next few days would bring.

Chapter Twenty-Three
Phoebe

Heavy rain had begun its assault on Romney Marsh shortly before they arrived home from Lydd on that Saturday afternoon. For the rest of the weekend, damp clothes hung from racks suspended from the kitchen ceiling, and Phoebe, with her aunt and Harry, stayed within the home as much as possible.

Monday morning brought with it a break in the weather and a general agreement that the vegetable plots would be all the healthier for their watering. However, as she reached to lower the clothes airer, Phoebe felt rather dispirited. By late afternoon *Louisa-Ann* would once more be setting sail to Wissant, this time with Marie onboard.

"You'll miss your aunt," Janey observed from her place at the fireside where the porridge pot simmered. She lifted it from a trivet, placing it further from the heat.

"I will," Phoebe admitted. "Her family need her though, and I know she is eager to see how Jesse is."

"It's good he's got someone to fuss over him," Janey replied. "And talking of fussing, I don't know where the girl has got to. It's not like her to be late, and I can't help worrying her mother has taken a turn for the worse."

"I'm glad she chose to live at home until the baby is born." Phoebe pondered the reason for Mary's absence, "Perhaps Lizzie is in labour?"

"Someone would have sent word," Janey responded. "If she's not here soon, then I'll go to see what the matter is."

At that moment, Mary burst in, her face flushed, and clothes dishevelled. "I'm sorry. So sorry. Here I am late, and you've been so kind as to give me work and a room of my own when I need it."

"Slow down," Phoebe said, her voice uncharacteristically stern. "There must be a reason, and if you rush about like this then nothing will get done. Is it Lizzie? Is she having the baby?"

"It's her mouth," Mary babbled. "Her mouth getting sore and... you said it might be, but we took no notice, Mrs Farrers... You were worried it might be the pox and Ma said it was nothing but her being too old to be carrying a child."

Phoebe felt her body stiffen and her skin chill. "Lizzie seemed so certain. What do I know of carrying a child? The weather has been so hot, and she is close to her time..."

"Oh Lord above! Not Lizzie, not when she's due any moment..." Janey cried out. "We should have taken more notice of her having a fever."

"And the fever, has it lessened?" Phoebe asked.

"She's not so hot, but the sores in her mouth are bothering her, and she can't get comfortable."

Standing in her roomy kitchen, with its high ceiling now free from the drying clothes, Phoebe pictured the scene in Lizzie's three-room cottage with her four offspring and husband. The windows were small and the ceilings low, and when the wind blew the wrong way, the smoke from the fire would fill the room.

The pox had not entered the cottage before, but Janey had told her that it was spreading amongst the wall-workers with whom Mary's father worked. The maid had spoken of her uncle being ill only weeks

251

before, yet others had been spared. Phoebe knew that every day Lizzie packed up slices of bread and cold meat or cheese and took them to her husband and sons who had been toiling since dawn on the seawall if the tides permitted. *While she was there, Lizzie would mingle with the men, and it was there too – the pox silently and stealthily moving between them…*

Mary sneezed.

Janey and Phoebe looked at each other in horror – a fleeting glance before the housekeeper almost screamed at the maid. "Lord, help us! I pray that I'm wrong in thinking… I won't even say it, but Mary you must leave now. I daren't have you bring the pox into Mr and Mrs Farrer's home. Go back to your ma and do all you can for her. Anything you need, I'll bring it. Leave now, Mary."

The girl blanched and without even checking for Phoebe's approval, she turned and fled.

Janey fell silent, then moved back towards the fire and began to ladle the porridge into bowls. Footsteps could be heard on the stairs and the breeze caught the curtain hanging at the open window. "It was only one sneeze," Phoebe said. "Perhaps the dust…"

"What happened?" Harry asked as he entered the kitchen.

Hardly knowing how to express the horror which had just unfolded, Phoebe told him about Lizzie being ill, and Mary coming into their home and sneezing.

"We don't understand how it spreads," Harry responded. "But it's best that Mary stays away. Besides she is needed at home."

"I'll help more here," Phoebe replied. "Janey, if there is anything you need to do to help your sister… meals… washing… then I can do more here, and together we can feed Lizzie and her family."

"I'll keep my distance, just in case…" Janey reassured them. "But I will go and see her husband up on the wall and find out how the rest of them are." She looked at the dirty pan, and the bowls containing the uneaten porridge.

"Eat first," Phoebe ordered. "Then Tante Marie and I will clear up and prepare the vegetables for dinner."

"You're a good sort, Mrs Farrers," Janey said, reaching for a light shawl. "And you, Mr Farrers."

The memory of Mary sneezing in the kitchen was fresh in Phoebe's mind as she prepared vegetables while Marie set about making bread dough. "I should have told her to stay away when we heard of Lizzie's fever," she said over and over.

"It is not for us to judge if someone has the pox," Marie replied.

Janey returned from speaking to her sister from the open doorway of the cottage and she had nothing to allay their fears, "Lizzie's mouth is full of blisters and even as we spoke, I'm sure pocks were appearing on her face. Her cheeks are flushed and she's turning this way and that. It's impossible to get comfortable with the baby ready to come at any moment. All we can do is take round a pan of broth and a loaf of bread, so she doesn't need to fret about feeding the family."

While Janey fried leeks and Marie kneaded the dough, Phoebe swept and dusted the parlour and hallway. *It was just one sneeze,* she told herself. *And no one knows… No one really knows how smallpox passes from one person to the next.*

"Let's go to Warren House," Marie suggested after their midday meal.

She can see that I need to do something useful, Phoebe realised. *Besides, the weather is fine, and the countryside refreshed after the rain. We will both enjoy the walk. Then, on our return, it will be time for her to go.* "Yes, we must do something," she replied. "I cannot sit here waiting for you to leave and feeling sadder as the time nears."

They set off at a brisk pace, with a basket containing wine and honey tucked under Phoebe's arm, resting lightly on her hip. Once on top of the seawall, the walk was invigorating, with the sky a fresh blue, and the sands a wide golden band stretching along the beach. Marie waved to the wall-workers who were becoming familiar figures, and occasionally they exchanged a passing comment or a greeting. Over the Channel, the sea and sky melded in the heat haze, and there was no hint of the French coast.

With Phoebe's distress on hearing about Lizzie that morning, it might have seemed that going to the hospital for those suffering from infectious diseases was a poor choice for an outing. Yet in visiting the imposing building in its lonely roadside spot, she felt as if she was doing something useful. Every one of the nurses or nuns she met would spare the time to pass a few words, and she felt calmed by their presence. This day was no exception. Sister Florence was tending the herb garden to the side of the property and straightened herself as they neared, a wide smile spreading across her round face.

"Honey and wine!" Phoebe said, as she placed the contents of the basket on a bench. "How are you, Sister? Did you welcome the rainfall?"

"Thank you," Sister Florence gave a nod of appreciation. As she did, a blonde curl escaped from under her wimple and bobbed about. "We did! It saved us from having to water our vegetable plots and the air is so much fresher within the upstairs rooms."

"And how are they... those who are here...?"

The nun gave a shrug and the smile fell from her face. "We lost a young man from Dymchurch this morning. He was only twenty-five years of age and leaves a wife and two children. Spare a thought for him and his dear family in your prayers."

"I will," Phoebe replied.

They left shortly afterwards, sobered by the news of a recent death, and humbled by the moments spent in the company of this good woman who had dedicated her life to God and the care of others.

Once back in Dymchurch, Marie's leaving them was imminent. She insisted on brief visits to those she considered to be Phoebe's English families, first Peggy and Giles, then Owen and Bess. Back at Walker House, there was time for a rushed cup of tea and a piece of spiced apple cake before Harry was carrying Marie's bag downstairs and out of the front door.

By now, the offshore breeze blew briskly, and they chose to use the main road as they headed towards Wall End and *Louisa-Ann.* Having passed through the village, they walked mostly in silence. Above them, gulls swooped and screamed, and wispy clouds raced, while on the beach, waves crashed upon the seawall.

The party was suddenly alerted to a new sound, caused by man not nature. At first the rattling of a cart on the road went unnoticed but as it neared them, the trio turned and stepped onto the verge. They watched it curiously, for as well as the driver and cart, a young woman and a boy ran alongside.

"It's Mary!" Phoebe cried. That moment when recognition came, it dawned on her that this cart carried the most precious cargo – a woman and her unborn child who were clearly destined for Warren House.

"Oh Mrs Farrers – Mr Farrers – there's no doubting it now." The words burst from Mary before she gulped at air. "She's covered! Covered in spots. But it's worse than that…"

"Worse?" Phoebe echoed.

"She thinks the baby is coming and… it's a terrible thing, Mrs Farrers… She's lost all her fight. Ma doesn't seem to care if she lives or dies, and the child with her. She's too old you see… too old for all that."

Phoebe glanced towards the cart, already some distance away with the boy still racing along at its rear. "It's the illness talking, Mary. In a few days, when the child is born and the pocks are beginning to heal, then she will start to feel more positive."

"She was already struggling – getting breathless for no good reason," Mary said darkly. "Before she fell for another baby, I mean. I'm worried for her, and don't know if I'm going to be able to work for you Mrs Farrers. I think it's going to be me at home looking after the baby day and night, and you'll have to find another girl to help my aunt in the house. I'm sorry. I really am."

They hurried along as this was expressed, and Phoebe, horrified by these revelations, could do no more than offer empty platitudes, "It will all seem better in a few days. Let's hear no more of you leaving us and feel positive that your mother will recover in body and spirit. It is no wonder she says such things when her body is so cumbersome."

"I fear nothing will change," Mary replied. "But I had best make speed. I can't leave my brother on his own."

"Does your father know?" Harry asked.

"He doesn't, but my neighbour has gone to tell him and my older brothers. They're at work on the wall."

"And you'll return to Dymchurch?"

"No, Mr Farrers, we'll wait right there until there is news of the baby."

Harry glanced towards Wall End where *Louisa-Ann* awaited Marie. "I'll leave you now Tante Marie and return to the village. Someone needs to tell Janey, and I'll take her myself to Warren House. Then, when they are satisfied that Lizzie is as comfortable as she can be, I'll bring the three of them back to Dymchurch. They can't stay through the night. I fear that Mary and others in the family will be showing signs of fever within a day or two."

Mary scurried off, and Marie said her farewells to Harry. As a parting gesture, she admonished him over not visiting Wissant that year, and he insisted that he was already looking forward to seeing the whole family next year. They parted, leaving the two women to take one of the many paths up the bank of the seawall. Here they would meet Walter and Joshua at Wall End, where the fishing boats nestled on a bank of sand and shingle with the water licking around their hulls.

On nearing the vessels, the men could be seen preparing to launch *Louisa-Ann* into deeper water. They gave a nod in the direction of the approaching women and continued with the task in hand. Marie was unusually quiet. *She will be thinking of the long journey ahead and wondering if by the time I visit Wissant next June, it will be with a child in my arms,* Phoebe decided.

However, Marie's next words were to take her niece by surprise, and to leave her momentarily speechless: "You must have the baby. Lizzie's baby – you must have it as your own."

Take the baby as my own? The baby who will be born in the pest house and most likely by the early hours of the morning. I cannot take a baby. It is not mine to snatch. The image of a scraggy, unwanted child entered unbidden into Phoebe's mind and there it remained. At that moment, her heart swelled with a longing to hold the tiny scrap to her, to nurture it and love it as her own. The desire to mother a child was stronger than she had ever known it to be, taking over

257

her whole being, making her limbs tingle and sending a sense of joy running through her.

Her reply showed none of this immense depth of feeling. "I can't," she replied, her tone flat. "I cannot take another woman's child."

Chapter Twenty-Four
Harry

The sun had made a spectacular show of setting that evening, and as Harry stabled his horse, the last of the light spread above the horizon, now mellowing to a soft yellow. He had left his housekeeper and maid sitting on a bench outside Warren House awaiting news of the pending birth of Lizzie's child. "Lucky that I had some blankets in your cart," he spoke to the chestnut mare as he scratched behind her ears. "It's going to be a long, lonely night for them, and no point in getting a chill."

The village street was quiet, with gentle light and muted conversation radiating from within the inns and taverns. Harry walked slowly, his mind on the events of the evening: *Marie has gone. I hope she doesn't suffer seasickness like Phoebe.* He smiled to himself. *No! Marie won't suffer; she wouldn't allow it to happen! What a shock it was when she arrived here, and I'm still thankful her outpouring was in her own tongue. I don't know what she said, but it wasn't good – that was clear enough. Phoebe and I have settled our difficulties, and I know Marie is happy about that. I'm happy about that! But the other thing... it's been three years since we married. They managed to find some asparagus, even though it was becoming a bit tough, but it's not enough, is it? There's some reason why Phoebe doesn't fall for a child, and I don't know that asparagus is going to make any difference.* He imagined a nurse going to the door of Warren House to announce the arrival of the infant. *It's no way for a baby to come into this world. How will they cope? We can only pray there are no difficulties.*

There was the glow from an oil lamp at the parlour window of Walker House, and Harry's eyes being focussed on that, it came as a surprise to see Phoebe perched on the brick wall separating their land from the road.

"Was there any news when you arrived?" she asked without preamble.

"None," he replied. "They are determined to wait through the night."

Phoebe looked up and down the street, as if to be sure they were alone. "Marie made the most shocking suggestion," she said.

Harry waited.

"She said we should..." Phoebe's tone was hushed... awed. "She said we should have the baby as our own."

The past weeks had thrown one surprise after the other upon Harry, but this revelation slapped him just as hard as all the others. *Have the baby as our own? How can we take a baby? You can't just go and take whatever you want – not without repercussions.* "The baby?" he repeated, "Lizzie's baby?" the words sounding weak and by no means expressing the thoughts tumbling about in his mind.

In the twilight, they walked up the front path, hand in hand, and entered the house. Phoebe drew the curtains at the parlour window, and they sat together on the sofa, fingers entwined, and backs rigidly upright despite the cushioning.

"I know."

Silence hung heavily in the air around them. Harry attempted to find something helpful to say... something to bring hope, but in the end, he merely asked, "What made her say that? What made Marie say such a thing?"

"It was Mary... she told us that Lizzie can't care for the infant, and she fears that she will be expected to take the role of mother to her new brother or sister."

"Because of the pox?"

"No. Lizzie was already struggling," Phoebe told him. "But I never knew of it. "

Harry pondered on this before responding, "I didn't know she was ill, but it wasn't my business to be told." He stood and walked to the brandy decanter, then stepped away, recalling the times he had turned to the fiery liquid in the past weeks, and his vow to abstain. "Would you like some wine?" he asked, already walking to the door.

"I don't know what I want," she replied. "Thank you. I'll have a little."

Harry walked through to the kitchen and absentmindedly poured wine into their best teacups. He shrugged and faltered. *Does it matter?* Then he tipped it into glasses and carried them back to the parlour. On his return, he saw that Phoebe was examining the stitching on the neckline of the nightdress she was making for Ellen's new son. "I must finish this tomorrow," she said. "There is no excuse for it not being completed."

They spoke a little of other matters – inconsequential things – while both aware that the other's thoughts were full of Marie's parting words. Eventually Phoebe asked, "If it were true that the baby would be too much of a burden for Lizzie, then would you mind us having a child that we raised as our own? Or if not this baby, this time, then perhaps another?"

Harry thought of his upbringing with loving parents, then of his father's death and the stepfather who had come into their home, causing nothing but misery. He remembered making the decision to leave his village and set out to find a new place to live. Romney Marsh had certainly not been his choice of destination, but events had conspired to force him to stay in Dymchurch and, in doing so, he had been cared for by a couple who treated him as their own son. In turn he loved them as his parents. Phoebe's family were across the water in Wissant, and her English mother buried in the churchyard just along the road. Here in Dymchurch her aunt and uncle took the role of her parents.

Then Harry recalled John Waller's words when they spoke recently: '*You've not got a father here, or an uncle or… well, you know how it is, coming from off the Marsh. But since you've been here, there's been me and Owen looking out for you. Him and Bess, they've been your family here in Dymchurch, haven't they? My team on the wall – they're all part of the family too.'*

"If we can raise a child, give it love and keep it safe, then that's what is important," he said. "But as for this baby, we must wait and see what the next few days bring. It isn't even born yet and I fear it may not survive."

"It may not," Phoebe agreed. She leaned towards Harry, and he wrapped his arms around her. "I hope it does." Her words were muffled, but he heard them and embraced her a little tighter.

In the darkest hours of the night something woke Harry and he lay in bed, alert to the slightest sound. A creak on the stairs… The rustle of a long skirt against the bannisters… *Ah! Janey is back. I wonder what her news is.*

Dawn came and with it the morning chorus from the birds. Harry woke early and was aware that Phoebe no longer slept. Once more there was movement on the stairs and they both listened to Janey making her way down to the kitchen.

"She came back in the night," Harry whispered.

"There will be news then," Phoebe replied.

He could imagine the thoughts racing about in her mind, as they did in his. Not long after, they dressed quickly and descended upon the kitchen as Janey lit the fire.

"Look at the pair of you, up at the crack of dawn," Janey admonished. "You'll be getting under my feet now."

"I've come to help you," Phoebe responded, pulling an apron off a peg. "There's no Mary and you have barely slept."

Harry, as always, took a quiet pride in his wife. She could have sat at the gateleg table by the parlour window and rang a bell for Janey to serve her morning tea; instead, she was filling the kettle with water and began to spoon tea leaves into the pot.

"We'll all sit down together and then you can tell us the news. The baby was born, I assume?" Harry stepped into the larder and took the jug of milk from the slate shelf.

"She came before midnight," Janey told them.

"She," Phoebe repeated. "A little girl." She reached for the cups and saucers, setting out four.

"We only need three." Harry replaced a set on the dresser. "I'll go and draw some water from the well, and by the time that's done, the tea will be brewed.

Soon Janey was telling them the little she knew. "There's not much to say," she apologised. "The baby came quickly, and they said she seemed healthy, but I've not seen her, of course. We heard a cry, Mary and me, from where we waited outside. They came to say she had taken a feed, but Lizzie took no notice of the poor mite. Wouldn't even look at her."

"She must be so sore with the pocks and exhausted from the birth," Phoebe said. "She's in no state to care for a baby."

"Can the nurses manage?" Harry asked.

"They have no choice," Janey replied. "No wet nurse will take a child who comes from the pest house, so they have to make do they best they can."

"We can only pray that Lizzie makes a quick recovery and is able to look after her daughter," Phoebe said. "I wish we could do something to help."

"Oh, Mrs Farrers, you do help." Janey smiled, despite her weariness. "No one could wish for a better employer."

They spoke about domestic matters for a few minutes, planning the early morning chores between the women, and then discussing the possibility of walking to Warren House to make enquiries. In the meantime, Harry would go to work and hear their news when they met for a midday meal.

"Does she have a name?" Phoebe asked tentatively, once more thinking of the baby.

"A name?" Janey pondered on this for a moment, perhaps trying to recall if a name has been mentioned over the past weeks. "No, there's no name. Not that I can recall. Lizzie's been that despondent over the little one that I don't think she will have bothered to name her.

"Oh…" Phoebe took a sip of her tea. Harry, who knew her so well, recognised that his wife's mind was alive with all the possibilities.

Shortly afterwards, Harry left for work. He carried with him a feeling that he was waiting for something and knew the women would be unsettled as they went about the morning chores. In his forge, he struggled to concentrate on any one job, and failed Matthew in his attempts to train him. Eventually, Frank Smith took over and suggested that Harry ride the horse out to Chapel Farm where they required a price for some work on tools in need of repair.

Sitting astride his chestnut mare, Harry found her movement soothing and by the time he reached the farm, he was able to focus on the job in hand. Upon his return, he spotted Janey walking along the High Street. Once more his thoughts were on the baby girl who had been born just twelve hours beforehand, and her pock-covered mother. He then considered Phoebe and he feared that already she was forming an attachment to a child she hadn't met. Leaving the horse in its paddock, Harry called out to Frank and Matthew that he was heading home and left.

Arriving not long after Janey, Harry interrupted an unusual scene: Phoebe preparing the midday meal, while the housekeeper was seated at the table with a cup of tea in front of her. "I saw you by the grocer's," he said, as Janey stood. "You must be exhausted. Please sit down."

"No, thank you. I'll stay standing. I don't feel I can settle when there's something I've been pondering on since the early hours of the morning." Janey walked towards the window and looked out past the scullery wall and the woodshed to the fruit

266

trees. "There's something that needs talking about now you're both here."

"Oh?" Harry replied. He glanced at Phoebe and waited.

"I've got something to say and hope you'll forgive me for speaking about private matters that shouldn't be mentioned by the housekeeper," Janey began, having turned to face them. "But there's things a person can't help seeing if they are working in someone's home, especially in the laundry."

Phoebe coloured. Harry frowned, knowing that this was women's talk, but for some reason he was needed.

"I can't see Lizzie, as you know, but we spoke a lot in the weeks before the baby was born. She was worried for the child and the rest of the family. Lizzie was convinced that she wasn't strong enough to care for an infant, and that her time on this earth was nearing an end. I told her that once the baby came, she would begin to feel better, but she was determined to find a solution."

"This is why Mary said that she will have to care for the child," Phoebe said. "She told me when we met on the road – when Lizzie was being taken to Warren House."

"Mary gets all sorts of ideas in her head," Janey replied. "And if Lizzie's fears are to be listened to, then the girl may well end up as mother to her sister. But Lizzie and I spoke of something different…" She faltered. "We wondered if you might take the baby?"

"While Lizzie is getting better?" Phoebe asked, not daring to suggest that she may not recover from the pox. Pus filled pustules would be covering her body now and as they broke the risk of infection within the sores was high.

We have already discussed this, Harry thought, *but Janey could not know that Tante Marie would have thought of this very scheme before she left. I can see Phoebe daren't hope Janey speaks of a future with the baby beyond the next few weeks.* "She would need to be fed," he said, not letting himself think further than the practical details.

"Lizzie may recover from the pox, and I pray she will," Janey answered Phoebe first, "But I am speaking of adoption, not a temporary solution. The child may die, of course, and this talk is for nothing, but she was born strong and with a fine pair of lungs." She gave a brief smile. "As for Mr Harry's question, we would need a wet nurse for it's unlikely Lizzie can provide for her daughter."

"Adoption?" Phoebe repeated, she looked at Harry, her eyes alight with hope. "Imagine that! Our own baby."

"Families come in different forms," Harry said, remembering his earlier thoughts on the matter. "If we can be parents to a baby who needs us, I'd willingly raise her as our own, but she has parents."

"A mother of forty-four and a father nearing fifty years." Janey shook her head. "I worry for Lizzie. She was struggling with her housekeeping at Cluny House before the pregnancy. Getting up the bank to the seawall or the staircase in the house has her struggling to breathe. Over the next few days her life will hang in the balance."

"And if she lives, you are sure she would give up her child?" Phoebe asked.

"I'm almost certain of it."

"How was she today?" Harry asked, consciously steering the talk away from the possible adoption.

"They say she just lies there, and they give her the baby to feed but she's not looked at her."

"She must!" Phoebe said, her voice earnest. "Lizzie must look because until she does, she won't know if she can give her up."

Janey appeared to consider this before she responded, "Of course she must."

This talk is all about Lizzie, Harry realised. *But the child has a father and there has been no word of him visiting, or even taking the child home with him. And there is something else – something the women have not mentioned, but it has to be discussed.* "Surely Lizzie will have plenty of time to see her daughter and decide. The baby won't be removed from Warren House, will she? I understand that her arrival puts the nurses in a desperate situation, but she must stay?"

"They say she shouldn't," Janey replied. The nurses believe she has some… natural protection. I see it like a bit of help to see her through the next few days, but she should be removed. I've told Lizzie's husband that we need to find a wet nurse, but it will be a job to find anyone who will take on a child fresh from the pest house."

The tea in the pot cooled and the pan of fried vegetables began to burn. "I forgot the dinner!" Phoebe wailed, grabbing at a thick cloth as she raced to the fire. She had been tending it sporadically while they spoke, although understandably her thoughts were absorbed with the future of the baby.

"A bit of burnt onion won't do us any harm," Janey said as she reached for the plates on the dresser. "I'll fetch the meat from the larder, and a nice jar of pickle."

For a moment the women bustled about. Then the three of them settled to eat while pondering on the events of the last few hours and the days to come.

"Perhaps a wet-nurse would provide milk and we... or Mary... or whoever has her can feed her?" Phoebe voiced her thoughts.

"It's not natural," Janey answered, "But it could be the only way. I was just thinking though... it's Mary... I fear the girl is coming down with the pox. She wasn't right yesterday."

Harry saw a look of horror flash over his wife's face. Then he recalled that she had mentioned the maid sneezing. Just the once, Phoebe had told him, but it was enough for Janey to send Mary home.

"Then it's up to us to find someone to feed Lizzie's baby," Phoebe declared. "I'll go to speak to Ellen. I've got the nightgowns for her newborn, so I needed to call in anyway. It seems the best place to start."

We are caught up in it now, Harry realised. *I speak of waiting and allowing Lizzie time to consider this, but the nurses are burdened by caring for a baby, and there is no time to be wasted. When I return to the forge, the women will be busying themselves in preparation for the arrival of this little girl, and I fear for the heartbreak Phoebe will suffer – we all will suffer – if Lizzie changes her mind.*

"Speak to Ellen," Harry agreed. "But the baby must stay where she is for a few days. Please give her mother the chance to begin to heal from the birth and the pox, because only then can she decide if she can bear to part with her daughter."

"The nurse I spoke to said they will keep the baby for a week," Janey said.

"A week!" Harry felt relief flood through him. "Life can change so much in a week. We can prepare for her to return home with Lizzie or to come here." He stood and placed a hand on Phoebe's shoulder, "In the meantime, we must not think of her as ours, but plan for her to be with her family or for us to help temporarily.

Chapter Twenty-Five
Phoebe

Alone on the seawall track, Phoebe didn't know how she could endure the trek to New Romney. Her limbs felt like jelly and her head swam. She paused, refusing to allow herself to sit, and stood facing the sea before taking long, deep breaths. The warm, salty air flowed into her body where she held it for a moment before slowly exhaling. Gradually the dizziness faded, and the strength returned to her legs.

"I must do this and trust I am protected. No one should take a child from a good mother, without being certain it is for the best," she murmured to herself. "Not without being sure it is what the mother wants."

Guilt weighed heavily on Phoebe. She loved and respected her husband, and it did not come easily to defy his wishes. Three days had passed since the nameless baby girl had been born, and for three days the message had come through Janey that her sister, Lizzie, felt unable to be a mother to the newborn. On the second day, Mary had been admitted to Warren House as her fever worsened, and on the third, Harry had been to see Lizzie's husband.

"He wants us to take the child," Harry had told her. "He is fifty years of age, and fears that he will not live to support this child beyond the first few years of her life. Lizzie is in poor health. It is a wonder that she has survived the pox so far."

"We can fetch her then?" Phoebe had asked, her eyes bright and expression eager.

"Not yet," Harry had remained firm. "It's too soon. They may change their minds."

Knowing that Harry only wanted to spare her from pain, Phoebe walked on. There had been a tentative agreement that the next day, the fifth after the birth, the baby would be collected from Warren House and brought home to Walker House for Phoebe and Janey to look after. To arrange for the precious bundle to be handed over in the garden of the pest house carried risks, but what Phoebe now planned was foolhardy to say the least.

"I have a name for you," Phoebe whispered to the baby she had not yet seen. "And a basket, and a soft shawl…"

Phoebe and Janey had been busy, with housework and hearty meals taking second place to collecting a growing pile of linen clouts and laces to secure them, soft caps and nightgowns, as well as bedlinen. Their priority had been to seek women who could provide the vital milk needed to nourish the infant. No new mother would consider feeding the newborn from her breast, so all Janey and Phoebe could do was beg for a small cup of the precious milk and hope she would suckle from a cloth dipped in it.

Phoebe's thoughts roamed to Ellen who had readily agreed to give milk, and to Anne, mother to a robust six-month old boy, who was also willing to help. "We are ready for her," she murmured, picking up her pace. "But it wouldn't be right, not without…" Her words trailed away, and she was lost once more in her thoughts.

Before long, Phoebe was approaching Warren House and, as always, she took a path trailing through the herb garden and vegetable plots. Then it came – the unmistakable mew of a newborn child, and for a moment the young woman was overwhelmed. It felt as if her heart would burst, and her arms ached to cradle the baby to her. Tears welled, and she dashed them away. The crying ceased and at the upper window a figure of a nurse could be seen with a swaddled infant in her arms.

Raising a tightly knitted shawl to cover her mouth and nose, Phoebe now marched towards the kitchen door, stepping nearer to the pest house than ever before. Poised at the open doorway, she immediately caught the attention of a kitchen maid whose eyes rounded in surprise.

"Mrs Farrers! You shouldn't…"

"This time I must," Phoebe began. "Can I speak to the nurse in charge please?"

Flustered, the maid fled from view. Moments later, a nurse appeared, her capacious apron wrapped around a slim body and only a hint of her dark hair under a mob cap. "Mrs Farrers? Are you ill?"

"Not ill," Phoebe reassured her. "But I need to come inside, please. It's about the baby – Lizzie's sister, my housekeeper, insists that Lizzie can't keep her daughter. Her husband says the same. It is agreed that we will collect the baby tomorrow. Harry and I have no child and we will raise her as our own, if that is what they want. But I can't do it... it would be wrong to take her without seeing Lizzie and seeking her blessing."

"You want to come in here?" the nurse responded, her surprise evident, despite Phoebe having made her intentions clear.

"I do. And if Lizzie agrees, I will take the child now."

"While Lizzie's pocks are mostly healing, there are several on her back which are causing concern for us. I cannot tell you that she is free from infection." The nurse glanced back, as a clatter of pans came from within the building. "And there are four others here whose fevers still rage – their sores are yet to fully come out. The threat of infection is high."

"I understand the risks," Phoebe said. "My maid is here as well. How is she?"

"Her spirits are low," the nurse admitted, "although the pocks are not as bad as many we treat here. I am sorry to say that concerns for her mother and sister weigh heavily on her."

"Then let me see Lizzie, and if she is sure she can part with her baby then both she and Mary will be burdened less?"

"You understand the potential danger to yourself and to your husband?" the nurse wavered.

"I understand."

"Follow me..."

Phoebe could have reached and touched the peg tile roof. She ducked, unnecessarily, and stepped inside, entering a long, low room. Before finding her bearings, she was forced to sidestep and allowed a nurse to dart by with a basket of laundry. Then, while her eyes adjusted to the dim light, the first thing Phoebe became aware of was that the two women at work in the kitchen had both turned towards her, silent in their astonishment. She gave a weak smile although it remained hidden beneath the cloth held at her mouth.

At first it seemed that this area stretched the whole length of the rear of Warren House, but then she noticed various doors, and realised there was more tucked away: *a pantry... storerooms perhaps... and... Oh! A staircase – I would have expected that to rise through the centre of a big house like this.*

In a cauldron-like pot, broth simmered over a smouldering fire. The cook, fleetingly distracted by a newcomer in her domain, moved a heavy kettle, wrapping a thick cloth around its handle and balancing it on a trivet. Meanwhile the maid resumed her kneading of bread dough, making a dull thud on the long wooden table as she manipulated the ingredients. Thick with woodsmoke, the air was stifling. Phoebe sniffed – onions and chicken stock. It didn't smell of death.

"This way." The nurse led Phoebe through a doorway to one of two rooms at the front of the building. "You'll have to wait here."

Standing in the centre of the square room dominated by a vast fireplace, Phoebe was struck by it being so cluttered. A desk with ledgers had been placed where it benefitted from the light filtering through the front window, and on the opposite wall a narrow bookcase displayed a selection of reading matter. A wooden trunk squatted in a corner, and three easy chairs were placed so they faced each other in a cosy semicircle. One of these was piled with squares of cloth and other delicate items in natural shades of linen and wool. Another had an open cloth bag on it, with someone's needles and yarn partly on display.

I imagined it to be more orderly. Phoebe frowned. The third chair contained a wooden box with a roll of material in it. The bundle appeared to move a little and then the reason for the disarray dawned on her: *She is here! This is where they keep the baby...my baby.* Heart pounding, she stepped forward, and knelt before the swaddled infant, as a sudden sensation of love and longing enveloped her. The child slept, oblivious to the momentous occasion. Her eyelashes rested on her pale cheeks and wisps of dark hair strayed from under the knitted bonnet. In her slumber, she moved against her shawl and a tiny hand, each fragile finger topped with perfect little fingernails, appeared. Phoebe realised she was holding her breath, lest she should disturb her, and allowed herself to relax a little, unable to take her eyes off the infant. *I could stay here all day, just watching you...*

"If you are certain, then Lizzie will see you," the nurse said from the doorway.

Phoebe stood, still looking at the baby, "Shall we take… does she have a name?"

"There's no name. Her mother feeds her but won't look at the poor child, nor think of naming her."

"Then we must," Phoebe declared. "I can't take her if her mother hasn't even looked at her. No one should give away a child without having the chance to see it and know for sure…"

"You're right," the nurse admitted. "You take her."

"In the box?" Phoebe asked.

"No, just scoop the baby out and hold her against you. Take care to keep a hand under her head."

Leaning down, Phoebe slipped a hand under the swaddled infant, supporting her along the length of her arm. Easing the baby out of the box, with her left hand resting against the knitted bonnet, she held her against the bodice of her dress.

"You need a rag." The nurse handed Phoebe a laundered square of linen. "You don't want to be mopping baby sick off your dress."

Taking the rag, while acutely aware of balancing the baby, Phoebe tucked the material into the front of her summer dress.

"Come on then." The nurse led the way to the staircase in the rear corner of the building.

As Phoebe ascended the stairs, each one taken cautiously, a corridor came into view. Cradling the baby close, she followed the nurse while noting part-open doors leading to rooms, and a simple wooden ladder rising to the attic where she believed the nurses slept. It was a spartan space with no unnecessary ornaments or furniture.

They walked the length of the house before entering a room with a window to the front and another with a view along the coast to Dymchurch. Four plain iron bedsteads, four side tables and four small trunks were the only furniture. In each of these beds there lay women all sharing one thing in common – their faces, and any other areas of skin on view, were sore and blistered. A couple of them turned a little, their eyes following the progress of a newcomer into their midst. They seemed too weary to show any surprise, and merely closed their eyes. The third was not much more than a girl, propped up on pillows, a thin blanket drawn to her chin. At first Phoebe didn't realise this was Mary, who should have been so familiar to her.

"Oh! Mrs Farrers you shouldn't be here!" the girl cried out.

"But I had to," Phoebe replied, hiding her horror to see her maid so changed.

The last figure lay hunched on her side, her back to the room and facing the side window. She gave no reaction to the outburst from her elder daughter, Mary, although Phoebe knew she was awake.

"Lizzie, Mrs Farrers is here. She wants your blessing to take the baby – your baby daughter."

The figure moved slightly. "She can take the child," Lizzie replied, her voice quiet but firm. "I said all along that I'm not strong enough to manage."

"Lizzie," Phoebe began, "I'll take your baby and love her and care for her, but they say you haven't even seen her. She's beautiful and I have her here now. I can't... I can't take your baby without you looking at her and being sure."

"The baby must be taken from here, and Mrs Farrers must leave too," the nurse spoke firmly. "You've just fed her, and this is the time for her to go before she starts fretting."

"How will you feed her?" Lizzie asked, still making no effort to turn, yet with those words she showed that she cared.

"I have found two women who will give me milk, and I must do the best I can," Phoebe told her. "Please look at your baby and if you want to keep her, then I will take her home and care for her until you are better. But if you want to give her up then she will be baptised as mine and Harry's – she needs all the protection we can offer."

Slowly, Lizzie began to twist her body. As she did so, Phoebe's heart began to pound, and a lump formed in her throat. Within moments she would know if the child in her arms would become her daughter. Lizzie didn't pull herself up, but with her head remaining on the pillow she faced Phoebe and the baby.

"Here she is." Phoebe pushed back the bonnet and swaddling to reveal more of the infant's face and, crouching forward a little, she repeated, "Here she is. Your daughter."

"She's a sweet thing," Lizzie admitted. "My choice is nothing to do with the pox. I'm not well. I've not been right for a year or more. Take her and give her the love and time that I can't." She paused as if allowing her breathing to steady, then continued with a determination Phoebe could not fail to admire, "It doesn't mean that I think nothing of her. I'll see her about the place and be glad she's cared for."

"Thank you, Lizzie," Phoebe attempted to contain her joy. "Thank you for this gift. Do you have a name for her?"

Lizzie, still gazing at the baby, replied. "No. It's not my choice."

"I was thinking of… Esther?"

"That's lovely." Lizzie's eyes began to close, then sprang open. "I'm tired now. You did the right thing bringing her to see me."

Phoebe adjusted the baby's bonnet and shawl, marvelling at her soft skin as she pulled the woollen cloth back into place. She turned to Mary who was watching the scene unfold. "You'll be better soon, and I'll need your help now there will be a baby in the house."

"I hope so Mrs Farrers." The girl began to cough, and Phoebe scurried from the room.

As she followed the nurse once more, this time retracing their steps to the front parlour, Phoebe's body felt light, as if released from the burdens she hadn't realised were leaning so heavily on her young body.

"You don't want to be carrying too much, so a few things to help you on your way," the nurse said, taking a bag and adding a couple of cloth squares, a clean shawl and a linen gown. "Just in case she gets wet, although I changed her minutes before you arrived. She's had a feed too. If you're lucky she'll sleep all the way back to Dymchurch, but she'll be after her milk soon enough."

"Thank you. I'll go straight to my friend Ellen, or ask my housekeeper to go," Phoebe told her. "I can plan it all while I walk home."

As they hurried through the kitchen and out by the back door there was a sense of being ushered from Warren House now arrangements had been made.

"You'll be in our prayers – you and the little one," the nurse said as they parted. "Stay healthy."

Passing through the garden, Phoebe shook her shawl free from her face and breathed in the fresh air. She absorbed the scents of lavender and thyme in the herb garden, and the blowsy blooms on a climbing rose Then she was pressing against a picket gate and free of the pest house altogether. With the soft bag swinging from her elbow and her daughter snug in her arms, Phoebe couldn't help a smile from spreading over her face as the sense of exhilaration deepened.

"We are going home now, Esther!" she said aloud. "What do you think of that?"

The baby merely snuffled, delighting her new mother.

Part of Phoebe wanted to linger and rejoice in this moment, but she knew she must hasten to Dymchurch, then to Ellen whose precious milk would feed the infant. After a while she became aware that however light her baby was, her muscles had been tensed in the same position for some time. Pausing, Phoebe allowed her left arm to support Esther and, having dropped the bag, she flexed her free limb for a moment. Then she gathered the bag, tucked her right arm under the sleeping baby and momentarily allowed herself to look across the sparking sea towards Wissant.

"I've done it, Marie! I have a daughter at last!"

Taking a deep breath, loving the freshness of the sea air, Phoebe flashed a grin towards France, and turned to towards Dymchurch, intent on quickening her pace. A lone figure was approaching, his features indistinguishable, but Phoebe soon became certain this was Harry. Guilt and excitement conflicted in equal measures, as she tightened her grip on Esther. Harry would be concerned... horrified... by his wife's decision to step within Warren House. "But he will understand," she said to herself, her words spoken with a determination that he would eventually approve. Then to the sleeping baby, "And he will love you as I do, and be the best papa."

Harry met his daughter midway between Wall End and High Knocke, on the seawall which was bound up with the history of his time in Dymchurch. "I had a feeling you had gone there..." he said. "And here she is!"

"Our daughter!" Phoebe replied, offering a tentative smile. "Our daughter – Esther!" This was a time to put aside any concerns for the immediate future. For that moment, the new mother allowed herself to relax and relish the pleasure of introducing the sleeping child.

Harry leaned forward to see the tip of an upturned nose, delicate lips and the wispy curve of her eyelashes. He nudged at Esther's shawl with his fingertip to reveal more soft skin and the tip of a delicate ear. "Hello Esther!" Then he looked at Phoebe and said, "Thank you."

"Thank you? I didn't…"

"You did! Perhaps not in the usual way, and I doubt many fathers are presented with their daughter on the Dymchurch Wall, but here she is and that's all that matters," Harry explained. With this he turned to face the village and, placing a hand in the small of Phoebe's back, they began to walk. "Time to take her home, I think. I don't know much about babies, but I assume she'll be wet and hungry before long."

"I don't know much about babies either!" Phoebe retorted, "But I'm sure you are right!"

Epilogue

Toke Browne, with his breeches brushed, his shirt fresh from someone's washing line, and his waistcoat newly darned by his loving mother, strolled along an earth track to the seawall. In his pocket he had eight barley sugar twists wrapped in brown paper. The autumn sun shone on his chestnut waves and his freckles had been washed clean that morning. He almost bounced up the grassy bank of the wall and once on its summit, he cast his eyes about to see if he recognised anyone.

It's Mrs Farrers with her baby. Doesn't she look smart in her summer dress and straw hat? I wonder if that's her ma she's with. Fancy having the time to go walking just for the fun of it.

Toke neared the women and glimpsed Esther's long eyelashes and rosy cheeks as she slept cocooned against her adoptive mother's chest, snug within her arms. Phoebe and Bess glanced at him as they passed; he lowered his head, partly in respect and partly in shame.

The tide ambled on the lower reaches of the beach, while on the dry sand a group of men were working on re-enforcing the sturdy upright oak posts on a knocke. *There's a job that must make you feel proud to be a Marshman.* He stood and watched them for a moment, in no hurry and enjoying this rare afternoon free from work. Glancing back along the length of the seawall towards the centre of Dymchurch, Toke saw a horse approaching at speed. *Must be a gent – one of them Lords of the Levels or someone with some silver coins in his purse. Oh! It's young Mr Bannerman. I don't recall his first name, but I like him well enough.* George Bannerman nodded at Toke as he cantered by, and the boy doffed his cap.

Sauntering along the wall, Toke held his head high and his back straight. This was to be a momentous day for him: a girl he had met while buying some thread for his mother had agreed to take a walk with him on her afternoon off. He was confident that his mischievous smile, coupled with the gift of barley sugars, would win him his first ever kiss that afternoon.

Another horseman approached, and without giving a second glance, Toke dropped down from the wall and onto the sands. A sense of self-preservation was strong in this boy who was fast becoming a young man. Although knowing himself to be hidden from the rider's sight, Toke held his breath while his heart pounded.

One day, Mr Chapman… not yet, but one day I'm going to tell what you did. How I waited while you sneaked under the stalls and snatched the prize cup. You were as quick as a flash and as bold as a… as bold as a lion. Toke had never, and would never, see a lion, but he liked the comparison and smiled to himself. *I'm going to tell*

Mr Farrers or Sir Rupert Bannerman that you told me to take the cup from you and hide it at the farrier's cart. And how I had to bring a bit of sacking as a cover. It was itchy, that sacking was, when I had it stuffed down my shirt. I thought you were clever, but now I know you are a cruel man.

Pressed up against the seawall, the wheals on the boy's back raged. They had been inflicted upon him just two days before by a whip in the hand of Aaron Chapman. *All I did was ask if there was any other special jobs I could help you with and said I was grateful for the shillings, all ten of them. You never said I wasn't to talk about it again, but I know now. I won't ever… I won't ever speak to you about it. But one day I will talk and tell what you did.*

With these words expressed, albeit only to himself, Toke found his confidence returning. He peeked along the length of the wall and saw his adversary had now passed by. Then he ran along the beach and up a ladder, returning once more to the path along the top of the wall. Reaching into a pocket, his fingers found their way past the paper wrapping and delved amongst the barley sugars. One delicious twist of sweetness was retrieved, and Toke popped it into his mouth, relishing the flavour as it began to melt. He brushed the dirt from the back of his waistcoat and the seat of his breeches the best he could, inwardly thanked the housewife from Donkey Street for the clean shirt, and picked up his pace, determined not to be late for his entrance into the world of courting.

The End

About the Author

Romney Marsh writer, Emma Batten, loves to combine her interest in local history with creative writing. It is important to her that historical details are accurate in order to give readers an authentic insight into life on Romney Marsh. She enjoys giving author talks about her journey as a writer, planning unique writing workshops and meeting her local readers.

The Whitsun Gallop is Emma's eleventh novel.

Books
Reading order and publication dates

The Dungeness Saga (also featuring Lydd and Ashford) set in late Victorian times through to WW2:

Still Shining Bright* (2020): Cora and her daughter, Emily, are brought ashore to Dungeness by lifeboat. With no home or possessions, they rely on the kindness of strangers, and Cora must use her wit to survive.

Reckless Choices* (2021): A chance meeting on a train upsets Emily, while on the streets of Ashford someone lurks waiting to make trouble. As tensions brew within a close family, the young woman makes a rash choice.

Secrets of the Shingle (2016 & 2020): A mystery set on the wild, windswept wastes of the Dungeness peninsula in the 19th century and seen through the eyes of a naive young teacher.

Stranger on the Point (2018): Lily sets off to discover the remote coastal village her mother called home. A wrong turning takes her to a place where her arrival brings hope. The story of a determined young woman's quest to fulfil her worth, as shadows of WW1 live on.

The Artist's Gift (2019): This tells the story of a fictional young woman, widowed through the war and living amongst real life events during the Second World War. Inspired by the bombing of Lydd Church.

*Prequels to *Secrets of the Shingle*

Stand-alone novels:

A Place Called Hope (2005, reworked 2019): Set in the 16th century, this tells the story of two young women living through the decline of a remote settlement named Hope on Romney Marsh.

What the Monk Didn't See (2017 & 2021): The story of New Romney and the 1287 storm, which changed the fortunes of the town forever. As the storm breaks out, a monk climbs to the roof of the church tower. It is a superb vantage point, but what doesn't he see?

The Saxon Series introduces West Hythe, Lyminge and Aldington in 7th- century Anglo-Saxon times:

The Pendant Cross (2020): For a few days a year, the Sandtun (West Hythe) is used as a seasonal trading settlement. While they await the boats from Francia, friendships are made and hatred brews. Meanwhile four monks travel by night carrying a precious secret.

The Sacred Stone (2021): An earthquake uncovers a Roman altar buried in the foundations of an old fort. An ambitious thane and his priest are determined to secure this prize, and their actions have repercussions on the people of Aldington.

The Dymchurch Series is set in Georgian times.

But First Maintain the Wall (2019): Harry is passing through the village when the seawall breaches and events force him to stay. As an outsider, he struggles to be accepted and a tentative friendship is forged with a young woman who seeks answers to her past.

The Whitsun Gallop (2022): On the day of the annual Whitsun Gallop, the people of Romney Marsh gather. It is a day to parade their best outfits, make merry, and wager on which gentleman jockey will glory. When the prize cup is stolen under the eyes of local dignitaries, a chain of events is set in place, rocking the secure world of Harry and Phoebe Farrers.

For more details take a look at Emma's website:
www.emmabattenauthor.com